The Square

Rosie Millard

Legend Press Ltd, The Old Fire Station,
140 Tabernacle Street, London, EC2A 4SD
info@legend-paperbooks.co.uk | www.legendpress.co.uk

Contents © Rosie Millard 2015
The right of the above author to be identified as the author of this work has
been asserted in accordance with the Copyright, Designs and Patents Act
1988. British Library Cataloguing in Publication Data available.

Print ISBN 978-1-7850799-2-4
Ebook ISBN 978-1-7850799-3-1
Set in Times. Printed in the United Kingdom by Clays Ltd.
Cover design by Gudrun Jobst www.yotedesign.com

Rosie Millard is a journalist, writer and broadcaster. She was the BBC Arts Correspondent for ten years, since then she has been a profile writer at *The Sunday Times*, columnist for *The Independent*, arts editor of *The New Statesman*, theatre critic and feature writer. She makes TV and radio documentaries and appears as a commentator for a number of national TV shows. She is Chair of Hull City of Culture 2017.

Rosie has also written *The Tastemakers*, an exploration of the British contemporary art scene, and *Bonnes Vacances!*, a comic memoir about taking her family around the French Overseas Departments.

Visit Rosie at rosiemillard1.wordpress.com
follow her @Rosiemillard

To my dearest parents John and Rosemary Millard, who love reading. Please ignore the bits in this book where people's clothes come off. Thank you.

Chapter One
Jane

Roberta climbs the steps and rings the door bell. In a disinterested way, she wonders who might answer. Patrick, the dishevelled husband? Jane, the trim, pressurised wife? It certainly will not be 'Boy' George. He will be where he always is. Upstairs, hiding in his room. Trying to squeeze another thirty seconds before being called down for his weekly ordeal.

Roberta is attempting to interest George in the complexities of the piano. Actually, no. She's just trying to get him to learn to play. George is not very interested in the piano. George's parents, however, are. Roberta has been teaching George for nearly two years.

Every lesson, Jane comes into the room that has been officially designated as the 'music room' and leans on the lovely Blüthner grand, with its blond wood and real ivory keys. She taps her fingers on the top of the piano in time to the music. Then, at a pause, she always asks about Grades, and more specifically when Boy George is going to take his Grade Two. Every single lesson.

Although most of her pupils have pushy parents, Jane is without doubt the pushiest. Just as well her son is so resilient, she thinks.

She glances across the Square; the perpendicular lines of the terraced houses face her, the grand facade of a palace. Built for the Victorian bourgeoisie, fallen into disrepair, divided up, broken down, reunited, refurbished, they are serving descendants of their original class once more. She is not disdainful of the Square; she is grateful to have found it. Everyone who has children on the Square hires Roberta. Perhaps it's not so surprising. The cellular living spaces indoors are perfect for music. Outside, the identical white facades of the houses, and their uniform black front doors make the Square look like a giant keyboard.

"Ah, Roberta, how lovely." Patrick swings open the door, and grimaces in a friendly way. Roberta, as a regular visitor, can be grimaced at. Roberta smiles back. He's one of the fathers she's warmed to. Cheery, not given to complaining. He is a man who has gone to seed, however. That belly. Pity.

"Sorry, sorry, Roberta."

He rolls his eyeballs at her.

"Der Führer is on the rampage."

That'll be Jane.

Roberta takes her shoes off. Has to be done. Nobody even asks her any more; it's part of the accepted greeting and entering ceremony these days. As if everyone lives in Buddhist temples.

"Boy! Roberta is here!" yells Patrick in stentorian tones in the vague direction of George, and disappears in order to make Roberta her customary tea.

She pads into the music room and unclips her bag, taking out her own notes. She finds George's book on a coffee table, under a copy of the *Daily Mail*, and props it up on the piano. After a few minutes, the door opens and Boy George trails in, a diminutive version of Patrick, smiling at her hopefully.

"Hi."

"Hey." George sits down at the piano, ruefully stuffs his mobile device in a pocket, and considers his book. Then he looks at the keys. What is the relation between the two? He wishes he could know. He wishes, as if by a magic spell, he could suddenly just play. He puts his fingers on the instrument, and sighs. He wonders, doubtfully, if someone was holding a gun to his head, say a Nazi, whether he would suddenly be able to remember the piece from sheer panic.

"Now, shall we do some warm-ups? Remember? Shall we start with Hanon?"

George nods. He wants to please. He wants to be liked. He likes Roberta, too. He just cannot be bothered to do the necessary tasks in order to master this instrument.

Laboriously, he opens the papyrus-coloured score and commences the deceptively simple five-finger exercises followed by keyboard neophytes since Hanon wrote them 200 years ago.

A tray bearing a mug of tea comes into the room, followed by Jane. She is blonde, bobbed, bony. She smiles brightly, but no-one is deceived.

"Roberta. Lovely to see you, here's your tea. How are you? Now, I have told George he has got to buck up. I'm sorry, but this week's practice timetable has not gone to plan. Has it, George?"

George shrugs happily. He stopped playing the moment his mother came in the room.

"If you say so, Maman."

Jane chooses to ignore this carefully weighted snub, and smiles again at Roberta.

"Piano has a tough trajectory," says Roberta. Think about something other than Grades, she wants to say. Let the child learn how to enjoy the music. But Jane will not. Grades are the holy grail. Roberta suspects the mothers of her pupils gather together on a regular basis comparing notes. Why is it so important? Don't ask. It just is. Learning the preludes and fugues of J.S Bach is improving. Baroque music is good for you.

Roberta never sees it in this way. For her, music has always been a code, a discipline which gives the world some

9

meaning. She plays a Bach prelude every morning. Every evening, not too late (neighbours), she plays a fugue. There are forty-eight in the series. After she finishes the book, she starts again.

"... and so I said to George, if you pass Grade Two, I'll buy you one."

Roberta smiles. She has no idea to what Jane is referring, but can only guess it is a bribe involving an electronic toy of some distinction.

"Great idea. Come on George, let's see what shape these pieces are in."

George sighs, shifts on his stool. Thursday afternoon piano lesson is just one of the rather duller hurdles in his week.

"*Ça va*, Roberta, my dear. Here we go again. Encore."

The patterns of Hanon emanate rather feebly from the Blüthner.

Jane leaves the room. Goes into the hall. Looks in the hall mirror. Sees a middle-aged woman with crow's feet. Thinks about when she was pushing George, fatly huddled with earmuffs and a scarf in his buggy, aged two, to Martha's Music Group. "He has real musical talent," Martha used to say, when George was minded to pick up a glockenspiel stick and wave it. So much for Martha.

She looks at her face again. Those lines. Thinks she might invest in Botox. If only it wasn't so bloody expensive. If only it wasn't so frightening.

She wonders vaguely when Patrick is going to find out about her affair, not whether he is, but when he is. She feels that she must hold the present together with all her might, as if it is a vase which is just about to break into a thousand fragments.

At least everything, for the time being, is calm. Earlier that day, it had not been. It makes her heart race to think about it.

Several hours earlier Jane's lover, Jay, texted her. Says

he is coming over. Well, she had suggested it. *How are you darling?* was all he had written. *Come over*, she had messaged him back, immediately. *Patrick is at work. George is at school. Can't wait to undress you.*

Fine, he replied. *Is it safe?*

Oh for God's sake, Jane thought. What do you think? *Patrick is at work*, she texted, again, irritated.

Then she goes to put on matching underwear.

Jay arrives.

She sees his shadow through the glass of the front door. Even through opaque glass, she desires him. He steps into her house. Mercifully, and rather uniquely, after he enters the house, she takes the precaution of putting the chain on the door.

There is then a frantic scramble between Jane and Jay, as if they are backstage at a show, in the wings, and must change their costumes instantly. Except the promise ahead is the more thrilling performance of having sex.

They cannot wait to get into another room, there is no time. There is no time for their desire to wait another second. There is no time even to speak. They are still in the hall, and he is pulling her cashmere jumper up, over her head, and at the same time, pulling down her trouser zip and then her trousers. She is getting out of her bra and at the same time, pulling his shirt roughly out from the back of his trousers, scratching him, yanking the starched cotton away from his body.

And then, as her breasts are bared to the light and Jay's pursed lips bear down upon her puckered nipple like a lunar pod landing, dreadfully, unexpectedly, Jane hears Patrick's key rattle in the lock. Patrick is outside. He is coming home. Everything goes into slow motion. Seconds yawn as she, Jane, computes the noise, figures out that he, Patrick, her husband, is in the Square, he's outside, he's standing on the doorstep of the house, their house, their shared home, where he will discover her, his wife, Jane, without a bra, and that he will also discover him, Jay, their neighbour and her lover, ready to suck her breast, his stiff cock within seconds of fucking her, up against the wall of their hall.

There is no time for a game plan. Even if they had one. There is no time for anything. Time has slowed down, but there is no time.

It is sheer unadulterated adulterous panic in the hall. Jay whips round, takes the stairs two at a time and hides in – where? Jane has no idea. He just hides. Upstairs. The houses in the Square are all the same. He knows the layout.

The door opens, is caught by the chain. She hears Patrick calling through the door.

"Darling? Are you there? My afternoon meeting was cancelled."

She squawks a response, pours her arms into the cashmere, jumps back into her trousers, charges into the music room, finds a CD, shoves it into the machine, shoves her bra behind it, scrambles her fingers over the buttons, presses Play and turns it up. Music, blessed music floods the house.

Absurdly, it's the piano pieces for George's Grade Two.

Jane adjusts her top, zips her trousers, opens the door, smiles. The above actions have taken about eight seconds. Patrick is bemused.

"We never, ever chain the door, darling, what's going on, why?"

"Oh, I got a letter from, you know, from Neighbourhood Watch today," says Jane, casually guiding him into the music room, and shutting the door firmly.

"Which said we should always chain the front door."

Her blood is thundering in her ears. The CD is thundering in the room. Jay is upstairs. It is all she can focus on. Jay. Upstairs. Actually, he is about twelve feet away. She feels as if the roof is going to lift off the house. Or perhaps the doors will fly open, or the walls fall away, like a doll's house, and she will be discovered. And then it will all be over. George's music crashes on.

Has Jay got the initiative to use the music as cover? He'd bloody well better. She gestures to her unusually unkempt appearance.

"I was just about to take a shower," she shouts, over a short study by Bartók. "Then we'll have tea, shall we? Lovely to have you back so early!"

And then, deliverance. The unmistakeable sound of the front door closing, very quietly. He doesn't hear it. She hears it, because she has been yearning to hear it. Thank God, Christ and all the saints and fucking hell. That was close.

She waits a moment, then opens the door of the living room gently, to find the hall completely empty. The music hammers on.

"Just let me take that shower, darling," she calls easily over her shoulder to her husband, the cuckold, who is sitting looking at the front cover of *The Mail*.

"This is the most dreadful rag, sweetie. Don't know why you love it," he shouts.

She pads towards her upstairs bathroom.

In the shower, she finds herself shaking, and then laughing. She feels as if she has been in a farce by Alan Ayckbourn.

Two hours later, the same music comes out of the room, only this time being played, far more slowly, by an actual child.

Jane looks at herself in the hall mirror again. As guilt, closely followed by relief, washes across her body one more time, she allows herself a small conspiratorial smile before briskly taking the stairs up to her bedroom.

Downstairs, things are not going well. "Try this piece," says Roberta. "The lit-tle boys of St Paul's," she sings as George's fingers with bitten nails slowly achieve the broken chord, "they pull all the app-les down".

Patrick comes into the music room. His socks have large potatoes in the toes. He peers over Roberta's shoulder at the page of music.

We're never going to get anywhere, thinks Roberta, if

these two don't leave me alone. Children are no problem to teach. It's the parents you have to watch out for.

"Isn't that marvellous, Roberta," he smiles at her. "A piece about St Paul's when St Paul's itself is just around the corner! Well, a mile or so off, but still." He sighs. "Grew up in Barnsley. Never quite lost the magic of living in London. *Sic monument requirit*, and all that. You?"

"Oh, very dull," says Roberta. "Maidenhead."

She smiles up at Patrick.

"Come on, George. One last time and then that's your lesson done with."

Patrick pads out of the room again, picks up an envelope from the doormat, opens it, unfolds the letter within and reads it. "Jane? Darling!" he shouts.

A strangled cry comes from upstairs.

"Have you seen this letter? From the Residents' Association? Darling?"

"What?" she says, on the landing, newly near.

"Oh, sorry. There you are. Just picked this up. It's from, oh, you know, the neighbourhood lot, it's just arrived?"

He waves it in her direction.

Roberta comes out of the music room, signals that the lesson is over.

"Goodbye, Roberta," he says to the piano teacher's departing back. She waves abstractedly at him and steps out into the Square, checking her watch.

"See you next week. This letter?" continues Patrick.

Jane arranges her face carefully. She may need time to think.

"Oh, is that the thing about the chain?"

"No. There's a meeting. Something about railings around the Square. It might be to do with all those car thefts recently. Would you like to go?"

She pulls a face. "It's probably about security. They are very hot on security at the moment. That's why I had the letter, that earlier letter, you know, the one I was talking about, about chaining the door. Did they mention chaining the door?"

"Don't think so. But I'll go to the meeting. It's only at Jay and Harriet's. Not exactly far, is it?"

That's Jay as in Jane's lover. He is also the head of the Residents' Association. He lives five doors down.

George is still in the music room, looking at a photograph of himself sitting in a sandpit. He notices something behind the CD player. He puts a small hand into the crevice, and pulls at a piece of frilled material. He suddenly finds himself pulling out a lacy, coffee-coloured bra. He raises one eyebrow.

He puts it in his pocket, and saunters up to his room. There, dominating the space, beside his single bed and small desk, is his Lego City; its construction a work of devotion and time, its shape of a style answering only to him, its benevolent architect.

He lies down and picks up a tiny brick, positions it on a fluted column, considers it, removes it.

Then he rolls over, pulls out the bra from his pocket, surveys it. Quickly, he puts it on his head. The two conical shells poke up like absurd ears, the lacy strap making it into a sort of Easter bonnet. He hears his mother coming up the stairs. Quickly, he stuffs it back into his pocket.

Chapter Two
Tracey

Belle grabs the long pole with weights on it at either end and brings it up to her shoulders. She grunts with the effort and peers at herself in the mirror, under the giant radiance of neon lights that flood the gym. It is a basement gym, but the lighting is specially designed to mimic sunshine and rid members of depression brought on by Seasonally Affected Disorder; a possible side effect of exercising in a sun-free basement.

She takes the pole back down again, switching the position of her wrists as the 20kg weight crashes back down on the floor. After a few seconds, she lifts it up again. She is meant to do thirty such lifts, three times. Well, scrap that idea. I'm not really old enough for a major work out. I'll just do thirty lifts, once.

She continues to survey herself. Her spots aren't looking good, but her hair is fine. Do people do that? Focus only on one thing, like hair? And ignore other things, like spots? She's glad she doesn't have other worries. Such as fat ankles, the ones which sort of join up with your calf. What was it that her friend Cathy called them? Cankles? Cathy doesn't have Cankles. Nobody in the Populars at school has Cankles. Everyone has long hair. A few spots are fine. Short hair and

Cankles, however, are not fine.

She abandons the free weights and moves to a bench below a long horizontal pole fixed with chains to a long stack of metal slabs. This could almost be a medieval torture chamber, thinks Belle. In a dungeon.

As she pulls the weight down towards her collarbone, she considers her options for the evening. Slight lack of funds issue, but she could probably bleed her father Larry for a tenner. Some of the Populars seem to have self-replenishing wallets; they never lack cash. Cathy says it is because their parents feel 'so guilty'.

"For what?" said Belle.

"Oh, only the divorced ones. For leaving. For being stupid, and breaking everything up," remarked Cathy, methodically, robotically brushing metre-long tresses. "I have to do this 100 times a day you know."

Alternatively, she could stay in. She pictures the evening. Organising her shoes. Practising the piano. "Belle darling, do practise the piano." She can hear her mother NOW in her silly wheedling voice. Forget the piano. She never practises. Hates Roberta, that silly teacher. Okay, so how about the shoes. Organise her shoes, then a long Facebook session. That's a better idea.

She sighs, swings her body off the device, stands up in the effortless motion that belongs to the under-twenties, and trots into the room where a dozen other women, each with their pubic hair waxed into trim little shapes; one, a heart, one a pencil-thin line, one a diamond, are changing, smearing on body lotion and texting on their phones.

"I'm trying to give up wine," says one chubby woman to another. "That's the killer. Red wine."

Belle showers, dries, dresses, pulls her hair into a scrunchie, leaves the gym, arranging a coat over her neatly honed body. Although nobody can detect what her shape actually is. This is because Belle, like all the Populars at her exclusive London day school, when not in her uniform, chooses to exist in a thick array of fleecy fabric. Wide terracotta colour trousers with a drawstring tie at the waist. Huge, greyish greeny sweatshirts. Black coats so wide they are tantamount to capes. Furry scarves of mushy blue. Today, she has accessorised this sleeping bag of clothes with flat boots and a hat with earflaps.

Let Tracey, her mother, wear as little as possible, high heels and tiny micro skirts, bright miniscule tops with weeny spaghetti straps, short sleeved jumpers even in the winter. Tracey likes uncovering. Belle likes covering up. All the Populars do. It is their style. That, and virginity. The Populars are all sworn to chastity.

Larry, who had matured when promiscuity was a new pill-fuelled concept, had almost choked on his breakfast when he learned about this.

"My God," he had said. "Sworn to chastity? I'm glad I'm not growing up in your era. I don't know how I would have coped!"

"Larry," Tracey had said, soothingly. "That's enough. I think it's remarkable. Really, I do. It's a very good thing, Belle, that you and your friends are all so focused."

Yeah, right, thinks Belle, that's the New Mum. The Post-Lottery Win Mum. She knows her mother would never have said such a thing before the Win.

'Focused.' It's all part of the private school belief system. That's the sort of language teachers use. At least her dad hasn't changed.

She marches home, swaddled, mummified in fleece. Focused.

She walks up the road to the Square, past the large council estate on the corner. A young man is practising wheelies in the street on his bike.

"Oy!" he calls to her.

"Sexy legs!"

Belle speeds up, but turns slightly, in spite of herself. Something about him looks familiar. He cycles up behind her under the electric lights of the estate which are always on, no matter what time of day or night.

It's Jas, a boy whom she has known since they were both children. They used to have swimming lessons together at the local pool. They were at the same primary school, before the Lottery win.

About five years ago, Belle can't really remember when, her parents won the Lottery. God knows how they did. I mean, of course they chose the right numbers but Belle has no idea what formula was used, whether invented numbers or proper things related to their birthdays, she has no idea. It was all like a dream.

She remembers her former life, before two million pounds entered it, only in vague pictures. Living in a tiny house, wearing uniform from the local primary and having play dates with people like Jas. Jas is no longer a boy. Now he is tall, hooded, accessorised with sports equipment and jewellery.

"Belle, whassup?"

"Oh. Hi Jas. Alright?"

She looks at him. She remembers he used to make her laugh outrageously. There is absolutely no way she could ever introduce him to the Populars, even if she wanted to. Even if the chaste thing didn't matter. Or her family. He might live around the corner, but it is far away for Belle, now.

"You are looking soooo good," says Jas, swinging his legs on his bike.

She looks at him, envisaging a scene where she might kiss him.

Her stomach flares up with a strange excitement at the idea. That would horrify her mother. Kissing someone from the estate. She quite likes it. She'll keep the idea as a weapon.

"Thanks, Jas," she says, waving to him and walking on, returning to her enclave of privilege. Jas shrugs, turns on his bike, rears it up, balancing on the back wheel as if it is some form of stallion.

Belle walks up the steps to her front door. Ting-a-ling. She's forgotten her keys. Anya, the au pair, opens the door. Romanian, Bulgarian, Croatian? Who knows. All Belle knows is that she is bloody jealous of her cheekbones.

"Good evening, Belle," says Anya, who is Polish and proud of her almost perfect English and her superficially perfect manners.

Belle acknowledges the woman, deposits her bag, cape-coat, hat, gym bag and scarf onto the floor in one grand gesture of entitlement and ascends the stairs. She loves the fact that her mother employs workers for her benefit in the house.

Anya, falling in behind, automatically picks them up. She knows this is expected of her. It is just one more thing, however, which she will be glad to leave behind. Anya has told nobody but she is intending to go back to her home in Lodz quite soon.

Belle runs lightly upstairs, heading towards the top of the house. Children in the Square always sleep at the top. Everyone on the Square arranges their homes from roof to cellar in the same way, as if there was a strict pattern guide.

At the bottom is a small room either used for laundry, or the au pair. Or, in some cases, both. The rest of the basement is devoted to the kitchen. The kitchen is always vast; a cavernous space which has been 'knocked through' from front to back. Knocking through is obligatory. Everyone does it. Nobody wants to repeat the dreadful episode of The Family Who Didn't Knock-Through, and therefore could not eventually sell up.

"They were completely stuffed," Jane would say by way of explanation. "Nobody was interested, apart from a family from Hull who offered way, WAY below the asking price. No knock-through, you see." To avoid this hideous and shaming fate, everyone knocks-through.

The paint scheme of each kitchen is doggedly bright, as if the kitchen were a primary school. A small blackboard on the walls, indicating vital elements for the next shopping mission, continues the illusion. These are always foreign and aspirational. Fenugreek. Persimmon. Star anis.

Belle likes to occasionally adulterate the blackboard with more everyday items such as Elastoplast or Tampax. Once she even put nit lotion down. Tracey always rubs them out as soon as she sees them.

Opposite the blackboard is the obligatory 'island'. Every kitchen has one, a marooned stone rectangle surrounded by a cluster of chrome stools. Somewhere on it there will be a single, commanding tap. There might be a recipe book propped up on a lectern, like a religious text.

Beside the island is a colossal, humming fridge and a vast six-burner appliance capable of feeding an entire church choir, should one drop in. This is known as the 'range'. It is not used very much. Hot meals still tend to come from the microwave, or local restaurants, whose takeaway menus are pinned to a cork board.

The entire room glories in laboratory-style cleanliness. There is an entire cupboard devoted to cleaning implements and chemicals. There is a bespoke bottle for the kitchen's myriad surfaces, each of which has been quarried, quartered, buffed and bullied into a properly gleaming state of submission.

Kitchens in the Square are a miracle of processed nature. Marble, granite, steel, quartz, slate, with accents of wood and chrome brought together in one glorious assemblage. The kitchens are like a geology lesson.

At night, the au pairs creep out of their small rooms. They enter these bright, soulless places and erect computers upon the marble islands. They perch on the chrome stools and talk via Skype to their families in languages which to Belle's English ear sound like falling water. Alone and undisturbed, they explain to their fascinated relations how things are in the Square, a place full of money, nerves and giant, unused ovens.

After the kitchen, on the next floor up, is the living room. The living room, or as Jane has it, the music room, is the domain of soft furnishing, Indian cushions, large sofas, monochrome wedding photographs, and antique chairs on which nobody sits. There is never a television or games console. There is never a computer. Hence, these rooms are usually deserted. Occasionally drinks parties are held in them. Sometimes a solitary child is forced to enter them, dawdling, for the obligation of meeting grandparents for an obligatory kiss, or music practice.

Belle goes up to the second floor. This is where her parents sleep. All parents in the Square sleep on the second floor, in 'master' bedrooms with ensuite bathrooms and vast beds in which Belle suspects sex never takes place.

There is a spare room on this floor permanently held in a state of tense readiness for the sake of the relations, whenever they descend, which is hopefully never, and then, at last, the top floor.

Belle's domain. Tiny rooms, low ceilings, poky sash windows. The floor where the servants used to live. Except kids aren't the servants in the Square. They are the masters.

Belle kicks open the door of her room. It is full of small, winking appliances. Digital clock, scales, monitors, speakers, music systems. An electric guitar. A long electronic keyboard. These items softly glow amid drifts of giant, fleecy clothes in earthy colours. The floor looks as if it has been inundated with a tidal wave of mud.

"You don't have a wardrobe. You have a floordrobe," her father says jovially.

In the middle of all this winking sludge sits her younger sister. Grace.

"Get out," says Belle. "Now."

"Aw, why?" whines Grace.

"Because I say so," says Belle, with inescapable logic.

"Well, anyway," says Grace, flouncing towards the door. "I've got news for you."

"Oh yeah?"

"Yeah. No piano lessons. Any More. No more Roberta. Mum says so. Says we are all having to Pull In Our Belts. Tee hee!"

As she darts out, Belle casually throws a copy of the final edition of Harry Potter at her disappearing form. It misses, cracks onto the door. The spine, already bent in a dozen parallel lines, breaks.

"Thanks, Mum, for cancelling my piano!" she shouts down the stairs. She's very pleased about this.

She hates her piano teacher Roberta. Silly cow, making her play all that, what was it? Hanon. Sounds like knitting.

She hears a vague response from downstairs.

"What? What?"

Tracey is coming up the stairs.

Her head is entirely obscured by a giant cheeseplant which she is laboriously carting up through the house.

"Belle, it is normal to say hello to the rest of the family when you come back from the gym. I had no idea you were here until just now."

"I said hello to Anya."

"Yes, but I am talking about your Family."

"I thought Anya was meant to be a member of the Family," retorts Belle. "Why on earth are you bringing that vile plant up?"

"Oxygen," puffs her mother. "I don't think you have enough oxygen up here."

Belle has no response to this.

"Read about it in *The Mail*," manages her mother. "Putting plants in your room helps your brain develop. So I thought you could have a spell with Charlie. He's been in the garden for far too long."

"Charlie?" echoes Belle.

"Yes," grunts her mother, heaving pot and plant on a table. Quite a lot of soil falls out of the pot and lands on the carpet.

"Damn. Gosh, that was heavy. Charlie the Cheeseplant."

She strokes a leaf.

"Had him in our first flat."

Belle isn't interested in her mother's memoirs. She's not interested in having a giant, dusty, soily cheeseplant in her vicinity, either. Now that piano practise has been magically removed from the equation, she is however quite keen to go out. She senses she needs to close down the piano conversation.

"So, no more Roberta? Ever? Thank God."

Tracey holds up a manicured hand. She is always perfectly groomed. Even before the Lottery win, she was beautifully turned out.

Tracey is part of a beauty product pyramid scheme which relies on people flogging cosmetics door to door. It used to be her sole income. She still does it, from time to time. The positive effect of this is her physical perfection. The negative side is that such a job wholly relies on the market. And people aren't investing, much, in beauty at the moment.

"I have arranged a small break with Roberta, Belle. Just until Easter. Then, hopefully, things will have picked up, and we can continue. Will you continue practising, though?"

"Yeah, yeah. When can I go out?"

"Tonight? You can't."

"What?"

"Sorry. We have the Residents' Association meeting tonight and you need to stay in and look after Grace. We have all been waiting for you to get back from the gym."

"What? But, Mum!"

"Too bad."

"What about Anya, for God's sake? She's meant to be here to look after Grace. That's the whole reason she's here! She IS the au pair. I'm just a blood relation."

"Anya is coming with us."

"What?"

"Anya is coming with us. Belle, will you stop saying 'What'? You heard me perfectly well. Anya is coming with us, because she needs to learn how a proper meeting is held. It's for her Business Studies Course."

There is a pause.

"What?"

"She says she needs to see the minuting and so on. Frankly, Belle, she's very switched on. A bit more than you are. Don't you have any interest in how a meeting is run?"

Belle rolls her eyes at her mother. She smiles and waves her arms in the air.

"Oh, Mum," she says.

"What, darling?"

"I can really feel the oxygen surging up here! It's amazing!"

"Thank you, Belle. We'll be back at nine."

Belle goes into her room, winds an olive-coloured scarf around her neck and picks up her electric guitar. If her mother wants her to do music, she'll do music. Her kind of music. Four floors down, and about ten minutes later, the front door slams.

Chapter Three
The Residents' Association Meeting

Harriet is standing at the island of her knock-through kitchen, laboriously putting small pieces of smoked salmon onto Philadelphia cheese which has been spread onto tiny circular pancakes. The fish is slippery and flaky. It does not fold out of the plastic wrapper in flat long flaps, but must be forked out in small shavings. This is because it is discount smoked salmon. Harriet's fingers are covered in fish grease accented by a smear of Philly. They slip on the handle of the fork, making the tines poke into the soft mound of flesh between the first finger and thumb of her other hand.

"Bugger."

She blows a strand of hair out of her mouth and raises her head, lips open, as if she was a turtle surfacing for air.

"Jay?" she yells, and then continues, not waiting for a reply.

"Have you got the Cava? Or Prosecco, or whatever it is? I left some in the fridge!"

Can't afford Champagne. Can't afford nice flat pages of proper, decent smoked salmon. Probably having a holiday in a bloody tent this year, thinks Harriet crossly, eating cream cheese out of the white plastic oval with a spoon.

Harriet is Jay's wife. She is a large woman. Her body speaks of luxury and indulgence, of not stinting. Her breasts are voluminous. They cause her jumper to form an unbroken matronly reef across her chest. Her stomach sticks out, a collapsed box. Her haunches are dimpled, carrying a shape of their own unrelated to the line of bone buried deep within the copious flesh.

She and Jay came to the Square in what they now regard as the Good Old Days. The days when you could really get plastered on proper 'poo. When everyone had taxi accounts, and private schools, and decent holidays in Tuscany.

Harriet isn't sure she really likes the current mood. A former teacher who gave up work when their only child, Brian, was born, she is wholly dependent on the money her husband earns. And he hasn't been earning as much of late.

Harriet is having to be careful. She doesn't like being careful. She doesn't want to be careful about things like smoked salmon, or buying new bags. She likes having a new Mulberry handbag every winter. She doesn't like camping. She doesn't want to go on holiday to live in an Amish-style sense surrounded by tents and truly appalling food. She wants Italian villas, olive studded bread and the Widow Cliquot.

She eats a canapé and reflects that she doesn't, really, like hosting meetings for the Residents' Association on the Square either. But Jay insists. Says it's good to 'be neighbourly'. Jay loves his neighbours. Harriet doesn't realise quite how much he does.

The door bell rings. She hears the sing-song welcome and the thud on the floor above of people taking off their shoes.

She pops another canapé into her mouth.

"Last one," she says. Then she puts the plate of discount smoked salmon canapés onto a tray, and moves heavily to the sink to wash her hands. As she does, she makes sure to throw away the wrapper for the discount salmon. Can't have anyone spotting it.

"Well, maybe one more."

She eats a third, then stomps upstairs with the tray of canapés.

Upstairs in the living room, Harriet observes that Jay has got out all the antique Chippendale-style chairs which are really only in the room for decoration and has assembled them in a circle.

It's as if the house had been turned into a posh old people's home, thinks Harriet as she enters with the tray.

Everyone is standing around the chairs, as if they are about to play a game, and are waiting for a sign.

Tracey and Larry are there, smiling ferociously at their Eastern Block au pair. Tracey is wearing something tiny, Harriet observes. That's because she is so thin. Harriet doesn't hold it against her, she likes her friend, who had after all come from absolutely nowhere (but then won a shed load of cash), she just wishes she had her figure.

The door bell rings again. It's the single mother from across the road. Harriet has no idea what she's called. Sophie? Karen? She's about fifteen years younger than Harriet. Then Patrick and Jane arrive. God, Jane looks good, thinks Harriet with a surge. How does she manage it? It is confusing. She sees Jane at plenty of occasions where there is food, but she must simply never eat. And how does she have time to appear so perfectly coiffed? She always makes Harriet feel messy, and dowdy.

Two other couples arrive. Harriet is pleased to see Jay dealing with them, handing each a glass of Cava, proffering canapés.

Jane advances on Harriet, eyes shining, smiling furiously. She has kept on her shoes, a spectacular pair of snakeskin mules with a vertiginous heel. Harriet wishes she was wearing heels, and not her Converse baseball boots, which she thought made her look young, but now she feels like mutton dressed as lamb.

"Hello Harriet," smiles Jane, high above her. She nods, as if she is taking a school register.

"Here we all are."

Yes, we are, thinks Harriet. We've had this Association

now for six years and all that's actually happened has been an annual Christmas drinks do and the enforced closure of a youth club for young disadvantaged people on the corner, the shutting of which was hailed as a communal triumph.

People start to perch on the antique chairs.

"So, what are we talking about today?" asks Harriet, dully, to Jane.

"Oh, don't you know? Hasn't Jay shown you the agenda?"

"No, has he written one?"

Jane, momentarily flustered, puts her chin up and looks at Harriet like a small bird.

"I don't actually know. I would think so, wouldn't you?"

Harriet spots the tall figure of her son in the hall. Respite.

"Sorry, Jane, just a moment." She moves away.

Brian. Her lovely son. How could Harriet have known that by the time he reached maturity, his name would become totally outmoded, a name of yesterday, redolent of football managers and tabloid editors. He tolerates it pretty well, thinks Harriet. Although, maybe it is the reason he spends so much time on that bloody computer. Maybe he has an ovatar, or whatever it's called. A different name, anyway.

"Hi, Mum," says Brian, leaning down to kiss her. "Residents' meeting tonight, is it? Lucky you. I'll go out."

She raises her hands helplessly. "Sorry, darling."

"Ooh, look at Dad, texting," says Brian, gesturing into the room of people now all sitting bolt upright on the circle of chairs, waiting. "Thought that was rude, Dad!" he calls into the room. "Texting when there are people around. Naughty!"

Jay leaps back as if he has been kicked by a large horse.

"Brian! Right, everyone, sorry, " he says, folding his device, but not turning it off, putting it into his pocket like a pack of cards he might at any time bring out again with a flourish.

"Shall we? Ahem. Welcome, all," says Jay, as Brian leaves the house, a wry smile on his face.

"Now, I have written out an agenda. Don't worry, it's very

short. It essentially deals with the railings around the Square which are in disrepair. The council won't pay for them. I think the notion is that we will. And the notion is that we should, because otherwise the Square will become riddled with foxes and other undesirables."

"Such as?" says the Single Mother, whose child attends a playgroup in the foyer of the council estate next door.

"Litter," says Jay firmly. He knows what the agenda of the Single Mother is.

Jane stretches her legs, arches her feet in their very high heels, and looks at them. She slides her phone out of her pocket, checks it is on silent, and under the cover of her Prada bag, taps out a brief message.

Jane is texting Jay. Jane is sitting opposite Jay and texting him. Small snippets of erotica. About what she will do to him when they next meet. It turns her on. It is her fantasy, and she loves the outrageousness of doing it amid the formality of the Residents' Association.

She presses send. Presently she hears a tiny buzz from the pocket of Jay's trousers. She arches an eyebrow and knowingly takes a sip. Oh, God, she thinks. Cava. It's not Champagne, but who cares. She's having a good time.

Harriet sits, plumply, on her antique chair and watches Jane. She wonders what she is doing behind that bag. She wonders why Jane is so amused by a discussion about feeding the foxes in the Square. She starts thinking about what time everyone will push off, and what they might have for supper, she and Jay.

"Excuse me," murmurs Jay. "Sorry. The office." He quickly pulls his device from his pocket and attends to the text. Reads the message, squares his shoulders, envisages Jane in their downstairs shower room. Kneeling before him. Sucking him off. That was what her message was about.

He shakes his head slowly, breathes in. He can feel himself becoming excited, can sense Jane watching him intently from across the room.

"So, the railings," he says.

Harriet watches everyone nodding, agreeing that what the park should have is a continued line of proper railings topped with forged Historic Finials. Rather than the current status quo, which is a smattering of Historic Finials, modern stuff, and chicken wire. Only this will cost £26,700, and the council, given the urgent call on its budget from other deserving causes, non-railing related, has declined to stump up.

Harriet leans back.

All at once, Harriet falls back through the Chippendale chair. Or rather, the back of the chair snaps, with a dreadful cracking noise, and Harriet falls off it, backwards through empty air, onto the floor. There is a horrified silence from the Association. Shattered pieces of curved antique wood lie on the carpet, like dismantled treble clefs. Harriet lies on the floor, her skirt up above her knees.

Eventually, someone speaks.

"Well, I'd say that chair is totally fucked," says Larry, through a badly disguised snort.

"Will you shut up," hisses Tracey, elbowing him. "Oh, Harriet, gosh, can we help you?"

But Anya, the au pair, is already there, helping Harriet up, a calm arm under her elbow.

Harriet looks at the assembled group blearily, as if she has just burrowed out from under the carpet. Her face is burning.

"I am so sorry," she says. She gives Jay a deadly look. "We never normally sit on these chairs, do we darling?"

She doesn't know where to exist. Her back and bottom are hurting, but they might as well belong to someone else. She doesn't want to take responsiblity for her body at the moment, to rub it, to care for it. She wants to leave it and the meeting and the room. She wants to sink down into the ground. Or fly out of the window. She leans on a sidetable, with what she hopes is a publicly rueful expression.

Jay is quietly gathering together the splintered back of the chair, putting the pieces on its embroidered, dusty pink seat, carrying the whole thing out of the room and putting it in the hall, where it will stay, like a child who has let everyone down and must be sent out to sit on the naughty step.

Just where everyone will pass it on the way out, thinks Harriet. And remember how bloody fat I am.

"Ooof. That was a shock! My arse," she says loudly and comically, showing that she doesn't care, as she walks across the room and descends into the soft billows of a sofa. She cannot look at Jane.

Larry comes over to her. She likes Larry, and she likes Tracey, his unthreatening wife. Yes, Tracey is thin, like Jane, but not in an opressively commanding way like Jane, whose thinness makes Harriet feel sad, and greedy. Larry pats her on the knee.

"Are you alright? Wine?"

She's very grateful he is willing to be alongside her.

"I'm fine. Thanks, I will."

He walks to the other side of the room, returns with a glass and a plate.

"Canapé?"

How can you offer me something to eat when you all know I am too fat?

"Lovely."

Larry sits down beside her.

"Shall we continue with the meeting?" says Jay, gently. His previous mood has altered. He is now irritated that Jane thinks so little of his carefully planned agenda that she can send him texts about oral sex during the discussion of it.

"Item 3.4. Railings around the park. We could try a fundraiser. But nobody here has the cash, do we?" says Jay.

"You said it," snorts Larry. He turns to Harriet. "We are so strapped for cash I'm thinking seriously of selling Belle's collection of electric guitars. On eBay." He grins at her.

Harriet is delighted by this. The news that Larry and Tracey have a lack of money, even though he is probably massaging the truth somewhat, after all, they are Lottery winners, but still, floods Harriet's body with joy. She turns to him, smiling, her undignified collapse momentarily forgotten.

"Oh, really? Are you broke too?"

"Oh, utterly. I never know when I approach an ATM whether it's going to pay out or not."

"Same here."

"Yes. And there's a new tense game to eating out," he continues, "namely Will My Card Work?, when the bill arrives."

"But that's just the same as us," says Harriet delightedly. "I never thought. But isn't Tracey doing brilliantly in Beauty at the moment?"

"Nah," says Larry. "No money in nails."

"Oh, poor Tracey," says Harriet. She is sorry for Tracey and Larry, in one way. In another, she is not. I mean, they must have spent all their winnings on their house, which is capital in another form, surely. And then there are the school fees, and that isn't obligatory, is it? Anyway, they haven't got much to throw about. Which shows her own situation isn't completely of her own making. How can it be, if other people are in the same state?

"So is that it?" says Jay, with reference to the railings. People start to talk about other things.

She starts to relax.

"Jay, could you pass around the canapés?" She's not going to get up. Her back aches anyway. Her husband moves into action. He brings the plate over to the sofa, proffers it to her as if he is holding out a Frisbee.

"Darling?"

"No, I mustn't. Come here, though," she hisses, bringing his ear down to her level.

"When is everyone going? How much more of this is there?"

Jay stands up. "Look, everyone, is that about the evening wrapped up? Is there anything more to discuss? Er, fences,

33

foxes, feral youths?" Everyone laughs.

"Marvellous. So, that's that. Until the Christmas party, I suppose."

Harriet waves from the sofa. "Bye, all. Sorry about the furniture acrobatics."

His mouth full of blini, Larry waves at the assembled party.

"Hang on everyone. I've been thinking. Wait a minute!"

Everyone sits back down again.

"Well, you know we need money for these railings, or whatever. And we haven't got any. So, I was thinking. Why don't we have a fundraising event this summer? Come on. We could flog all our old stuff, you know, have a posh car boot sale."

"Like a jumble sale?" says the Single Mother.

"No," says Larry. "Not at all. More like a circulation of goods. Like they do in Manhattan."

The mention of New York City has an almost alchemical effect. People start listening. If it's alright for Manhattan, it's alright for them.

"A Stoop Sale, they call it," continues Larry. "Everyone gathers their stuff together, puts it on their front door step. Good stuff, you know, nice things. Then people just go around the place and see what they want. The Square is perfect. We could have drinks and things in the middle. You know, turn it into a real community event, for the railings. It could be good. It could be great!"

"I could have a half price cosmetic sale," says Tracey.

"How about a cake sale?" says Jane.

"How about a dog show?" says Patrick.

"Yeah, except nobody has dogs, apart from people in the council estate," whispers Jane, quietly scathing.

"We should get the children involved," says the Single Mother.

"Absolutely," says Larry, bustling forward on the sofa. "Very true. Hang the sale. Why don't we get the children to

34

do something special? You know, a bespoke performance. I know. How about a Talent Show? Get them off their lazy backsides. We all spend so much time and effort on them. This is payback time!"

There is general laughter around the room.

"There are probably enough of them to make a string quintet."

"An orchestra, more like!"

"What, alongside the dog show? Brilliant!"

More laughter.

"How about a fashion show, does anyone have connections in the fashion world?"

"I think a Talent Show is still the best idea," says Larry, although it was his idea.

Harriet looks around the room. The notion of a plan has galvinised people to fish for their diaries, tap dates into their phones, checking addresses, dates, chatting eagerly.

The Eastern Bloc au pair comes over.

"Is your back alright now?"

"Oh, yes, of course. Silly. Those chairs! Made for a different world, weren't they?!"

"Sorry?"

"The chairs," says Harriet, standing up. "They are about 200 years old. They were constructed, you know, made, for people who were very different from us. Much lighter."

The au pair smiles at Harriet. In her home city of Lodz, to be fat and well-fed is still a goal. It is also difficult to get furniture made before 1967.

Larry stands up.

"Look, everyone, I'll send round a list of possible dates, although the end of June looks like the best option. We don't want to clip the beginning of the summer hols, and you know how early schools break up these days."

"Well, we've probably got until the end of July, term goes on until then," pipes up the Single Mother.

"No, not for private schools, actually," smiles Jane.

"Oh," says the Single Mother.

"We'll also need lists of who can do what," continues Larry, breezily. "If it is going to be a Talent Show, then obviously everyone has to think about what talents they have. I mean, ones that can be publicly displayed," he says, laughing loudly. "And we will need to have a list of people willing to do things like lend chairs, or whatever."

There is a general noise of contented approval.

"Do we want to involve the vicar?" asks Larry. Nobody says anything.

"Alright, nothing religious," he says hurriedly. "Do we want to involve Philip and Gilda?" Groans all round. Everyone knows Philip Burrell. 'Famous in the Sixties, infamous in the Seventies' is how Larry usually defines him. "A total pain in the arse," is Patrick's way of describing Larry. The only actual professional creative in the Square, Philip Burrell is a self-defined artist with a capital A. Determinedly 'eccentric', he never surfaces before midday, wears paint-spattered boiler suits and walks ten times around the Square for exercise one way at 3pm, and ten times around the Square the other way the next day at 4pm. Never married, he has however had a string of Bohemian-style lovers through his life, which he is always very proud of, and mentions often. The Tate has infrequently flirted with buying his work, but never actually done so. His current amour is Russian. Gilda wears fairy tutus and ostrich feather boas and considers Philip the world's greatest artist. Nobody is quite sure what she does, although it was rumoured that she had a live art show in a Mayfair gallery once. Philip has a gallery in Paris and one in Dublin, apparently for 'tax purposes'.

"Well, we should ASK them," says Jane scornfully. "They won't come, you know. Because they are Proper Artists. This is just amateur stuff. They'll look down their noses at us."

"Well, let them. They're harmless," says Larry. This is his default position on most people, unless they are known supporters of the Labour Party.

"But remember, it has to be good. We have to raise money, you know. I think a Talent Show is the best idea. I know, it was my idea, but still."

Everyone laughs. They're a pretty talented bunch, after all, are they not? And their children certainly are.

It is time for the evening to draw to a close.

Harriet, confident now, approaches Tracey.

"I have to go to this event at the Book Fair tomorrow," she says, as Tracey waits for Anya to join them.

"Are you free? Shall we go together? If you want, I'll collect you at 6.30. I won't tell you what it is, but I think you'll really like it."

Tracey nods, enjoying the feeling of being organised. "Alright, Harriet, thanks."

Jay is putting on Jane's coat for her in the hall. She stands patiently, preening herself under the attention. The detritus of the chair lies behind them on the stairs.

"You could organise it, " he says. "You could present it, honestly. You're a natural at this sort of thing. And George could give us all a recital on the piano."

"What, wheel the Blüthner out into the Square? I don't think so!"

"Well, get an electronic keyboard."

She smiles at him, thinking about showing off her son.

"How thoughtful you are," she says, revealing dimples Jay has never noticed before.

Jay rolls his eyes at her.

"You are adorable. And very naughty. That text."

Jane smiles proudly, steps out of the house, following her husband across the Square to her house. Turning men on in her mid-forties. She has it, she has to admit to herself. Whatever it is, she has it.

She looks up at the houses around her. Their long rectangular windows present an ordered pattern. Each has two window panes above two window panes, like a maths lesson. The repetition is severe and uncompromising. She tosses her head, pleasuring in the way the glossy weight of her hair takes a split second longer to follow the movement.

The living room in Jay and Harriet's house is empty. Jay is in the shower-room toilet, thinking about when Jane will be kneeling on the terracotta tiles before him with her head thrown back. Down in the kitchen, Harriet is polishing off the plate of smoked salmon blinis and wonders whether she could allow herself a cigarette. After a minute or so, she decides she will.

Chapter Four
Philip

At No. 12, the Square, Philip Burrell stands, naked in front of his window. He is confident that nobody can see him, but what if they could? It's not illegal, is it? To stand privately in front of your window and look at nature? Philip Burrell is sixty-eight. He flexes his wrinkled buttocks and takes a Full Warrior yoga stance, looking down with pleasure at his still elastic thigh muscles. He notes his penis dangling between his legs. A fine warrior. Still pretty much of a beast, considering.

He stands tall again. His eye falls on the cherry trees opposite his house. He can't bear the cherry trees, at least for eleven months out of twelve. Weedy things. Not at all like the magnificent London plane. 'Lollipop trees' he calls them, dismissively. They have taken over the city, and he rails against it.

There is only one time he will accept their existence and that is during their blossoming period. That is the moment. He loves it when they are covered with creamy flowers.

This morning, however, he looks at them ruefully. The trees are not full of blossom. They are covered with rather ugly red leaves. Small birds hop about in them, searching for insects. He wanders over to his dressing room and reaches for his towelling robe. He always spends the morning naked but for his towelling robe. It is one of his habits.

"Habit," Philip has a tendency to say, "releases my mind into another place. All of the great aesthetes throughout history were creatures of habit."

He enjoys the habitual goings on in the Square too; the trees, blossoming at the right time, birds, flowers springing up in the central garden. He likes the parallel human regularity. The bin men on a Wednesday. That piano teacher, turning up like clockwork for her pupils in various houses during the week. The men from the council, weeding the beds. They almost feel like characters in a drama. Philip performs the Tree stance before his window, standing on one leg, feeling almost at one with the actual trees in the Square, and then as he sees Tracey leave her house with her young daughter, he brings his foot down from his thigh and watches her. He finds Tracey quite alluring. All those tarty outfits she wears. He likes it. Likes seeing her exposed thigh and shoulder. She's the one who won the Lottery a few years back, he thinks. Not a silly amount of money, but enough money to buy a house here. She's not the sort of person who would usually live here. Shows, too. You can see she isn't used to having money. At least, she's the only woman in the Square who dresses like a bitch on heat. He knows she has a husband, that Larry chap who is always laughing, no wonder. He won the fucking Lottery, didn't he?

Nevertheless, Philip still wonders vaguely if she might allow him to fuck her, whether she would be repulsed, think he was too old. Maybe not. Women behave differently around artists. He discovered this to his great pleasure several decades ago. Ask them to take their clothes off and they are only too happy to oblige. Not that he does life drawing, or nude portraits any more, Christ no. But he is a famous artist. And he is quite confident that normal rules don't apply. He considers Tracey again. Well, maybe some day.

He turns lightly, heading downstairs to the knock-through

kitchen, where he knows Gilda will have his tray ready for him. Coffee and a sliced mango. Philip will never let anything touch his lips but coffee and fruit until midday.

Outside, Tracey is holding the rear car door open for her daughter.

"Twelve times twelve," says Tracey to Grace.

There is a pause.

"Well?"

"Is it 112?" suggests Grace.

Tracey smiles. She holds her small daughter's hand.

"No, not quite. Bit more. 144."

"Do we HAVE to do this?" asks Grace. "Mummy?"

"No," says Tracey with relief. "No, we don't."

She never enjoyed doing times tables herself. She does like taking Grace to school, however. Three more years. Then she'll be at Secondary, like Belle, at which point Grace will be lost to her. That will be it. No more daily journeys to and from the school gates with conversations about the intricate details of Grace's day, about who has fallen out with whom and where her library card is. Taking her daughter to school makes her feel connected with the rest of the place, with the High Street and the library and the swimming pool. If you just drove in and out of the Square all day to deliver your child to The Prep, which is ferociously exclusive and expensive, you would feel as if life was a sort of planet of plenty, thinks Tracey, who knows full well from her clients who buy cosmetics from her that it is not.

Today, however, they are driving. Grace hops in, hand on her head to steady the boater. For some reason the children at The Prep have to attend school as if life was stuck in the 1950s; the girls uniform consists of grey pinafore, long black socks, boater with black ribbon.

"Put your seat belt on," she says.

Tracey gets in the front, pulls her skirt down towards her knees. She hopes she'll be early. Then she won't have to run the beady eyed gauntlet of the school gates. All those women with husbands who work in the City, dressed in their silk shifts and tweedy jackets, makeup so subtle it looks like it's not even there, hair beautifully blown. It is the handbags which are the signifiers, though. Soft, buttery leather bags. Purple and green and black, with clinking accoutrements to announce their presence; silver locks and heart-shaped key fobs and gilt chains, and huge stitched handles which fit just so under your arm. They possess a sort of magical charm. Tracey fears she will never exude such magic. Even though she and Larry had got enough cash, just, to buy their way into the Square, she still feels as she feels most days, like a fraud.

She wishes Larry worked at Goldman Sachs or Merrill Lynch, or any one of those places which seemed to carry people off into environs of untold wealth. She could never admit to the women at the school gates exactly what her husband did. Or what she did. Imagine. Admitting to flogging cosmetics. It made her stomach quail to even think about it. No, she usually just dropped Grace off and stayed in the 4x4, waving madly as her child turned into the enclave of privilege for the day in her grey pinafore.

She looks in the mirror, sees Grace's merry little face under the brim of her hat.

"I like your hair today, Mummy."

Tracey's insides melt with love for the child. "Thank you very much."

As she signals left to turn into The Prep's private road, two miles away Philip Burrell is putting a forkful of melon into his mouth while he considers whether Tracey would allow him to lift her skirt up one morning.

Gilda watches him anxiously.

"Do you think that is ripe enough?"

"Darling it is ravishing," says Philip in his low, sonorous voice. "As are you."

Gilda smiles, looks down. Her eyelids shimmer like butterfly wings. She glances up at Philip through a haze of black filament. She is wearing false eyelashes. On the top of her head is a tiny, winking tiara. Gilda usually dresses up, but this is quite a lot for a weekday morning, even by her standards.

Philip raises one bushy eyebrow. He has no hair on his head, but quite a lot of it on his face.

"On behalf of Magnus," she says by way of explanation for her glamour.

Magnus is Philip's dealer, a beefy man with no wife but a calculator for a brain. He is the link between Philip's overseas galleries, and his studio here at his London home. Ask him the percentage of anything; VAT in Singapore, Capital Gains Tax in France, death duties in the States, he will work it out in a split second. Magnus can juggle figures with dizzying skill and speed, and does so for great effect. Particularly when closing a deal.

"I'll knock the VAT off," he tells a hesitating customer. "That will save you £23,000. Done?"

Philip marvels at how he does it. He marvels in particular at how Magnus has carried Philip with him, year after year, taking pieces all around the world, selling, selling, always selling and always closing. Much to Philip's pleasure. He knows his dealer makes 50% from every deal, but as long as the figures are high, Philip doesn't much care whether Magnus takes a big lump, or not. Actually, he'd rather he did. Keeps him on his toes. And the figures are high. Philip has never earned so much money in his life. In fact, he now earns so much from his art that he can almost laugh at the notion, once his closely guarded ambition, of being an impoverished artist who had a work of art in the Tate collection.

"Ah, yes, of course. Is Magnus coming for lunch?"

"Had you forgotten?"

He had, but no matter. He would be dressed by then, and ready for lunch. Whether Magnus was there or not was immaterial.

He should, however, see what Magnus thought of his latest idea.

"I'll be in the studio for the rest of the morning. Treasure? Lunch? Can you organise lunch? We will have the usual."

"Of course."

The usual was a rough loaf of artisan bread. Salted Napoleon butter. Brie. Grapes. Vine tomatoes. Wine. Perrier.

Philip enjoyed lunch. He would sip Perrier and dab at his mouth fastidiously with a red-checked napkin, almost as if he was on one of the foothills of the Pyranees. In a Renoir film.

He gets up from the table, pushes his plates towards Gilda.

"Delectable. And delicious. *Comme vous.*"

"Oh, you are calling me *vous* this morning, cherie," she says playfully, batting her lids fronded with long nylon strands.

"Well, I see no reason why we should not be formal, at times, with one another."

She loved him when he was like this, play-acting.

"Go on, arsehole."

They also loved being rude to one another.

He raises another bushy eyebrow and walks towards the studio, swishing his robe.

Flick. The long row of halogen lights leaps into brilliance.

The studio is white. White walls. White floor. White frosted window, so nobody can see in. Long white trestle tables are set out along the space, which is on the ground floor of the house. The rooms everyone else on the Square has as their formal sitting rooms, Philip uses as his studio. He likes that, feels it to be revolutionary.

"Stupid arses," he is wont to say. "With their fancy cushions and their bloody pianos. Whereas I have a workshop in my house. A workshop!"

This is where Philip makes his sculptures.

Philip Burrell makes simulacra of holes on famous golf courses around the world.

"Everyone has their favourites," he would tell people curious to know exactly what he is sculpting.

"Everyone has their particular hole. Whether in Augusta,

or Hoylake, or Wimbledon Park. They show me what it is. I look it up on the internet. Then I recreate it for them. Sometimes I put a box underneath it. Sometimes I put it in a frame. Once I had one on wheels."

Each golf hole is perfectly recreated in wood and clay and chicken wire. Each bump and hollow and bunker, built and painted with painstaking care, right down to the tiny pin in the middle bearing a minute triangular red flag. Sometimes there are tiny trees around the edge. Occasionally, a water feature. Philip is very glad that, firstly, he was so good at Lego as a child, and secondly, that golf is such a bloody global obsession. Oh my goodness, when the Chinese discovered the joys of golf, and came into money, that was a big moment for him. He made at least a million in one year, on the Chinese golf market alone. Alone!

Along the trestle tables are golf holes of various degrees of complexity and in varying stages of completion. He has an assistant, a rough lad who comes in and helps him with the initial pieces, does the sawing and the sanding, but that is simply to help with the workload.

Philip likes to think that he, Philip Burrell, is behind every single stage of this Wonderland recreation of the beauty of the links course. Or the suburban course, hell, he doesn't mind too much where the bloody course is, although he is rather fond of the 18th at Dornoch up near Inverness. And he loves the 6th hole at Clonakilty, County Cork, because it goes over a bloody road. Typical Irish.

Philip walks between the trestle tables, white robe flowing, like a priest preparing for some sacramental offering. He touches his small creations as he does, blessing them. They have propelled him into a life of comfort and pleasure. Cherry blossom is all very well, but for real hard cash you need a proper idea. And recreating famous golf holes for clients around the world who will pay upward of £50,000 per sculpture is it.

And now he has a new idea, a rather wonderful one. He

can't wait to tell Magnus about it. He thinks it will propel him into a new stratosphere of wealth.

The front door slams as Gilda leaves the house in search of the artisan bread.

Chapter Five
Philip

Magnus lounges on the doorstep, having rung the bell. Where the hell is Philip, he thinks. He checks his phone for the time, and waits. Magnus hates waiting. Hates it. Magnus is an important dealer with a roster of artists and a clutch of galleries in the UK and abroad. In turn, each gallery has its own roster of smaller dealers, and what used to be called a Rolodex, before it all went digital, of high net worth clients, to whom he sells directly. Then there are the Art Fairs. Magnus enjoys the Art Fairs. There's Miami, and Basle. And Basle/Miami, which is when the Basle lot come to Miami. Magnus does a lot of journeying between Basle and Miami. There's also Frieze, which is accurately named as it is not only in November but also in Regent's Park, London.

Magnus has a dressing room full of perfectly cut suits for Miami and Basle, and cashmere coats for Frieze. He has a laundry service which delivers immaculately ironed shirts to him on a weekly basis. He has ties. He is about the only person he knows who still wears ties. And handkerchiefs. It goes without saying that his shirts all use cufflinks. He is beautifully turned out. He needs to be. He has dozens of artists, of course, on his books. But Philip is one of his most precious.

Magnus flogs Philip's sculptures all over the world to golfing fanatics who pay thousands to have their favourite hole immortalised in plywood and paint. Surely he owes it to them to do the deal in a smart suit. He never forgets that Philip is the goose providing the hardware. So he dresses up to see Philip, even though he internally shudders when he thinks of the dust in Philip's studio and how it will probably cling to the fabric on his jackets.

The door swings open suddenly, causing Magnus almost to fall inside, over Gilda. Magnus is rather fat, and balance is sometimes an issue. She smiles up at him triumphantly, her blue eyelids flashing under the paste jewellery on her head.

Oh why are you wearing a tiara, you crazy old thing, thinks Magnus. Of course, he doesn't say this.

"Gilda. Darling. You look ravishing. Ravish me!"

"Ah, Magnus," she cries, her Russian accent even more pronounced, leaning up into his neck, grabbing his whole spherical middle, almost lifting herself off the ground.

"Yes, well not actually on the doormat, darling," says Magnus through lashings of something he eventually identifies as Joy by Jean Patou. "I mean, ha ha, yes, well."

Somewhat ruffled, Magnus puts her down. Gilda beams, and adjusts her tiara and a strange neck collar which Magnus thinks might be made of jet but is probably black plastic, sourced from a charity shop. She is wearing flowered cropped trousers, a McQueen top detailed with harlequinesque diamonds, and golfing shoes made by Prada. The entire ensemble looks as if Gilda has just stepped out of a theatrical clothing emporium, or is trying to represent a painting by Watteau. Well, nothing's changed, thinks Magnus. Gilda always dresses in a gigglish combination of thrift shop and high-end designer. It sometimes works.

"Come through," says Gilda theatrically. "And see what Philip has in store for you."

"Lunch, I hope," says Magnus.

"Oh, there's more. Much more."

"Morning," says Magnus, stepping through the hall and greeting his star artist.

"Afternoon," says Philip to his dealer. They always talk like this. Philip has changed out of the long white robe and is wearing one of his white boiler suits, and a bow tie raffishly decorated with red hearts. Philip is the only other person in Magnus' life who wears ties, but they are always bow ties. If you ever ask him why he favours the bow tie, he will always have the same answer.

"For the same reason as a gynaecologist does."

Today, however, he merely bows solemnly and gestures for Magnus to follow.

They walk downstairs through to the knock-through kitchen and sit at a scrubbed pine kitchen table, which is decorated by an array of daisies casually popped into Robertson's jam jars.

Unlike everyone else on the Square, Philip and Gilda don't approve of the latest style in contemporary kitchens. They do not wish to live alongside stone counters, islands, bar stools, wine fridges and taps of instant boiling water. Their kitchen is dominated by a giant wooden dresser, displaying bone china tea cups and painted jugs, sourced at bijou flea markets in Sitges or Quimper. The wooden chairs are painted. The floor has rush matting on it. Nothing matches, deliberately.

Along one wall are a set of black and white photographs of Gilda looking titillatingly raunchy, in stockings and suspenders, accessorised with a balcony bra and stiletto heels. One of them also involves a feather boa which she is holding tautly between her legs. They were taken by a *Sunday Times* magazine photographer, when Gilda was quite a lot younger. Everyone on the Square longs to visit Philip and Gilda's house in order to check these pictures out.

Nobody ever has.

They are therefore spoken about with the hushed reverence usually associated with high religion, or high porn.

Philip stands in front of the black and white photos, and

holds up a bottle of wine with a quizzical air.

"Yup," says Magnus, who has a bad drink habit. Used to have a bad drugs habit too, until he was taken to one side by the director of the Basle Art Fair and told in no uncertain terms that if he carried on giving coke to the artists, he would be banned from the Fair, both in Switzerland and in Miami. For life.

"I'll get on with the bread and Brie. Bring Magnus back in ten minutes, my dove," says Gilda, tying an apron around her somewhat solid middle.

"Come up to the studio," says Philip.

The two men walk into the long, airy room where Magnus is confronted with a new object on the trestle table before him. It is a lot larger than the golf holes. A lot larger. It is higher, too, and altogether more complicated.

"Marathon courses," says Philip with a flourish.

Magnus stares at the table. He looks carefully. The piece involves a snaking long grey route weaving around various hillocks, skyscrapers and across Tower Bridge.

"The London Marathon," whispers Philip. "Run by 40,000 people a year, every year. Don't tell me one of those bastards isn't going to want to have something like this in their boardroom. Think of the scope, Magnus. Think of it."

Magnus is thinking of it. He can see the commercial opportunities at all his galleries across the world. Is there a marathon in LA? He fervently hopes so. He knows there is one in Geneva because a former girlfriend once ran it. Christ. She moaned about her hamstrings for about six months before, and six weeks after, until Magnus dumped her.

"Then there's Berlin and Boston and Chicago. There's even one in Las bloody Vegas," says Philip. "Gilda researched them all for me. There are about 200 of these bastards."

Magnus looks at Philip. Philip returns his look equably.

"How much?"

"Yes, how much?"

"I am a famous artist. Probably the most famous artist in

the country. Certainly the most famous artist in this city."

Yes, well, thinks Magnus. As long as you keep bringing in the money. And there might be quite a lot of money in marathon courses. Maybe even more than in golf holes, frankly. Although the manpower needed to make them, and the time, and the materials... I need to take soundings on this, he thinks. Consult my Board. But Philip is already slapping down virtual figures for Magnus to salivate over.

"£150,000? I think possibly even more. Quarter of a million? Look how fucking big it is, Magnus. It will cost me, though. This took over a week. If I get an order book going, I'll have to hire not only that boy from the estate but also all his friends to help me build it, you know."

"It's tempting. Very good. Very good. Makes golf holes look pretty basic by comparison."

Philip raises an eyebrow.

"Although basic is what they are, of course, not," says Magnus hurriedly.

"Let's talk about it anon. Shall we have lunch?"

"Yes, yes. Of course. Gilda will be expecting us."

Just as Philip and Magnus have a formal manner of speaking, they also have a formal way of eating lunch together. Magnus knows the routine. Gilda will have laid the table as if for a three course meal. There will be proper cutlery, and napkins, and two glasses per setting. Good, thinks Magnus, for whom eating is an important event.

Before sitting down, guests must stand with the two hosts alongside the chairs, and bow their heads while Gilda recites a humanist prayer.

Magnus and Philip take their places. Gilda takes the tiara off before leaning forward and incanting the prayer.

"As we eat, let us turn our minds to every individual we know and wish them plenty, love and comfort on this day and every day. As we celebrate, let us turn our minds and hearts to love, always love, of everyone in this world."

Philip and Gilda draw back their chairs, and sit down.

"Excuse me," says Magnus, stepping back, taking leave to go to the downstairs cloakroom. As he stands before the toilet, urinating, his eye wanders as always over the bas-relief nature of the cloakroom. Tiny sculptures dot the surface of the walls. It was only after he had been going to Philip's house for a while that it dawned on him these sculptures were not strangely shaped coat hooks, but plaster cast mouldings of Gilda's genitals. Well, he had always assumed they were Gilda's. They might be another woman and Gilda together, or another woman/women completely.

This time, as he casually gazes at the assemblages of labia, clitoris and vulva he notes that there is indeed a discrepancy of size. Maybe there are a whole lot of women here, he thinks, washing his hands and drying them on a towel which reads Royal Hotel Newquay. The Burrell downstairs toilet is of course another fevered talking point on the Square, which nobody had seen but everybody wanted to. Jane once called it the Burrell Collection, which she thought was very funny indeed.

Over the Brie and artisan bread, which Magnus pulls apart fastidiously and crams into his mouth rather less politely, Gilda brings Jane into the conversation. She had bumped into her on the way to the bakers'.

"I met Jane on the way to Craven's," she announces, putting her small hands flatly onto the table. Magnus notices how perfectly she has painted each tiny nail. Pearl pink, with a shimmering white tip. French manicures. Christ, he hasn't seen a French manicure for years.

"Oh yes," says Philip, abstractly.

"Jane?" says Magnus.

"Bitch who lives on the Square. No, not the bitch you are thinking of. Another bitch. Not the one I fancy, ha ha."

Magnus hates it when Philip descends into bawdiness, but like everyone else, he puts up with it. He looks at Gilda. She is looking down, staring at her hands. She is quite used to the way Philip sometimes insists on talking.

"Anyway, seems as if Jane is organising a big fundraiser for us here. To get new railings or something."

"Fundraiser! As if there's not stacks of money in every single bloody household here. Christ Almighty." Philip grew up on benefits in an impoverished household near Truro, and would like everyone to remember it.

"Nightingale. May I continue?"

"I'm listening," says Magnus gently, covering one of her tiny hands with his. He's rather fond of the mad old bat, in her tiara.

"Anyway. The idea is to have a Talent Show."

There is silence around the table. Philip raises his chin.

"Talent!" he says eventually. "What, what on earth do this lot know about talent? Laywers and bankers, the lot of them. There's only one real talent in the whole bloody place, and you are looking at him."

Gilda puts a hand on his cuff. "We know, darling. We know. But you know, sometimes, you have to let people have a go."

She's quite clever, thinks Magnus. In terms of dealing with Philip, she vacillates between being a child and the persona of a mother.

Philip snorts. "What did she want us to do, then?"

"Oh, I don't think anything. She just wanted to let us know it was happening."

"Nothing? You share a neighbourhood with someone who had their own stand at the Frieze Art Fair, and you don't want to have a sniff at their talent? She didn't want me to be involved? Christ Almighty. They are lucky to have me on their doorstep, bloody lucky."

"Well, I think she is open to suggestions, my shooting star. Why don't you suggest something? I mean, why don't you give a talk?"

"Yes, yes," muses Philip. "A talk, maybe that's the thing."

Magnus has had enough artisan bread and Brie. He has also had enough wine. He now has a strong urge to leave this lunch and this chat about the neighbours, and get back to his office where he can have some decent coffee and do some serious thinking about the marathon pieces, how much he could get for them and how the hell he will exhibit them. All of that will be left to him to work out, he knows it. Philip Burrell may have started out in a garrett doing everything himself. He certainly doesn't do that now. He pays 50% to his dealer and expects his dealer to sweat blood for it. Magnus feels that before he can leave it will be incumbent on him to solve the Talent Show conundrum. Philip clearly wants to be involved.

"Well, you could sell an old piece. What about one of the golf holes that nobody wants? You know, that one of the 4th at Augusta which was commissioned by the man who went bust. We've still got that in the gallery. You could have an auction for it. Might raise thousands, you know."

He stands to leave, catches a glimpse of the photos of Gilda in her underwear, remembers the moulded genitalia and is struck by a bright idea.

"I've got it. Why don't you offer tours around your house? £20 a head. You'd clean up. Probably make enough to redo the whole bloody Square, and then some."

Chapter Six
Tracey

It's true. There isn't much money in nails. Or, indeed, door-to-door makeup sales at the moment.

At the appointed hour, Tracey is ready. She is not a woman who is late, hates it. She looks at Belle and Grace, her daughters. She worries whether they are ever going to live up to the aspirational female attributes of their names. Each is intently focused on a tiny hand held screen.

"Dad's going to look after you tonight. What about your prep, Grace?" she says.

"Talk to the hand, Mum," says Grace, not looking up.

"What?" Tracey hates that phrase. "I am asking you about your prep."

"No-one calls it prep any more. Too posh. These days, it's just called homework."

Stung, Tracey whips out a response.

"What, even at your posh school? It's called The Prep, for God's sake! How can you outlaw a word which is part of your own identity?"

Grace simply shrugs and carries on tapping the screen.

Tracey thinks of that school. The fees. The uniform. Her mind clicks through the whole morning routine. The mothers outside. Their perfect jeans. Their bags. Their bags.

Sometimes she thinks it would have been better if they had never had any money at all, never had such a giant bloody windfall, then they wouldn't have had to move house, sign up to the private way, BUPA, schools, bookshops not libraries, private clubs not the local pool, everything. Life might have been a bit easier.

The door bell rings.

"Prep, homework, I don't care what you bloody call it. You're doing it. That is Harriet and she is taking me out, so Belle you will have to be in charge for a while. Until Daddy gets home. Please make sure Grace does her homework."

"Oooh, Mummy's swearing," sighs Belle.

"That's £1 in the Swear Box for you, Mummy," says Grace with prim delight. Why are my children ranged against me, thinks Tracey vaguely.

"But we'll let you off," shouts Grace, "because we know you haven't got any money any more!"

She can't even put a quid in the kids' fucking swear box.

Which makes it two quid. Although she didn't actually articulate that curse, so it doesn't count.

The door bell rings again.

"Harriet."

"Tracey."

They embrace. Tracey grasps Harriet's bulk, inhaling her personal bouquet of tobacco and perfume. Harriet must be one of the last people in London, if not the UK, to still be a smoker.

"Alright, so what are we seeing?" says Tracey.

"You'll love it. We are going to the Book Fair and we are going to hear Alan Makin talking live," announces Harriet, with a grin.

"Oh, my goodness!" shouts Tracey, clapping nail varnish to lipstick. "Really?"

To the Max with Makin. God, she thinks. I hope Harriet doesn't think we are broke, because we are not. Just a bit skint. At the moment.

"Alan Makin, visiting our weedy little Book Fair?"

She is amazed that he is on the programme. Alan Makin is a star of financial daytime television. The man in a linen suit who says you should always keep a grip on your money. The man who advocates weekly budget sessions and spreadsheets and other things which just make Tracey's head ache. Yes, that might be useful. She's also excited to have the chance to see someone from television, just down the road in a marquee. As if they have been spirited directly from the airwaves. This is the sort of thing which happens in her life now. Her new life, her post-Lottery life. Christ, she is glad it happened to them.

"You are quite, quite brilliant," she says. "Do you know, I've always wanted to meet him. Bye, girls."

There is a hummed response from the screens. Neither girl looks up. Tracey leaves the room and opens the front door.

She smiles at a plump man in a very well-cut suit, walking quickly away from Philip Burrell's house. He smiles back, nods his head.

"Anyone you know?" says Harriet.

"No, at least I don't think so. See him quite often, though. I think he might have something to do with, you know, that artist Philip Burrell. His agent or something."

"Probably runs his gallery," says Harriet. "Selling all that stupid sporting stuff. Do you know I saw an ad for one of those golf sculptures the other day, it was going for £20,000. Loony."

Even though she's won the Lottery, Tracey doesn't want to grapple with the idea of people spending the equivalent of a year's school fees on a sculpture of a golf hole.

"Do you think I am smart enough?" she asks Harriet. Harriet surveys the tight skirt, the tiny cropped jumper with the words *Bien Sûr* emblazoned on the front, the leather coat. Dear Tracey, she thinks. She never gets it quite right. Well, that's what happens when money just falls in people's laps, isn't it. Wasn't brought up to know how to spend it.

Harriet conceals her thoughts, and smiles. "You're fine," she says. She is swathed in a giant pashmina and Ugg boots.

"So, is it true that you really always wanted to meet Alan Makin?" They step out into the Square.

Tracey arches her eyebrows. "Are you kidding? My mum thinks everything he says is gold dust."

"Well, I don't know if you'll meet him, but you'll certainly hear him and see him. I'm so glad I got you a ticket. Are you interested in his financial brilliance? Or do you just like seeing people off the telly?"

"Both," says Tracey. "I mean, it's not like we are stony broke, or anything, but… "

"Oh, I know… " says Harriet quickly, opening the car door.

"… Its just nice to know you are doing the right thing with the money that you have."

"Absolutely."

"Because, you know, sometimes you feel a bit, you know… "

"I know."

"You know."

"I know."

"Skint."

"Yeah!"

Why are English people so crap at talking about money, thinks Tracey. Ever since we, ever since she and Larry, since IT happened, talking about money has been more difficult, not easier. You'd have thought that having money, a lot of money, would make it better, but it hasn't. And now, what with the money they spent on the house and school fees and her cosmetics business slowing down quite a lot, things are beginning to look a bit tight again. Tracey doesn't quite know how that has happened, even having two million quid suddenly slammed into her life, but somehow, it has. Everything suddenly went up a notch. Bags, cars, houses. Piano lessons.

Harriet drives ferociously to the Book Fair, quickly smoking two cigarettes on the way.

"Love smoking at the wheel," she says. "Best place to do it. It always gives me a thrilling illusion of being in control."

Tracey smiles and quietly opens the window.

At the Book Fair, several hundred chairs are set up in front of a small temporary stage, on which is positioned a large easy chair behind a desk, with a microphone and a large name board. There is also a banner over the desk. Both read 'ALAN MAKIN, Taking You Through The Good, The Bad and The Ugly in The Finances Game!'

A steady stream of people are taking their seats in the tent. Most people are over forty. No students or teenagers here. These are all grown-up people with money issues, thinks Tracey. She hopes very much that she won't bump into anyone she knows. Or any of her cosmetics customers. God, that would be awful. She'd have to pretend she was there for professional reasons, make out that Alan had hired her or something. It would be so embarrassing.

She and Harriet take up their seats somewhere towards the back, and shiver out of their coats. Tracey starts to think the event might be quite amusing after all.

"This is great," she whispers to Harriet. "A night out, watching a celebrity but also doing something virtuous." It's fun to be out of the house, and at an event. Even if it's an event devoted to thinking about overdrafts. She notices that other people are quite brazen about being there, waving and shouting 'Hi!' to acquaintances on the other side of the marquee. Maybe, she thinks, that because there is a famous person in the room, they think they have become a little bit famous too.

At precisely 7pm, the lights dim, and Alan Makin springs onto the stage. He is a very fair man with aviator glasses. He is wearing one of his famous light-coloured linen suits. He waves at everyone.

Alan Makin's Unique Selling Point is that he tries to make

paying off debt seem thrilling.

"Good evening, all!"

Harriet turns round and pulls a face.

"He's a lot smaller than he is on the TV, isn't he? I hope I haven't wasted your time, sweetie."

"No," says Tracey. She is transfixed by watching someone from the screen existing in real time just before her eyes.

"Tonight, I am going to educate, entertain and inspire! I am going to help you all become better investors and to learn how to deal with debt. Because debt must be dealt with. Do we not agree?" thunders Makin.

The audience murmurs sheepishly.

"Doesn't it?" booms Makin.

"YES!" shouts the audience back at him.

"Tonight, we are going to understand THE WAY FORWARD." He steps one pace forward on the stage. Harriet and Tracey exchange grimaces.

"I am going to leave you wanting to TAKE ACTION!"

"I believe this is what's known as ecstatic economy talk," whispers Harriet, laughing.

"Who feels their debts are impossible to deal with?" continues Alan Makin, stalking the stage. A few people raise their arms, but it is only to take photos of Alan Makin on their phones.

"Who is trying to bury their head, and their bank balance in the sand? Like an ostrich? Who thinks they cannot live without going shopping? Who has been fooled by promises of 0% interest rates, and then finds themselves shelling out interest to credit card companies which comes in at 35%?"

Various hands go up.

"Ostriches, you are going to change your ways. Earn it first, then spend it," says Alan. "That's what you are going to learn tonight. Earn it, then spend it. Not the other way round."

He then dives into an anecdote. It is not a long and winding road. In Alan's expert hands, it is a short, straight road.

"Once upon a time I had more debt than I was earning

on an annual basis. Can you possibly imagine what my bank charges were?"

Knowing laughter ripples around the room. Tracey looks at the audience. Nobody looks obviously impoverished. They all look like people who would normally attend an annual Book Festival. She's feeling happy, in the presence of Alan Makin. He seems to be exuding a sort of glow. She nudges Harriet.

"He's rather adorable."

"I gave myself eighteen months to pay it off," continues Alan. "I was working at the Post Office. I took no trips. I bought no clothes. Whenever I travelled anywhere, I went on the bus. I sold my car. I worked every nightshift, holiday and extra hours that I could. I substituted for everyone on my team. Gradually, I shifted that debt. And do you know what it taught me? It taught me that nothing is worth having the stress of a huge debt. Earn it first! Then spend it! Not the other way round."

After the anecdotes, Makin encourages people to come up on stage. They sit on a stool, Alan sits behind his desk, and gives them a four-minute Money Makeover, as honed on his eponymous *TV Makeovers*, as explained by him in his *Daily Mail* columns, and as written about in his numerous books, sold at airports around the world. Because debt, as Alan is fond of saying, is global. Tracey finds herself wondering whether he is married.

"Do you think he's gay?" she whispers to Harriet.

Harriet tilts her head back, and surveys Alan.

"Could be. That suit. But no. I don't know." She looks at him through half-closed eyes, as if that will give something away.

"I don't know," she finally says.

Meanwhile, Alan, unaware of this scrutiny, is well into his stride. He deals with each person on stage in the same way.

First, he starts with praise:

"You should be proud of yourself. Your own business? Five children? A sculpture studio in the garden? Well done."

Then it quickly transmutes to humiliation.

"What? You have an overdraft of £25,000, and an addiction to catalogue shopping and a beach hut worth £60,000, and you can't make ends meet? Sell it! Sell it, unsubscribe, and don't look back!"

A middle-aged man grins and stumbles away off the podium.

A serious-looking woman of fifty is next up.

"Am I hearing you correctly?" yells Makin. "You are earning an annual income of £55,000 and you can't work out how to pay your tax bill? Don't avoid those letters coming in. Tax evasion is dealt with so seriously!"

She nods furiously.

Then she leans over and gives Alan a huge kiss. Being publicly humiliated by Alan Makin has clearly delighted her.

"Thanks, sweetie. Next!"

His next victim is a younger man with glasses, who confesses he wishes to build up a property portfolio.

"You want to do buy to let? With debts of over £48,000? You are out of control with your desire to own property. Take control of yourself!"

The man shrugs his shoulders and looks at his shoes.

"What is your overdraft like?" demands Alan. "Well, I've got about £20,000 in unsecured debt," he confesses.

"Talk me through your assets," says Alan.

"Err, house. Flat in Courchevel. Er, Car. Sports car. Merc. Err, plasma screen telly," says the man. He grins cheekily. "Although I don't know that I could call that an asset, since what's on is just rubbish."

Alan glares. He is the gag master around here. Plus, he gets a lot of income from his daytime TV franchised shows.

"Well, you need to simplify your life," he says. "Minimalism. That should be the life-changing mantra for you. Say it as you cut up those cards, as you sell the plasma TV, as you flog the ski flat. You need to be rational. You are way over-leveraged. Thank you."

However, the man doesn't want to leave the stage humbly.

He doesn't seem to notice that his time is up with Alan Makin.

"But I thought it was good to be aspirational," he retorts. "And keep money circulating in the market. Isn't that Keynesian? Isn't that capitalism?"

Everyone laughs.

Makin moves into aggressive mode with the speed of an accelerating BMW.

"You feel pretty good about yourself, don't you?" he says to the man. "Like you've made it. But you haven't. In fact, the little I know about you, and your money situation, I already would say you are way off making it."

Gosh, that's a bit below the belt, thinks Tracey.

"You come up here with your plasma screen, and your Merc, and you start to brag to us all about your ambitions to be a property mogul, and tell us how in debt you are. You are living in folly! And I will make you see it."

The man goggles at Makin.

All at once, Tracey stands up. She doesn't know how she is suddenly standing up, but she is. She needs to prick this man's balloon. She doesn't care that he is from the TV. She's had enough of it.

"What are you doing?" hisses Harriet.

"Mr Makin," shouts Tracey, waving urgently. "I have a question for you. Is this the point?"

Alan Makin looks slightly irritated. He squints out into the body of the marquee to answer her. He also looks at his watch. Tracey blusters on, aware of Harriet staring at her from somewhere by her right elbow.

"What's that?" shouts Alan across the hall.

"I mean, what is your definition of Making It? For you it might be wealth. Or fame. For other people it might be other things. Raising a family. Looking after an ageing parent. Being a great friend. Overdrafts aren't the end of the world, are they? I mean, are they?"

Everyone applauds.

Alan Makin looks thunderously at her. After the first thrill of adrenalin, Tracey is beginning to wonder how she can end this confrontation, and sit down again.

"He probably didn't mean to become overdrawn," she continues in a faltering voice, pointing at the man on stage. The man nods vigorously at her.

"No, I didn't," he shouts back to Tracey.

Cheers from the audience. This inspires her.

"Nobody in this tent did."

Alan gives him a withering look.

"None of us did," continues Tracey. "Debt just happened. Crept up on us. Somehow owing hundreds of pounds became owing thousands of pounds, and then tens of thousands, and then the figures stopped relating to actual money, and just turned into little black marks on a piece of paper."

Everyone has turned round and is now looking at her.

"All that happens from the credit card companies is that you get a bill." She pauses. "With the interest rate written down in monthly figures, so it looks terrifically small, and a nice message saying all you have to do is pay the minimum fee, which is minuscule. And then it offers you Increased Credit."

More nods, and a few claps.

"It doesn't have anything to do with making it, or not making it, or whether you are a success in life or not. It really doesn't. About whether you are a fantastic mother, or a fantastic wife." She pauses. Should she confess? "Do you know I have an overdraft, even after winning the bloody Lottery a few years ago!"

This gets a laugh.

"Oh, God Tracey," moans Harriet beside her. "Please shut up."

"Oh, I remember now. The famous Lottery couple. Looks like you need a Makin Makeover," says Alan, recovering his poise. "But not now. Next time!"

Tracey takes this as a signal to sit down, and does. She is shaking, slightly. Harriet looks at her, smiling tightly.

"That was weird."

"Sorry, Harriet, do you think that was rude?"

"No," says Harriet, whose face indicates otherwise.

"Really sorry, Harriet. I just felt... I felt for that man on stage."

"No, it's fine. It was funny. Not sure about the Lottery mention, but never mind."

Middle class people are so uptight about the Lottery, thinks Tracey. She then wonders, as she always does, how what Larry did, winning a bit of money, well quite a lot of money, on the Lottery, is really any different from winning a bonus on the Stock Market.

Alan shakes hands with the man on stage, and claps him on the back.

The agent steps up to the microphone. "Alan will be signing books here for everyone. Please form an orderly queue."

When they get back to the Square, Harriet drops her off and leans across the passenger seat.

"You were great," she says, exuding the bitter stench of tobacco over Tracey.

"Not too weird?" Tracey says, still worried.

"No, no. It was fine. Why don't you get in touch with Alan Makin, though. I dare you! You never know. He might have you on one of his shows. He could do a Makeover on you, and you could say all that stuff again, on TV. Apart from the Lottery bit, of course. But seriously, Tracey, he might help you out with your overdraft."

She thinks about it at night, lying in bed, surrounded by the evidence of her lucky, lucky win; the perfect house, the immaculate kitchen, a wardrobe full of shoes, quietly existing in the soft darkness all around her.

Chapter Seven
Roberta

She's knows she is lucky to have an allotment. She got it under the Austerity Enterprise scheme from the local council. It used to belong to some woman who never used it. She did use it, actually, but not for vegetables. She just grew sunflowers on it. This was regarded as inessential. It was taken away from her. Now it belongs to the piano teacher who plants vegetables in it.

Roberta's back aches. This has got to be the last row. Please let it be the last row. She looks back at the small pots. How many are there? Fifteen? Twenty? Surely she can put these all in the same row, can't she?

Are leeks a less deserving enterprise than sunflowers? Is a beautiful flower, which manages to swivel round and look at the sun every day, less important than a leek? The council certainly judged so, and Roberta, whose name was first on the waiting list, was the beneficiary of that judgement. Food before art.

She bends down stiffly and quickly picks up a little pot, holding it by its plastic rim. The ribbons of bright green in the centre of the pot wave encouragingly. Carefully, she tips the dome of soft compost into her gloved hand. It falls easily into her palm, the sandcastle shape contained by a web of thick white latticed roots leading to the fleshy cylindrical core. She dusts crumbs of soil from the long ribbons. Leeks.

She pushes the raised line of soil askance with her toe, and puts the leek into it. Still crouching down, she picks up the next pot. Squatting now, she swiftly decants the baby leeks, pot after pot, into the open ground, each in its allotted place. After three, she stands up, stretches, walks along and squats down to plant three more in their places. Allotted, on the allotment. At last the job is completed.

She stands up and walks along the row, treading down the rich black compost with her boot, walking carefully so the flat long emerald leaves aren't imprinted with its muddy sole. The light is nondescript, the sun absent. She hears children shouting on their way home from school.

They sprouted last year, tiny green hairs in miniature square containers made of card, their nursery the sunny, wind-free world of her kitchen table. A packet's worth. Then, she pricked them out into larger pots. Now she's planting them in the garden for the winter, a task as ancient as it is repetitive. She'll have leeks all season long. Braised, stirred with olive oil over a gentle heat, simmered with melted cheese tempering the blackened edges.

Hanon is repetitive too, considers Roberta. Repetitive exercises designed to strengthen the fingers and improve fluency. She'd rather play the piano than plant leeks. But this means a winter's free vegetables.

Eighteen months, for three rows of leeks. Does anyone ever think about this in Waitrose? Do they hell.

Later, back at home, washing the soil off her hands, stretching her aching back, she feels content with her morning. She considers the small leeks now securely wrapped underground. Completely free, bar the 30p for the packet of seeds. She got the compost from Patrick, who gave her a whole bag of it. Fifty litres. Why do they always measure compost in terms of liquid?

"Robs, old thing, we never use this, why don't you take

it?" he had said to her bluffly one day, after she had finished teaching and was bringing her cup into the kitchen before leaving. Patrick was dangling a bag from his hand.

"Bought by Jane in one of her mad gardening schemes. Lost interest after about a week, ha ha! But I know you have an allotment. Would you like it? I'll give you a trowel too, if you like."

She had slipped the trowel, its red unused blade and still shiny wooden handle, testifying that it had never been left out all night in a flower bed, into her coat pocket and awkwardly lugged the long, heavy plastic bag back home on the bus that night, slightly worried it might mix with petrol fumes and explode. Wasn't that how the IRA used to make its bombs? Fertiliser and petrol? She's not sure.

Food before art.

But that's not true, she thinks, sitting at her upright, playing Bach's Prelude No. 1 in C Major, the first of the Forty-Eight Preludes and Fuges. Art is food.

She breaks off, notices her answerphone winking at her. She gets up from the stool, rewinds it. This machine is about to be as defunct as a typewriter, she notes. She'll have to upgrade to something digital and seamless. She reaches the beginning of the tiny tape, presses Play.

"Hello, Roberta, it's Tracey here," says Tracey. "Listen, Roberta, I need to talk to you about Belle. I've been thinking, well, she's been thinking about her piano playing, and it's sort of made me start thinking, about next term's lessons. Can you call me please? Any time."

Roberta feels her stomach clench. She knows very well what that sort of message means. It means 'my daughter is fed up with her lessons and wants to stop, and as I have done my parental duty to introduce her to the piano, I want to stop too.' That's the start.

It is a piece in four movements. First, comes the theme. I want my child to stop learning. Then there are usually two variations on it. "Well, I'm not going to stand in her way,

68

because the effort has become too great." That's the first variation. "Of course (laughs) we all know she will regret it when she is thirty, but that's teenagers for you." This is the second variation. "As Oscar Wilde probably never said, education is wasted on the young, ha ha, now thank you so much for all your hard work, really. Thanks so much, Roberta."

Finally, the coda. "Of course we will recommend you to all and sundry, you have been absolutely amaaazing, good night." Exeunt, to rapturous applause and the scraping sound of a bank account, her own bank account, at rock bottom.

No more Bach tonight. She tucks her hair behind her ears. She stretches her aching back. She pulls down the file above her piano, opens it. On it is a list of names each written carefully in a column. At the top of the page, a large heading:

The Square. It's the list of all her pupils. So far, there are no purple lines through the names. Parents in the Square do not want to deny their children piano lessons. If Tracey prevails, she will be the first to do it. And her move might encourage others.

Roberta looks at the precious list of names. She thinks about Belle. Then she thinks about George. Boy George. Only a child, but with the singular cleverness and adult grace of the singleton.

After his lesson last week he had lingered by the Blüthner grand, standing there in his shorts, his finger tracing the bright walnut grain with its shapes of skulls and berries.

"Roberta."

"What is it?" she had said. "You did well today. Really well."

"I need your help."

She was slightly alarmed. Her relationship with George was uncomplicated, and this she found relaxing. What was the boy going to confess to her now?

"You know there is to be a Talent Show here. Later on," he eventually blurted out.

Her first thought was simply marvelling at how this community will stop at nothing to proclaim how amazing it is in every way. Her second thought was one of genuine curiosity.

"Oh, George, how fascinating. What will you show off to everyone?"

George sighed mournfully.

"Mother says I must play the piano."

Of course.

"Well, that might not be so ghastly. What would you like to do?"

"Well, I am much better at building Lego, but if Mother says it, then the piano," – he tapped Middle C with a small digit – "it must be."

"Why don't you do both?"

"What, build Lego to music? My dear Roberta, I don't think so."

"Yes, but, let's think, I know, why not show a film? With Lego characters. You know, on a stop-frame animation. And then play a piano as accompaniment to it. You could have a screen up in the hall, or wherever the Talent Show will be."

He gaped at her. She could see the idea take fire by the light in his face.

"Could I? Why, yes, I could," he said, as if she wasn't there. He was quite used to holding conversations with himself.

"It won't be in a hall, but we could have a screen out in the park. Right above the piano. Roberta, thank you. I will go and start crafting the screenplay right away!"

She started packing up her bag, smiling to herself. He might not be an infant Mozart, but he had initiative, she'll give him that.

"Righty-o. I'll have a think about what you might play to go alongside. I assume you will have some form of keyboard with you?"

"Oh, certainly. I think Mamma is letting this old thing out for the night."

A Blüthner? Outside? These people.

She stops musing about George. She calls Tracey. Before the call, she runs through the conversation in her mind, although she instinctively knows what she has to do. She must concoct a conversation so clever, so adroit, so full of acknowledgement of what the child has, what the child could have, that the parent will fear missing it. Furthermore, alongside this positive strand, she must also present a parallel sense of fear, a dark foreboding about what the child might be missing out on, the entire boundless and bountiful world of the piano repertoire, eternal and endlessly sustaining, a glorious future that Tracey, and more importantly Belle, can in no way even contemplate being part of once the appropriately named fall of the piano, in other words the lid, has been slammed down on it.

At the same time, she must subtly remind Tracey, the committed parent, of things that perhaps Roberta herself does not hold all that special, but she's pretty sure Tracey does because every single parent on the Square does. Firstly, there is the glory, the parental pride in the prizes that might be forthcoming, prizes for her offspring, the Grades taken, the applause, perhaps even a medal, of the words of marvel hanging in the air from peers that Belle can indeed justify thanks to the complete mastery of E Flat Minor (harmonic and melodic) and some Chopin preludes.

Now, thanks to George, she also has a Talent Show to add to the cornucopia.

She must remind her of Belle's Life Chances. Of her Personal Statements, pieces of writing to achieve a university place, in which commitment to an instrument – it doesn't really matter which, (but piano is the top, surely, along with the violin) – is proof of superior brain power and discipline.

Roberta clearly has not emphasised this enough in her lessons so far with Belle. So, a three point plan is needed. These are the things she must highlight. The value to the child. The acclaim to the parent. The fragility of the future.

These are the things that Roberta has to drum into Tracey's perfectly coiffed head, in order to keep the precious booking, which is worth £60 a week to Roberta.

She rolls her shoulders. Maybe she should cut her rate. No. She can hardly get by with what she is currently earning, no matter how many leeks she plants.

Up until now, she has – foolishly, she now realises – thought that music was enough for the appetite of families in the Square, but it is not.

She picks the phone reciever up.

Chapter Eight
George

Having ensured complete privacy by positioning the Do Not Disturb sign on the handle of his bedroom door, George pulls his mother's bra out of the pocket of his hoodie and inspects it, turning it over in his hands. What a construction, he thinks. All those straps and hooks and hard metal bits, covered with frills in order to look soft. If you're not wearing it, what could one do with it? He has no intention of giving it back to her. He assumes it's hers anyway. Doesn't know who else it could belong to.

He gets a pair of scissors from his desk. He wants to deconstruct it. Those pointed cups would look awesome in his *Star Wars* desert assemblage, quite honestly. They could be alongside the Pods and the Lunar Landing Craft. Actually, he thinks, breathing heavily, his mouth moving with the excitement, they would look like those sand dunes that C3P0 walks over at the beginning of... one of the films, he can't remember which one, but his mind is alive with possibility. Anyway, playing the piano to a film showing his Lego pieces in action would be awesome, he knows it.

He picks up the scissors and prepares to liberate the cup from the strap of his mother's underwear. It is harder than he thinks; he is not ready for the tough white plastic below the cup. How do ladies wear this sort of stuff? Doesn't it hurt them?

After a few minutes of concentrated effort, he is rewarded with two separate moulded cones of coffee-coloured lace, supported by seams and curved pieces of white plastic. He tosses away the straps in a bin. George likes his room to be tidy.

He enjoys knowing where everything is in his room, like a pair of scissors or a protractor. So he can get right down to work with whatever is uppermost in his mind, be it a Wombles book, or building his Lego. Actually, scrap the Wombles book. He liked the first two, but felt that after that, the series ran out of steam. His father insisted on reading all seven to him, however, so he was forced to listen for practically the whole of the Autumn Term last year, but did so from politeness rather than actual interest. He was aware that this book, the Wombles, was something his father had 'grown up with' and so had to be experienced again. Parents were like that, George knew. Always keener on things they had known when they were young. Well, not always a bad thing. It worked with Lego, at least. Because both his father and mother had played with it, and knew it, and weren't afraid of it, they were always okay about buying him more of the stuff. Whereas if it had been a new thing, he suspected they would have regarded it with suspicion, as they did with anything electronic.

He sighs, idly scratches his hair, positions Cup One beside his Droid Destroyer and looks at it. It sort of worked. If you could forget where it came from. Maybe if you built some sort of covering frame around it, to hold it in position, that might work. He'd attend to that later. He puts Cup Two in a drawer, replaces his scissors in the Deloitte pen holder (which he had been given by his father after a conference, along with a bag, a pen and a baseball cap), and saunters downstairs.

As he reaches his parent's room he wonders how many other bras his mother has in stock, as it were. He pushes open the door and walks in, inhaling the strange sensation of adult privacy which he found always lingered in the bedroom of a parent, anyone's parent, but most of all, his.

He toys with opening his mother's top drawer, running his fingers along it, but then sees the door of the ensuite bathroom is slightly ajar.

George loves going into his parents' bathroom, because it it is frowned upon by his parents, and he is never allowed to go there. "You have your own bathroom, darling," his mother would say to him. "That ought to be enough. Honestly! When I was young, I had to line up with my sister and we had to share a bath… " and on and on she would go like that.

But here he is, suddenly, in the forbidden room. It's exciting. George looks round, wondering which of the attractions he ought to experience first. First, he has a look at his father's electric razor. Then, he weighs himself. The needle reads two stone six pounds. Is that a lot, or not enough? He has no idea. It's fun, standing on the scales. I wonder how much I can make myself weigh, he thinks, jumping on them. The needle swings frantically to seven stone. It doesn't appear to go right back to zero, however, so he gets off quickly and kicks the scales underneath a towel.

He looks at himself in the giant mirrored wall beside the bath, opens the mirrored door of the cabinet above the basin. Then he stands in the middle, between the two, and waves his arms, marvelling at how the dual reflections go back into a sort of corridor of infinity. He always does this. It's a bit like being inside the Doctor Who title sequence.

After about five minutes, George remembers to examine the contents of the cabinet over the basin. As he did last time. And as last time, the cabinet seems to to contain a lot of very dull stuff such as Pepto-Bismol. And plasters, and athlete's foot powder.

There is another cabinet, however, on the opposite wall, which George hopes might prove more fruitful. He crosses the room and swings it open. It it is crammed with devices and products for every facet of Jane's complex beauty regimen. Eyelash curlers. Eyebrow dye. Bikini wax strips. Nose strips. Masks. And a lot of removers. Cuticle removers, hair removers, spot removers. Alongside removers, there are all sorts of creams. What is the difference between creme and cream, thinks George.

His mother certainly has a lot of both creams, and cremes. Looks like she has a special cream for every single part of her body. Face cream. Creme de Corps. Foot cream. Hand cream. Neck cream. Nail cream. Eyelid cream. Thrush cream. What can that mean, wonders George. Something about a bird, maybe.

He reaches in, sees something else in the cupboard. He pulls it out. It is a small pink battery driven device with two ears on it. He switches it on. It jumps around in his hand. Wasn't his mother mad, having electronic toys in her bathroom? Wasn't that dangerous? He had always been told it was dangerous to have electricity in a bathroom. He holds the toy, lingering over it, wondering why it quivers as it does.

He would quite like to keep it upstairs in his room, but something about its very pink, squidgy nature and unsettling suggestion of entertainment makes him think this is a private toy, or something medicinal perhaps, that his mother does not want to find by accident anywhere else in the house. He replaces it carefully and softly closes the cabinet.

He quickly uses the toilet, remembering to flush it. Forgetting to wash his hands, he tiptoes out of the ensuite bathroom and goes downstairs to answer the door bell, which he realises is ringing.

It's Anya on the front doorstep. George looks up at her, smiling. "My mother is… "

"… Not here?" says Anya.

"No. She had to go out for about two hours. She said I was not to answer the door. Oh, whoops."

"George. If your mother says you are not to answer the door, try to remember that. Never mind. It's only me. Now, you know your piano teacher Roberta? Who teaches you the piano."

George bows in assent.

"I was wondering, if she could come over today?"

"Today? But my lesson isn't until Friday. Plus I haven't practised."

"No, not for you. For Belle. Our piano is broken and Roberta is on her way over to our house, in order to give Belle her lesson. You know Belle, don't you? Grace's big sister. Would that be alright?"

George raises his eyebrows, as if shouldering the metaphorical weight of the household and all the decisions thereof.

"Should think so. What time?"

"In about half an hour."

"Good. Mother will be back by then, I should think."

He closes the door carefully and walks back into the house. He's not sure how he feels about sharing his piano.

Chapter Nine
Jane

It is so dangerous, but then danger is part of the allure.

"Is it the whole allure?" says Jay, lazily tracing his finger down her back. It is mottled and livid with red scratches.

She shivers with pleasure, rolls over and looks up at him.

"Of course not."

At Jane's house, Roberta is teaching Belle on the lovely Blüthner. But Jane doesn't know this, because she and Jay have stopped meeting in each other's houses. After the near miss in the hall, she has insisted on meeting for sex in hotels.

But it must be done in the proper, acknowledged way. Hotels. This is how the adulterous act. Booking a day room in a hotel. Several days beforehand. You can't just turn up and ask for a room, it must be done in advance. Otherwise you might be mistaken for a prostitute. You have to ring up a day or two beforehand and say, with great authority,

'I need a day room. I am travelling in from London, and I need to rest for a while.' After you have done this once, you then just ring up the same hotel and say, with the same authority,

'A day room, please.'

Does the hotel suspect? Probably. The hotel acknowledges she needs a day room. Jane pretends the hotel believes this need. The appurtenance of propriety to the necessity of the day room is crucial.

Although today, she acknowledged, was a bit more complicated than most. She had forgotten that George was going to be off on an Inset Day. She remembered, with a swoop of guilt laced with love, laced with guilt again, how he used to call them Insect Days. When she had found out that this term's Insect/Inset Day clashed with the day she had pre-booked in the hotel, her day, the day for her and Jay, she had toyed with the idea of cancelling, but knew deep down that she would be unable to. She couldn't bear to cancel her assignment for sex.

George would be alright on his own in the house for a few hours, she reasoned. He could be upstairs, playing with his Lego. Wasn't that alright? She needed to see Jay. Needed to be with him, alone. Wasn't it alright to put her needs, for once, above those of everyone else in the house? The pull of the appointment was greater than the presence of her own child.

She is addicted to her affair. She finds the falseness, the invented drama, and most of all the forbidden nature of it utterly intoxicating.

Running through town towards the day room, she prefers not to, doesn't even need to think about why she is doing it. She is not going to think about George, left alone in the house. She is not going to analyse why she is running across town.

She knows the reasons better than she knows her own body. Having an affair is not part of the story, of her life story. It is frowned upon and disallowed. But it's happening. She can't help it. At these moments of transgression, even though she cannot admit to anyone, sometimes even to herself that she is doing it, even though the whole thing is but a dramatic image of a partnership, in spite of this all she feels alive, that she is really living. It is a paradox, she thinks. She doesn't want to really acknowledge she is doing it, but the fact of doing it makes her feel more real than everyday life with Patrick.

Sometimes a man will wolf whistle at her. She will turn

and smile at him. You don't know where I am going, she thinks. Or maybe he does. Perhaps he's whistling because of unseen pheremones, or hormones, or whatever they are. When she is heading towards Jay she feels as if there's a great big neon sign above her head reading I Am About To Have Spectacular Sex.

La la la. Ha ha ha. As she crosses the road in front of Argos, she imagines the meeting in the hotel lobby, the kissing in the hotel lift, the running along the hotel corridor towards the hotel bedroom, the tearing of each other's clothes. The direct physicality, no prologue. She's not even there but she is already starting to sweat with excitement, envisaging the discarded clothes, how they heap up, the shoes, kicked anyhow along the floor. Somehow the fact they start taking their clothes off in a hotel corridor helps.

The hotel corridor is crucial. The wholly corporate nature of the scene is important because it makes it seem more unreal. It's as if they are in a play. Even though it makes her feel alive.

The hotel is good. When she is indulging in the hall of her house, kissing Jay beside the clutter of George's shoes, allowing her breasts to be touched beside a picture of Saint Paul de Vence which her mother had given them as a wedding present, it seems much more immoral. There is too much of the quotidian around her. It makes her feel suffocated, these reminders of her parallel duties, and it provokes unwanted feelings of guilt.

Jane feels guilty, of course, but it annoys her. She doesn't 'do' guilt. There is no guilt in a corporate hotel whose corridors are decorated with neutral pastel prints lining the walls in exactly the same point on each floor, and fire extinguishers at the corners, and perhaps a vending machine, and tall silver ashtrays yet to be made redundant, squatting in those little round points in the middle where people get in the lift. The whole thing is like a stage set.

Today, it's even more theatrical than ever.

"I dare you," says Jay, amused, on the phone before they meet.

"What?"

"I dare you… to turn up this afternoon with nothing on."

She pauses, inhales sharply, tosses the specially blunt cut fringe.

"Don't be completely mad. Are you mad?"

"Not at all. I'd like it. Under your coat. Nothing. You must be in the nudy-rudy."

She laughs.

"Are you joking? What if I meet someone on the way, someone I know? A parent from George's school? With one of George's friends? You know it is Inset Day."

He says nothing.

She blushes. She is embarrassed by her prudery, about whether Jay won't like it. She wonders if she is seeming middle-aged, not fun any more. Maybe she *should* go and meet her lover naked but for a coat. She then thinks of Harriet, Jay's wife. She is sure that Harriet would never do this, that is for certain. She envisages Harriet's curves without underwear, lumbering unsupported into a coat. That makes her mind up. She'll do it, if only because she knows Harriet would never.

"Would it excite you? Would you really like it?"

He says nothing. There is a small rustle at his end of the phone. It's a joke, of course. But she senses he would clearly like her to do it.

"Alright, I will."

She hears him breathing.

"Will you? Really?"

"Yes, but I'll have to dive into a shop if I spot someone I know. So I might be late."

She is sitting at her kitchen table. As she talks, her eye falls on the pinboard hanging on the wall. It is full of small pieces of paper headed with a crest and a Latin phrase. These are from George's prep school. They speak of term dates and sporting fixtures. George's imminent future is mapped out on the pinboard, beside a menu from the local Thai. There's a list of opening times for the local pool, over a very old photograph of her and Patrick standing in the Grand Canyon. Ooh-ah Point, it's called. Because that is the noise that people make when they are standing on it. Ooh-Aaah. She and Patrick are arm in arm, grinning.

She turns away from the pinboard. Jay is still talking.

"… and so I'll see you at two, yes?"

"Sure. But Jay?"

"What, sugar?"

She smiles at him down the phone.

"I've got a great idea too. Why don't you come with nothing on?"

Now it is Jay's turn to be silent. Then, a cackle of laughter.

"Darling, really? Must I? Would you really find that a turn on? I'm not sure I do, you know."

In Jay's mind the idea of a penis vulnerably dangling under a coat is not quite the same as the idea of a naked female body hidden behind the folds of tweeds or wool of London Fog. It is not erotic. It is rather embarrassing. Or just funny.

Jane laughs out loud.

"You might get mistaken for a flasher!"

"Quite. Oh, God Jane. I don't think so. I have to tell you, I'd feel a bit seedy, you know. Anyway, how on earth will I obscure the fact I have nothing on my legs? I'm in the office!"

"Go on. I dare you."

"Bare legs on a woman are sexy. Bare legs on a man tend not to be."

"Oh come on, Jay."

"I must insist on trousers."

"Very well. Trousers. But no underwear, and no shirt."

"Socks?"

"No."

He sighs.

"I'll have to go out of the back entrance."

He wishes he'd never brought up the whole fantasy. It has been a fantasy of his for quite some time, envisaging her dashing through town with nothing on but a coat. Because Jane has always been so perfectly groomed, certainly compared to his wife's rather chaotic appearance, it excites him to wield the power of ungrooming over her.

"I look like a mess anyway. Nobody will notice I haven't got socks on. But I may have to arrive by taxi."

How much harder it is for men to disrobe in public, she thinks. Bare legs, bare arms, these things are quite commonplace for a woman. Going out at night, they are almost requisite. When they appear on a man outside of the realm of exercise, he could be marked down as a nutter.

And so, just as the afternoon has commenced in earnest and people are sitting down to business lunches across town or collecting their small children from morning nursery, Jay and Jane are crossing town to see one another. Partially naked.

He is coming from work. She is coming from her house, where a child is now alone.

He leaves the office in his coat and trousers. A pale cashmere scarf at his throat disguises the fact he is wearing no shirt. He feels rather lost without boxer shorts. Lost but weirdly liberated. He feels his genitals brush across his leg in a not wholly unpleasant manner.

He hails a cab, and with a sigh of relief, clambers in.

Jane is walking briskly down the road. Bare legs, simple sandals, a knee-length mac. She has nothing else on. Her buttocks are goosepimpled against the shiny lining of the mac. The lack of a bra makes her nipples stand out. A man walks past her. She smiles at him. She is getting turned on by this, despite herself. Jay was right; this is exciting.

As long as she doesn't meet anyone she knows.

Oh, shit.

Here, walking down the road towards her, is someone she knows.

George's piano teacher. Roberta. No, no. Of all people.

Maybe she won't see her.

Roberta sees Jane, smiles. Stops.

"Hello Jane," says Roberta, who is full of inner joy because Tracey has rebooked a whole term's worth of lessons with Belle. "How lovely to see you. I'm on my way to the Square, actually, to teach Belle. And I was just thinking about George."

"Oh, Roberta, hello," she manages to say, keeping her hands in her pockets, checking with a tiny downward movement of her head, that her coat is buttoned up. "How are you?"

Rather than continuing to walk, Roberta decides to stand still on the pavement.

"I'm very well. Looking forward to seeing George."

"Roberta, I am so sorry. I am on my way to a meeting. And I'm a bit late. I've left George at home, actually. He's on an Inset Day, and I can't leave him for long."

She makes to look at her watch, realises she doesn't have one, puts her hand swiftly back in the pocket of her mac. She smiles hopefully at Roberta.

"Oh, not at all. Just wanted to say how well George is going at the moment."

"Great, great. Well, see you on Friday, then?"

"Right-oh. Bye."

As they part, Roberta looks at Jane's departing back and wonders almost subconsciously why Jane, always so immaculate, is wearing sandals, with bare legs, on such a chilly afternoon. Then she walks on.

Jane, walking in the other direction, is travelling very quickly now. Her armpits are clammy, sticking to the unmoulding lining of the coat, without the forgiving intervention of cotton to soak up the sweat.

Oh for God's sake, thinks Jane. This is madness. It's not erotic, in the least. It's stupid.

She arrives at the counter.

"I booked an, um, a day room," she says to the receptionist.

In the foyer, Jay, reading the paper, looks up and smiles.

Then he gets up, folds the paper, comes close and stands behind her.

"Hello darling."

He presses his body to hers. She can feel his hard cock in the small of her back.

"Room No. 314," says the receptionist.

"Thank you," says Jane in what she hopes to be the professional way of a woman who is about to have a meeting.

In the lift he unbuttons her mac.

"This is so mad. I bumped into the fucking piano teacher," she whispers into his ear.

"I don't care," he moans.

He leans towards her and kisses her breasts, fondles her naked arse.

"Oh my God Jane," he murmurs as the lift doors open.

"You really are naked. You did that for me?" He buries his face in her neck.

They step out onto Floor 3.

Then, in the corridor, it's easy. Because neither of them is wearing anything. He pulls her coat off her shoulders, surveys her standing there, totally naked, in sandals. Then, deliberately, he takes off his coat. Undoes his belt. Slips off his shoes. Pulls his trousers down, and off. There they are. Two respectable middle-aged professionals, whose conservative lives are of untrammelled comfort and pleasure, naked in the corridor of a Travelodge.

"I am going to fuck you in this corridor," whispers Jay.

"What? What? Are you bloody out of your mind?" says Jane, trembling, laughing. She grabs his buttocks, which are slightly cool to the touch.

"What happens if a cleaner turns up?"

Jay shrugs.

"Let her."

"Or him. Not all cleaners are female."

"Open your legs you politically correct darling."

She backs up against the wall, smiling nervously. Strands

of her perfectly cut hair cling to the slightly raised wallpaper, galvanised by static.

He grabs both her thighs and heaves her body up the wall against the raised wallpaper so her feet leave the ground.

"Do you think anyone has ever done this in this particular corridor before?" he grunts.

She cannot speak. She is fucking her lover in the corridor of the Travelodge. She can't think of anything else. Her brain is flooded by sexual excitment. She looks over his shoulder down the corridor, at all the demurely closed bedroom doors. What if one should open? She imagines she can hear a television, or some sort of music playing nearby. Someone is probably sitting on a bed, watching the racing. Or MTV. Maybe they are pottering around the room, turning up the air con, having a bite from one of the tasteless apples sitting in the display of the stainless steel bowl on top of the minibar. While two people about twenty feet away are indulging in sexual intercourse outside their door. Maybe this person is opening the minibar, and, discontented with the paltry array within, is considering going downstairs for a proper cup of coffee. She realises she would quite like to be discovered like this. Her back is rubbing up and down the wall. Feels like it's been papered in Artex. How she is going to explain the scratches away to Patrick is a problem she will have to assess, later. She then remembers how rarely he sees her naked body.

Jay groans, and slowly lets her down. She pats his sweaty back. She feels liberated, joyous, momentarily a different person, someone careless and untrammelled by convention.

"Thank you," she says, looking at him.

"Why?" he gasps. "For fucking you in a corridor?"

"For fucking me in a corridor. Makes me feel alive."

He laughs, kisses her shoulder.

"Let's go into our bedroom. Have you got the key?"

"Yes, but quickly. I only have about an hour left."

Chapter Ten
Jas

"Jas! Get up!"

Far away, he hears his mother's insistent cry, rolls over on the bed, clasps at his duvet for one last sustaining moment of soft warmth, then wakes up properly, swings his legs over the side of the bed, and stands up.

"Jas! Don't you have to be with Philip?" his mother calls.

"Yup!"

"Well you are going to be late!"

Yes, yes, he knows, he knows. He takes off his T-shirt, pulls on another, steps into a pair of boxers, walks over to his younger brother Javi. The boy is still sleeping, a beatific look of relaxation on his face.

Jas and Javi share a room so small you can almost touch both sides of the wall when standing in the middle of it. This has some advantages. Not going far to get dressed is one of them. Always having a bottle of Lynx at hand is another. Jas reaches, grabs the aerosol can, sprays it over Javi's bed. It has a satisfactorily immediate effect.

"Arrgh! Fuck off! Jas! Mum! He sprayed me again! Mum!"

"Morning. Wasteman," says the tormentor, grabbing his trousers and leaving the room, laughing.

Brushing his teeth, he considers his day, which is to be spent with his quondam employer on the Square. Philip.

Now there is a lucky bastard, muses Jas as he spits into the basin. How the hell does he get away with it? Not for the first time, Jas thinks about how jammy Philip really is. Walks around in a robe all morning. Has lots of money. Talks dirty, especially about women. Has porno pictures around the place. Dresses like a binman, or an electrician. Lives in a million pound house, or more. Gets people, people like Jas, to help him with his work.

And it's not exactly work like mending cars, or brain surgery. It is making models of golf holes, which sell for shed loads. Or rather, not making them because he, Jas, does the lion's share. And nobody tells Philip off for being rude and sexist because he is a famous artist. He sort of earns money for being eccentric. How do you manage to arrive at that, thinks Jas. How do you train for it? How, when you are starting out, or thinking about becoming an eccentric, do you know it's going to work? Or maybe that's the thing. Eccentric artists never contemplate the possibility of being normal, because they are not normal.

He finishes brushing his teeth, checks his hair, runs down the short flight of stairs to the living area where Brenda, his mother, is finishing her breakfast while watching a report on TV which is coming live from an award ceremony in Hollywood. A very excited reporter in a tuxedo is gushing over a never-ending array of American celebrities who are all looking very pleased with themselves and grinning over the giant golden objects they have just won.

"Look at that dress," Brenda comments on one of them. "Bloody marvellous. How does she get into it, that's what I want to know. Look at the size of them."

Jas looks steadily at the screen, where a succession of tiny women with giant heads in shiny colourful gowns are grinning and waving on a vast red carpet which surrounds them like a painting.

"Yeah, whatever," he says.

"Well, you are meant to be the creative one," she whispers, reaching up to kiss him. The report finishes. The presenters of the breakfast show, who are sitting on a bright pink sofa turn to each other and congratulate themselves on how wonderful the world of American award ceremonies really is, and how happy they are to be discussing it on a bright pink sofa.

"Go on. Win your old mum an Oscar," says Brenda, who is a care worker for the council with five people, all in wheelchairs, all living in separate areas of the borough, all of whom she is obliged to visit on a daily basis. Once she accounts for public transport and traffic, Brenda has no more than twenty-five minutes with each of them, in which time she must give them a hot meal and check they have taken their medicine. It's a sprint. She sighs, puts on her coat.

"That's show business, Mum. I am in the Art World, remember!"

"Yeah, well get out of it and go into the movies. Bye, babe. Gotta go. And babe?"

"Yeah?"

"Walk the dog."

Walk the dog, do some stuff, earn some money, spend it, walk the dog again. It's not great, but it's not a bad routine, thinks Jas. All he has to do is continue to put up with Philip, keep his head down and pretend to be interested in golf, a game which he will never play. Don't screw up. On the threshold of his twenties, Jas has realised that quite a lot of adulthood seems to involve the simple maxim of not screwing up. He is determined to abide by it.

He surveys the TV again. A man comes on, grinning, and starts bringing down huge figures on some sort of whiteboard behind him. He is very fair and is wearing a white suit, which Jas thinks is a bit ridiculous, as it's still quite cold outside.

"Good morning!" yells the man. "Are we ready to do away with debt? Looking after your pennies can be done, you know!"

It's Alan Makin doing his daily routine on the breakfast show.

No thank you, thinks Jas. I hate that bastard. Why should someone who clearly has a colossal bank balance tell us all how to do away with debt? You need someone who is skint to tell you how to cope with looking after your pennies. That would be believable. Using a rich bastard to do that simply doesn't work.

He checks his phone. Shit. He's going to be late.

He goes to the bottom of the stairs, screams up to his brother.

"Javi, you arse! Get up out of bed. I'm out. And walk the dog!"

He leaves the little flat, shuts the door carefully because it is warped, steps out onto the little porch with its slatted roof, runs down the wooden steps and out of the estate, heading towards the expanse of the Square.

Back in the house, Alan Makin continues telling the nation how to save their pennies. Quite a lot of this morning's advice seems to centre around eating soup, and walking everywhere. 'Ditch the car' is the Saving Slogan of the morning.

Jas steps into the green light of the place, which is as always incredibly quiet, as if the Square is actually wadded with noise-cancelling bushes, and everyone in their houses is doing something fascinating and absorbing. Silently.

He wonders if he'll see Belle again. Belle. Ding Dong, he used to call her. His old friend. Although now she is incredibly posh and, so much so, living just a few doors along from Philip Burrell. That is of course another way through, thinks Jas. Winning the Lottery, like Belle's old man did. He remembered the celebrations at his primary school, the day Belle's mum Tracey brought along a huge cake, saying to his teacher, 'Of course, it's not going to change anything.'

Not that she did, in fairness, change all that much. Apart from moving to the Square, obviously. As far as Jas could make out, she was still the same old tarty Tracey in her heels and short skirts. It was the daughters Belle and Grace who changed, started going to different schools and wearing boaters, behaving as if they had been born in the place, not just lucked out into it.

Winning the Lottery. Yes, that was an option. But was it an easier way through than becoming an eccentric character in the art world? Both seem quite impossible to Jas, whose generally benign view of the world is nonetheless bitterly tempered by a fundamental knowledge that, bar acts of God, being a Premier League footballer and winning the Lottery, (which is sort of the same thing), Britain is cemented into its positions of wealth and power.

He reaches the door, rings the bell, hears Gilda pad along the corridor. He loves Gilda. The door opens with a flourish.

"Mornin'."

She is wearing a red silk kimono, with a red ribbon around her forehead and long crystalline maroon earrrings. A slash of red lipstick on her mouth. You go, girl, thinks Jas.

"Jas," says Gilda dramatically. "My nightingale. How wonderful."

"Yep," he says, walking in. I'm only turning up for work, he thinks, but he still gives Gilda a nice smile and a wink. Funny how these arty people greet every day as if it's an event akin to walking down the red carpet at the Golden Globes.

He carefully hangs his coat up in the cloakroom. He comes here twice a week. The elements of the house: the pornographic pictures, the bits and bobs of Gilda's fanny in the downstairs loo, all that tat, hold no interest for him. He's seen them too often, and anyway, he can see all that stuff on the internet at any given time. No big deal.

He pokes his head around the studio door, taps his pocket to check his phone is off.

"Mornin'." says Jas.

Philip raises an eyebrow. Then he looks, too obviously, up at the giant clock on the wall. He says nothing. Jas feels obliged to acknowledge the gesture.

"Sorry I'm late."

In his robe, Philip walks grandly towards Jas.

"Well, I have to inform you that he has seen it. And he thinks it will work," he says, gesturing to the new sculpture on the trestle table. He leans over the piece. "All we must do is build quite a few more of them."

"Sorry, who has seen it?"

"Why, Magnus, of course."

Oh, yeah. The dealer. Well, that's good, thinks Jas. More work. He looks at the course of the London Marathon. Lots more work. This test model took him over a week to construct, and he knew all the buildings already. By the time he's built Berlin and Paris and New York, he'll have earned enough to buy a car by the end of the summer, if he plays his cards right.

"You will need to do some research for me. Can you do that, can you research this stuff?"

Of course I can. Do all your thinking for you. He doesn't mind being used like this, as long as he is being paid properly, but something inside Jas does rankle. I mean, he considers, everyone thinks artists are completely original. Isn't that what makes them an official artist? Bet Leonardo da Vinci didn't have someone researching stuff for him in his studio.

Jas has been brought up to understand that there are rules, like invisible areas of order around everyone. And in order to have authority in those areas, you have to be trained. Doctors had to do this, or that. Teachers similarly. Artists the same. You had to be able to draw. Only in Philip's case, you didn't. He can't draw and he can't sculpt. All he does is have ideas. Jas' job is to help him realise those ideas. Jas simply didn't know how he had become the world's greatest artist at the same time as not being able to do anything artistic. It was like magic. Or a con. Only Jas didn't like to believe it was a con, because that would mean he was working for a con-man, and that would be humiliating. He sighs. What is Philip cantering on about?

"… and so I need you to find out what these races actually are."

"What?"

"The five or six Masters. The great marathons around the world that the serious marathon community runs. That's what we'll be building. The elite races. For the elite runners."

"Are you sure?"

Philip glances quickly at Jas. He hates being queried.

"What? Of course I'm sure."

"It's only that… the Marathon Elite." Jas considers how well Philip's work will wash with sporting professionals. He thinks that Philip will go down quite badly.

"It's just that, well, I don't know that they will be all that interested in owning… " he gestures to the table "… one of these. Shouldn't we be doing stuff that rich people like, find the marathons which collectors might be running? What are our most successful golf holes, after all?"

He knows, because he has made them dozens of times. It's the ones in the rich areas. Augusta. Littlehampton. Hampstead. Virginia Water. St Andrew's.

"Alright, well find out where those ones are, then. The posh races."

"It's going to be Paris. New York and London," says Jas. "And maybe Florence. And each one is going to take us about two weeks to build, I should think. More, maybe. Think of all those Eiffel Towers. And I bet Florence won't be easy. Any quicker, and I'll need some help. Unless, of course, you want to do it with me." As if that was ever going to happen.

Philip snorts, and strides out of the studio, leaving Jas to get along with sculpting the 10th hole at the Royal Liverpool in Hoylake.

Chapter Eleven
Tracey

She starts off by putting his name into Google.

Stuff comes up. Testimonies, accolades, that sort of thing. Alan Makin, you have changed my life. Alan Makin, you have reorganised my budget, my bills, my world. You are a modern day Saviour.

She could do with having a modern-day Saviour in her world, she thinks. To have all the bills paid off. To have everything smoothed out. To be like her neighbours. Organised, efficient, adult, responsible. When they had won the Lottery, they had had some help from the people at Camelot, it was true. But once they had bought the house, had sorted out a new car and got the girls into private school, all of which had taken about a year, Camelot had moved on, onto other winners. People who had won more than she and Larry had. That was when the money problems started.

Eventually, she discovers his website, contact details, agent. MoneywithMakin.com. She envisages various possible gambits. *Hi, is that Alan Makin? I'm the woman who shouted out at your show the other night. Alan Makin, I spoke to you in the tent on the Common. Just wanted to say how inspiring you were. Dear Alan, I heckled you last night. Can you forget that, and give me a financial makeover?*

That's the one.

When she tells her eldest daughter of her plan, Belle is incredulous. "Mum, people just don't contact other people like that."

"What, by emailing them?"

"Yes! Nobody emails anyone, any more."

"Don't be ludicrous."

Tracey sighs. First nobody writes to anyone any more. Snail mail, used only for thank you letters and postcards. A few years on, nobody calls anyone else on landlines. Apart from Granny and salesmen from AmEx. Mobile calls are the next thing to go. Now it's emails. Belle makes her feel so old. The other day, she banned her from listening to Radio One. Marched into the room and switched it off.

"You are too old for that, Mum." Where does one go when you are told you are past it? You're never going to be younger, thinks Tracey. Now I can't even send emails, apparently.

"What do people do, then?"

Belle sighs, and shrugs on a voluminous sludge-coloured shrug.

"Facebook? Direct Message on Twitter? WhatsApp?" she says, leaving the room in her Doc Martens.

What the hell is WhatsApp? And DM Alan Makin? Really? Somehow, Alan Makin doesn't seem to be a Twitter kind of guy, she thinks. She emails him.

Two days later, a response.

It is both oddly formal and rather suggestive. *Tracey (if I may), of course I remember your 'heckle'. Very interesting it was too. Yes. Moving forward, let's move forward. Coffee? Thursday?*

Thursday it is. What to wear. She stands in front of her wardrobe, deciding. It must not be too short. Short skirts and financial acumen do not go together. She must not look flirty. Eventually she wanders up to Belle's room, and stands in front of her wardrobe. None of Belle's clothes are in the least flirtatious. She pulls on a black dress made of boiled wool.

It has a very below the knee hemline, almost calf-skimming. Perfect with flat heels. Good. Although actually putting the thing on goes against the grain with Tracey. She simply never would wear a skirt of this length. Furthermore, does she want Alan Makin to think she is a below the knee person who never wears stilettos? She's not sure she does. She abandons the boiled wool and goes back downstairs.

In heels, her pink tweed fitted jacket and its matching, not-very-mini, mini skirt, Tracey is finally ready to meet Alan Makin for coffee. She brushes her hair, checks her nails, runs her tongue over her teeth for stray lipstick marks. There are none. Her makeup, as ever, is immaculate. She is rather excited.

She slams the door and steps out into the Square. Walking briskly along in her heels, jacket, mini skirt, she feels the part. What part? She doesn't know. Just the part.

Jane, who would never need a financial makeover because Patrick earns hundreds of thousands of pounds every year in the City, probably millions actually, is carting groceries from the back of her Audi.

"Hi Jane," she sings out.

"Oh, hello. Going anywhere special?" asks Jane, somewhat sourly, Tracey thinks.

"Oh, no," says Tracey. "Not really." Just to meet a television star, ha ha.

"Well, actually I am." She pauses by the car. Jane, who had had no intention of stopping, is forced to stand still.

"It is quite special. I've got an appointment with Alan Makin."

Jane cocks her head at Tracey, birdlike.

"You know," continues Tracey, "the guy who appears on TV. Sorting out everyone's financial problems. Well, I went to see him with Harriet the other night and he now wants a meeting! With me! Don't think it's anything special," she says, deliberately downplaying it. "I mean, I don't think he wants me on TV with him," she continues.

Jane stands holding her groceries. There is a distinctly fed-up look on her face.

"Marvellous" she says faintly. "You'd better go. Don't want to be late."

Tracey clicks away in her heels.

When she arrives at Patisserie CoCo, an authentic Viennese pastry shop selling Austrian fancies to harassed Londoners who already have dangerously high levels of cholestrol, Alan Makin is in place.

"Tracey. My dear," he says, proffering a chair.

Tracey slides into it.

Alan looks at her, half humorously.

"You know you don't look a bit like a Tracey."

Tracey sighs.

"My parents thought it was a fashionable name. It was, when I was born. And it's turned out to be a white trash signifier."

She laughs, delivers the customary punchline.

"They were debating with the idea of calling me Sharon."

Alan laughs too. "Do you know, I have the same problem."

"What, that your parents were about to call you Sharon?"

"Yes! No, no, with being called Alan. A signifier not so much white trash, as date sensitive. Only men of a certain generation are called Alan."

The waitress appears, bearing cups full of speciality Viennese coffee dusted with bitter chocolate.

Alan and Tracey, the badly named couple, take their cups from her and settle, blowing on the coffee, ruminating on the social hurdles which come with having blue collar names in a white collar world.

"Makin is good though."

"Oh, that. Actually, confession Numero Uno. It's an invention. Works well with what I do. Makin' money."

He's quite fun, she thinks. Amusedly open, giving away trade secrets. Small and fair, with nice clothes.

She puts one of her hands over his wrist.

"What is confession Numero Duo? That you can't add up?"

Alan laughs.

"Oh, no. Figures have always been my speciality."

"Can you wave your magic wand over my financial affairs, then?"

He looks at her archly.

"So, let's talk about it. Don't be embarrassed. People give me their financial secrets every morning on national television. Right. How much money do you owe, right now? Including your mortgage?"

She squirms.

"We don't have a mortgage."

"Well that's a start. Excellent."

"We won the Lottery a few years ago."

"And you are coming to me for help? Well, well."

Tracey feels as if she has entered a Confessional box at church.

"So we bought the house and put the children into private school and now I think I need a plan, so the rest of it doesn't... fritter away. I've already got an overdraft."

"Do you think you have, shall we say, an entitlement to debt? Because everyone else is looking flash and spending money on your street. And everyone else is probably also in debt, so it's okay? Where do you live?"

"In the Square."

Alan nods knowledgeably.

"Oh, I know about the Square. And you bought a house there without a mortgage? I won't ask how much you won from the Lottery," he says, even though he already knows, because he has Googled her too.

"No, no, that's alright," says Tracey, slightly disappointed.

"How do you know about the Square?"

Because he has done his homework. Because he has just had a performance in a marquee in that part of town. Because he knows how things are, in places which are called by a singularity.

"Well, I've never been to it. But I assume it's full of bankers and lawyers and bankers' wives, no? With their Prada handbags and cars and au pairs and bonuses and beautiful haircuts?"

She thinks of Jane unloading the Audi.

"Perhaps."

"And you'd like to be like them? Feel ashamed that you aren't? So you take out that 0% finance on the credit card, right? To pay off another one? Then your salary stagnates, so you can't pay anything off bar the minimums?"

She looks at him. He is her confessional priest.

"That is exactly where I am right now. Sometimes I feel, I feel… "

"What?"

"That I am looking into the abyss. And it's frightening."

"It's also… not good for you. Is it?"

"Is there anything… to say?"

"There might be. Shall we talk about how things work, or shall we say *don't* work, for you? What is your mode of employment, if you have one?"

Forty minutes later, after experiencing an indepth conversation about selling cosmetics door to door, and how it really works, with commission spiralling back to a pyramid of Giza-like dimensions, Alan Makin looks rather dazed. Still, he's not averse to a challenge. His whole life, as those who have heard him talk know, has been about challenges. He rolls his sleeves up. He has enjoyed the morning. He likes this woman, with her clothes of a twenty year old and perfectly presented face, with her trashy name and her Lottery story, and her silly spiralling debts and her phalanx of brimming credit cards desperate for relief.

He knows how to help people like this.

He is also aware that her belief in him, Alan Makin, and in what he, Alan Makin, knows, is what drives his show, the belief that life can be effectively ironed out and started over again.

He thinks this is a worthy thing to communicate. He hates the bankers, the debt peddlers, the payday loan merchants. Despises them. He would like to save this woman from them.

"How about I talk to my team about something?"

"What, a makeover on your show?"

Alan shrugs.

"Perhaps. 'How I ran through my Lottery Millions' is a good start. Would you like to be on TV?"

Would she like to? She'd love to.

Over supper, back at home, she's walking about the room, humming. She's rather proud of her conquest.

"What, so Alan Makin took you out to coffee? You actually MET him?"

"Yes, Grace, I did."

"What did you wear?"

"The pink suit."

"Oh, MUM!"

"Well, Belle, it is actually a very smart suit."

"You know, Belle dumpling, not everybody wants to walk around as if they are in the London branch of an Amish sect," snorts Larry. "Some people like to recognise we are in the 21st century, and reflect that in their costume."

Belle pulls a face at him.

He turns to Tracey.

"How was it, then?" he says, amused.

"Quite good, actually. He's going to talk to his producer about having me on the show."

"Really? Did he ask you about the Lottery win?"

"No. He didn't seem in the least bit interested in that. Well, I told him about it of course, but he didn't... linger on it."

"It would probably make your experience seem too unusual. Alan Makin's show isn't about the unusual. It's about the bloody familiar, that's why it's a hit."

"You? On telly? Hee hee hee."

"Yes, Belle. Not everyone thinks I am an embarassment."

"When? When will you be on, when?"

"I don't know. Perhaps next week. Will you both stop texting at the table?"

"I'm not texting, I'm DM-ing."

"I'm not texting, I'm Instagramming."

Belle and Grace giggle and punch one another.

"Well, whatever it is, please desist," says Larry, ineffectually stifling a burp.

Tracey pushes her plate away. She doesn't want to be in this kitchen, her familiar home, a place full of burping adults and whining children. She wants to be back in Patisserie CoCo, putting her hand over Alan Makin's wrist, in a world which is smart and fast moving and free of financial snares, and full of important people having meetings and appearing on television.

The door bell rings. Anya, the Eastern European au pair glides away to answer it.

"What is the time? Eight? That will be Roberta. Your piano lesson, darling."

"But I thought you cancelled her! I thought that lesson we had over on George's piano was going to be my last one?"

"Well, I didn't actually. Cancel her."

"God, Mum! How could you! I hate her! I hate you!"

"Go on. Go and have your lesson."

"But I haven't practised. Oh, Mum."

"Well, darling. Roberta rang me and we had a long, long chat."

What did they talk about? Tracey couldn't quite remember, but she knew it mentioned various key things, such as The Repertoire, and Grade Five. Oh, and of course Belle's chances at university. Yes, that was it.

"Roberta reminded me that music always looks good on a Personal Statement, you know."

"I thought you couldn't afford it."

"We can always afford things for your education, dumpling," admonishes her father.

Anyway, things might be on the upturn, thinks Tracey. With the blessing of a television show.

Belle pushes past Anya who has returned and is silently tidying up the marble island. Belle glares to nobody in particular.

I could be at the gym right now, she thinks. Rather than doing bloody Hanon. La-de-dah. Why does Mum even want me to play the piano? It's stupid, stupid. A nineteenth century leisure pursuit. Not a single one of the other Populars plays an instrument. Honestly, not one. Well, Cathy plays the clarinet. And Maria the trumpet. But those are fashionable. Jazzy. Portable. Accessories, really. In boxes with shiny hinges and a handle. Whereas, the lumbering old piano. It's like playing furniture. She enters the living room.

"Hello, Belle. Shall we start with Hanon?" says Roberta, in her deceptively cool manner.

Belle pulls the stool out and settles down, huffing slightly.

Downstairs in the knock-through kitchen, Tracey hums as she hears the familiar patterns once more. Her phone buzzes. It's an email from Alan. *I've just been working things out. How about a meeting with the production team next Tuesday? 9.30? That would suit me fine. All directions on the website www.MoneywithMakin.com.*

She answers it with a single word, then snaps the phone shut with a happy sense of progress.

Chapter Twelve
Belle

The door bell rings.

"Mum!" she shouts. "Muu-uum!" Where the hell is she, thinks Belle, before remembering about Tracey's 'Production Meeting' at Makin TV. She puts the quotation marks around it even though she is only thinking the words.

She walks to the door, opens it. She blinks at the person several times before she realises who it is. Christ, it's Jas. What the hell does he want, is her first thought. Why am I wearing a flowery top, is her second thought. Belle does not like being seen in obviously female clothes.

"'Right, Belle?" says Jas.

She eyes him suspiciously. Hates the way he says her name. He seems to put a W into it. Bewul. Ugh.

"Jas."

"Er, Belle, I got something to suggest to you. Now, I don't know if you're interested in this, what with your house, and everything."

"But?"

"But, well, I wondered if you'd like to earn some money?"

Emboldened by her eyebrows rising, he continues.

"It all depends on, like, how good you are at making things."

Three minutes later, Belle and Jas are sitting at a bench in the middle of the Square. Jas is smoking. He knows better than to light up indoors, so they have come outside to talk. He'd rather, anyway.

Belle looks up at the vast canopy of the London plane above them. About 20,000 leaves are about to unfold, all at once, on the tree, but at present, there are just bright green buds on the dark twigs and branches, giving the sensation of a verdant mist. It is a spectacle which only lasts about a week.

Even though she is in her huge black astrakhan coat, she shivers, wrinkling her nose at the bitter smoke.

"Tell me again what you need me to do."

"I want you to be my assistant, for a week or so at least. At Philip Burrell's studio. You know, just over there, at No. 32. I want you to help me make models of famous marathon courses around the world."

"What? Like a sort of Lego thing?"

"No, out of wood and papier mâché and paint."

There is silence under the plane as Belle tries to envisage the plan.

"Why? Does he think this is art?"

"Yes! Not just him. He does this sort of stuff. It's his sculpture, his thing. He has a dealer, and collectors, and, like, art fairs. His stuff goes for a bomb, Belle. There's a lot of money involved. A lot. It is art, anyway," Jas continues, seeing Belle's incredulous face. "Sort of," he concludes quietly.

Belle would quite like to know how much money Philip makes out of this venture, but realises, correctly, that Jas wants to have his pitch without being quizzed on it. She lets him continue.

"I am Philip's main assistant. I help him make golf holes. Like solid replicas of famous golf holes. In miniature."

Belle is getting a bit confused. "I thought it was marathon courses, a minute ago."

"Yeah, well he does golf holes, mainly. They sell all over the world. I mean *all* over. For a lot. Tens of thousands of pounds. Then he had a brainwave and thought he should escalate to marathon courses. Why not?" Jas pauses.

When Philip is doing it, explaining everything in his studio, it sort of makes sense. He's not sure he is making sense to Belle, but he badly needs to convince her.

"Belle, Philip is an artist. One of the most important artists in the country. And this is his latest idea. Anyway, people want to buy his stuff. And I don't have enough time for it all. I need someone to, like, help me make it."

He does not want Philip to ask anyone else for help. Particularly that arsey dealer Magnus. Jas doesn't want the work to leave his grasp. He can see the amount of money hovering over the project, like the green mist above them. He intends to have some of that money. And why not? He's earned it, turning up three times a week and having lunches with Philip and Gilda. That's another card to play.

"You know Gilda? His girlfriend? Russian? Well, you'd meet her and see their house. It's pretty awesome."

"Is it true the place is full of porn?" says Belle, not wanting to seem too curious about it, but as a matter of fact, the porn at her arty neighbour's house was something that the Populars had urged her to find out about for months now, that would be something to have up her sleeve.

"Yep."

That did it.

"I'm in. When do we start?"

"Really?" He's really pleased. "Great. Belle, I knew you'd be up for it. I think you'd be great. Remember that project on the River Thames that we did together in Year Five? It's going to be a bit like that. It's going to be a blast."

She laughs. "What, with papier mâché?"

"Yeah, and chicken wire. Do you know anything about marathons?"

"No. Only that they are bloody long, and all the traffic stops for a day."

"Well, pretend you do. And when you meet Philip, don't,

for fuck's sake, mention the Tate Gallery."

"Why? Artists like the Tate, don't they?"

"Nah. Not this one."

Belle looks at Jas. He lifts his chin, smiles back at her merrily. He is pleased that his plan seems to have worked out.

She thinks about how they were together, working on art projects in their aprons at school. She wonders how different she would feel now, if a big hand marked Money hadn't picked her up and moved her away into the Square and private school, what she would be like now.

Jas looks at Belle. Success in one field has given him a notion about success in another. He wonders vaguely when he might be allowed to fuck her.

"Right, so tomorrow. I'll call for you. Nine? Philip likes an early start."

"Right."

"I'll have all the materials. We'll go to the studio and we'll start working. I think tomorrow we are going to start on Berlin."

"Right." She's quite excited.

"When do you go back to school?"

"I have two weeks. It's half term."

Blimey, thinks Jas. She has to pay for school and they hardly turn up. Two weeks! Well, that's a blessing, actually. They might get Tokyo done as well.

"Er, Jas, what's the fee? I am getting paid for this, right?"

He hadn't thought about this too closely. Philip would need to be consulted about how much this new assistant was going to be paid. He'd have to feel comfortable with this new person in his world. Philip was a man who didn't like surprises. He wanted to be surrounded by people who weren't going to criticise him. He liked to be able to glide about in his robe and not have people laugh at him, or roll their eyeballs at him. He was the unopposed king of his world.

"Philip will sort that out. But it won't be nothing. Honestly, Belle, you'll enjoy it. Just one thing."

"What's that?"

"Don't laugh at him. Take him seriously."

"Right."

He stands, grinds the stub onto the ground, clasps his hands together almost as if he is praying.

"Thanks, Belle. I knew you'd like the idea. Knew you'd be up for a challenge. So. Tomorrow, nine, right?"

"Right." She has already turned away, waves a hand behind her.

It's going to be hard to get into her knickers, thinks Jas. But he's sure he can manage it. At this particular second, he feels as if anything and everything is possible. He gives a little skip as he walks towards Philip Burrell's house where the chicken wire and wood are already marking out the course of the Berlin Marathon.

Belle shivers from the morning chill as she comes into the softly warm house, and almost collides with Anya. She is carrying a large bag of rubbish.

"Oh, sorry, Belle."

Belle decides she will smile at the au pair as she edges out with the sagging black sack. She's in a good mood. She'll get quite a lot of money from this venture. Money earned, rather than given to her. Is it different? Apart from the time spent getting it, probably not, thinks Belle. It's all numbers. But at least this means she'll be able to buy what she wants, when she wants it, and not have to bother being nice to her mother, or clear up her plate after breakfast, or tidy her room, all things which her parents seem to think go hand in hand with a monthly allowance.

Plus, it will be quite a laugh, working with Little Jas. That's what everyone used to call him at school. Alright, he's not so little now, but she'll still make sure he does most of the work. It's not going to be too arduous, she thinks. Bit of sticking and painting, it will be like being back in primary school again.

And then there's all that stuff in the house, she'll enjoy

nosing around there. Belle is very pleased. What looked like a rather dull period of time, stretching ahead of her, was going to turn out to be rather entertaining. And she would get paid for doing it. Belle tosses her large coat onto the bannister as she walks upstairs. It promptly slides off onto the floor. Well, Anya can deal with that.

Chapter Thirteen
Jane

Yes, but if it's going to go ahead, the Talent Show needs planning. Really good planning. Proper production. It must be smooth. Professional. Impressive. If a thing's worth doing. And so on. Which is why Jane put herself forward, volunteered for the position of Talent Show Producer. Yes, she wanted to be seen as a volunteer. However, now that she was in charge, had been given the task of organising it by Larry, whose idea it had been, it would be so awful if it was a damp squib.

She thinks of the event. She thinks of the audience. What happened if nobody turned up? If everyone just couldn't be bothered? That would be dreadful. That would be like nobody turning up to your birthday party.

Plus, there is the talent part of it. She thinks of George. George has a fairly fixed set of parameters for his enthusiasm and talents, thinks Jane with a frown. What could he do? Dressing up? She can't quite see him reciting a poem, plus it would be so dreadful if he forgot his lines, she doesn't think she could cope with the stress of that. Yet she wants to show her son off. I pay enough for his bloody education, she thinks. He's got to do something impressive. She only has one child. He has to fulfil all her dreams. Maybe he could play the piano, if I can dragoon Roberta in to teach him something which sounds complicated but is actually very simple. She remembers hearing Jools Holland say this about playing boogie-woogie. Somehow she can't quite see George mastering boogie-woogie in the matter of a month.

She has bought a large block of lined paper. On the frontispiece, she has written *Talent Show*. She looks at the pad. She's quite excited about the project. It's like being back at school when she was Head Girl. Since when, her expectations of power were somewhat thwarted.

It took her several years after arriving there, at her job in Freshfields, to realise that the City was not like an all-girls school. At the beginning, she was full of confidence, short skirts and swear words. After a while, she got bored with matching people drink for drink at the bar. It began to dawn on her that the City was not really a place to throw your weight around, if you were female. People, i.e. the men, simply didn't include her in the action. Women were acknowledged, but only on a token basis.

She hated to admit it, but she felt far more in control at home. In terms of a domestically-based event, something in the Square, people expect a woman like Jane to be in charge. They'll be looking to me to organise it, she knows that is why Larry had emailed her to ask if she could do. "Where's Jane?" people would say, if she wasn't in evidence. At least, she hopes they would say it.

She drums her fingers. Maybe she needs to talk over the options with Jay. The more she thinks about this, the more this seems like a good idea.

She once met a woman in her seventies who had had a rather racy younger life. This old woman had once said to her, apropos of having an affair, that she couldn't imagine how it would be done in the modern world.

"You are just so likely to get found out, that's the problem," she had said to Jane. "What with everything going on a screen on your phone."

The seventy year old woman had explained to Jane that her affair, being conducted in the days of the Poste Restante, took place via individual letters.

"Much safer," said the woman.

What a time waster, thought Jane. Imagine all that incriminating evidence. And what torment it must have been, all that waiting for the letter telling where and when to meet. God! Weeks could go by. Weeks in which day rooms could have been booked, and enjoyed. She had been polite to the woman, but some of these sentiments had clearly leaked out onto her face. The woman had smiled at her sympathetically, thinking of the hoard she now treasures. The shoeboxes in her attic, the yellowing papers, the ribbons, the faded napkins from forgotten cafes and lingered-over coffees, the short scrawled lines of erotica. *My darling. The softness of your thighs.* She allows herself to look at them, occasionally.

Jane doodles slightly on her pad.

Surely there cannot be an easier time or place than the present, in which to conduct an affair? Modern technology simply lends itself to it, so much so in fact that it could almost have been invented for it.

At any time of night, or day, there are so many ways to link up with Jay. She stares out of the window, looking without seeing the naked branches from the plane trees, outlined against the white sky.

Right from the beginning of the day, Jane is engaged in a virtual conversation with her neighbour and lover. She thinks about it as soon as she wakes up. I can message him while taking my morning shower, she muses. I shall tell him I am naked. He might respond with a silly something which will make me smile as I am on my way downstairs for breakfast. Sometimes, he will even text me while I am having a cup of tea with Patrick. I might text him back.

There is only one awkward moment. She doesn't much like him to text her while she is dressing George and getting his bag ready, that makes her feel uneasy and a little guilty.

111

But texting her while she is smiling at her husband, that is fine. More than fine. It makes her feel sexy and alive. Wasn't this how a modern woman was meant to be?

Of course the audacity of it is part of the excitement. And is it any worse, Jane thinks, almost as if the seventy year old woman is sitting right in front of her, is it any worse than writing secret letters in lavender ink and sending them to a Poste Restante, and keeping the replies, tied in a ribbon, in a shoebox forever? Of course not. It's just a bit more technical. And there are no incriminating replies to be kept in the technological age. She never keeps anything, of course.

She deletes absolutely every single sentence from Jay that arrives on her phone. Every one. She never emails. She never writes. He used to drop cards round, before she demanded he stop. She has nothing in her Prada bag, nothing in her knicker drawer, nothing in her wallet which might provide excitement and a household drama. She used to write things down in code, but when she came to re-read them, she had forgotten the code. She found she was just looking at a whole lot of silly scribbles, which made her feel sad as she had no idea how to understand them.

Birthdays, Christmasses, trips abroad; they all must go unmarked. Jane never sends cards, they never exchange presents. The quotidian stuff of love; the photographs, cherished letters, gifts, boxes full of memorabilia from set piece events, these are forbidden. Affairs must happen right in the middle of the slip stream, and must leave no permanent trace. Those are the rules. They must be washed away by life. They are not about posterity. That is their pull, and their pain. *Hey. What's going on?* she texts.

To her satisfaction, he replies immediately. She hates waiting for him to respond.

Jane. What the devil are you up to? Sorting out the Talent Show. Very bored. Head Girl To Action. Would you like a helping hand?

She looks at the text, helpless. She puts away the pad.

Since the fucking in the corridor, she has been counting the days until her next fix. After about nine days of chaste married life, she is desperate for a day room.

But she has no day room booked today. She feels like a cross child whose offer of play has just been snatched away. *Thought you were busy today. Darling. We have no room booked. Never mind. Let's have coffee then. And a chat.*

Jane doesn't want coffee, or a chat. She wants to be back in the corridor, being screwed up against the wall. Alternatively, she wants to be carried across the bland Travelodge bedroom, legs wrapped around his body, intoxicated. She wants him sucking her body. She wants to be delivered into him. Or he into her. Instead, she must look forward to a cup of coffee.

She feels like pouting. *Oh. Ok then.*

There is a pavilion in the middle of the square, where a Filipino woman sometimes serves instant coffee in plastic cups. Nobody understands when it is open, since the opening of the pavilion is at the behest of the council, which runs it on some hidden programme.

It's the perfect place to meet, because it is right under everyone's noses. If anyone asks, they are simply organising the Talent Show, thinks Jane.

She dashes to the mirror, puts a pair of earrings on, dabs perfume around, assesses her makeup, arranges a scarf. Just something she threw on. Today she is clothed under her coat. She steps out of the house and walks briskly into the Square, hoping that the fresh breeze will make her look windswept, casually sexy. She quite often looks at herself from a distance like this.

"Hello darling."

"Hi."

"So, how's the impresario?"

She sits down. The Filipino woman is not around. The shutter on the cafe is very firmly shut.

"Oh, Jay. I'm nervous about this. Everyone was so keen at the meeting, but now I don't know if this is really going to be a good idea. But I have managed to get myself in charge of the whole thing."

Jay raises his eyebrows, smiles at her teasingly.

"I wonder how that happened."

"Piss off. Well, now I'm tempted to just book a band, and bring in catering instead."

"Don't be crazy! That would cost a fortune. Anyway I thought the whole point was to have a fundraiser for what was it... railings? You can't go spending thousands on catering. Unless of course Patrick is up for bankrolling it."

Jane had forgotten about the fundraising bit. How tiresome.

"Oh, yes, of course."

"We can get stuff from here, at a pinch."

Jane looks dismally at the pavilion. There are cracked plastic chairs and ashtrays with half an inch of rainwater and some leaves swimming in them. It's far from Jane's idea, which concerns hog roasts and delicious canapés and a tent borrowed from the Sultan of Oman in case of inclement weather.

"I was thinking more of a hog roast."

"Ha! Hog roast? For a fundraiser? Do you know any millionaire pig breeders then?"

"I hate living with Austerity Measures."

"Come on! Now you are sounding like Harriet."

Jane's stomach clenches. She hates him talking about his wife.

"Oh, thanks."

"Well, you are. This is nothing. Imagine really having a hard time. Living through the War or some such, imagine how that must have been."

"I do. All the time. George is doing the Blitz as a school project. Every night he comes home demanding to eat only rationed food. Powdered egg and so on. It's driving me mental. I'm only allowed to give him a banana on Thursdays."

"Oh, that sounds perfect for the show. So what will he do? 'It's a Long Way To Tipperary'?"

"Good God, I hope not. I might get him to perform something with Roberta. You know, the piano teacher. Something classical."

"Well, that might be your choice. Would it be his?"

"No."

"Well?"

"If he had his own way, he would probably stay in his room building something with Lego."

"But you want to parade him. The Infant Mozart. The Child Prodigy."

This was true. Sometimes, Jay really did annoy Jane. She loved fucking him, of course. But today that wasn't on the menu. Today, he is annnoying Jane so much that she deeply resents even the space of air he takes up on his chair. She silently heaps disdain on his head. It was something she sometimes did. Took a sort of savage joy in doing so. She also did it to his irritating wife. Harriet. Who was out of shape, and ate too much.

"Something like that. Why, what are you going to do then? Are you going to do something with Harriet?" says Jane suddenly, terrified he might say he was. She opted to go for sarcasm by means of defence. "Something amazingly contemporary? A piece of modern dance?" she says, snorting.

Jay laughs, ignoring the obvious jibe.

"Actually, I think Harriet is planning to do a Bach Chaconne, in fact. Or something by Corelli. Nice baroque piece, you know. She's rather good at the violin. Very good, in fact. Grade Seven-ish. Did you know that?"

Jane isn't prepared for this. Harriet, having a skill. And in something really admirable, like the violin. Why didn't she know that before?

"La-de-dah."

"Why on earth does that matter to you? Surely it's good if we all bring our best talents to the night. I mean, you're organising it. Have you thought about who will present it, then?"

115

"Well, I actually thought, as I am taking all this time to organise it, and of course I will know what's on the programme... then it would make sense... if... "

She tails off.

"Oh, YOU will?! Of course, of course."

"Don't you think so?" she says, anxious.

"Oh no, you must. You'll be great," he says, putting an arm around her. "You must."

There is a pause.

Then, "When did she start learning the violin?" Jane asks. As if she cared.

"Oh, she learnt when she was a child. She's always played, on and off."

Jane pokes at some mud on the ground with her smart shoe. She wishes she was still at home in her office. She should really only see Jay if and when they have a prior arrangement, otherwise this sort of thing is likely to happen.

Instead of Jay telling her how fantastic she is, and fantasising about her being naked under a mac, or best of all, making love to her, all he has done is tease her about being Head Girl, and reveal that his wife has inner hidden Nigel bloody Kennedy status. Great.

She stands up. She needs to be made love to by him, but she will have to wait.

Jay stands up too, pecks her cheek.

"Look, darling, I have to go. Main Presenter, Head Girl, it's been lovely."

"Yes, so do I," she responds quickly. "I'm actually very busy."

"When are you not?" he asks.

Is it over? thinks Jane.

Chapter Fourteen
Tracey

Tracey rings the door bell in the converted warehouse.

"Makin's Makeovers?" says a female voice from the speaker.

"Yes, er, I have a meeting with Alan and his team," says Tracey into the plastic box.

"Fourth floor," says the voice.

The door swings open.

She walks up. Four floors. This can be her exercise for the day.

At the fourth floor, another door. Alan Makin is standing in front of it, beaming.

He is in a white suit with a thin beige stripe and a beige tie with thin white stripes. Beige European sandals. Thin cream silk socks. Cufflinks.

"Tracey! Marvellous. Come right in. Drink?"

Tracey finds herself grasping a cup of coffee, and sitting in a large, vaulted chamber alongside Alan's 'team'.

Vast pictures of Alan Makin in charasmatic mode grin down from the walls.

She suddenly notices that there is a large illuminated vitrine in the corner. In it is sitting a rather big iguana, on a stick. It does not appear to be moving.

"Oh, God. Is that thing alive?" asks Tracey.

"I should co-co," says Alan. "Gets through a bag of live crickets a week. The Munchkin, we call him."

His assistant giggles.

"Now," says Alan. "This is the Team. Helen, Joseph, Alex, Geraldine, this is Tracey."

"Hi," says the Team in unison.

Tracey manages a smile.

"What we thought would be great would be to do a sort of Makin Makeover on you," continues Alan. "See where you are going wrong, see where you are going right, straighten everything up for you. You know… The Woman Who Won The Lottery… and frittered it away." There is a pause. Tracey looks at him, eyes widening in alarm.

"In a nice way, of course. Nobody will look at it in a bad way. Really. They will empathise with you. Empathy. Very important in a television programme, isn't it, Team?"

The Team nods its head.

"Almost as important as Jeopardy. But you have that already," says Alan, smiling.

Do I? thinks Tracey, bewildered.

"Because," continues Alan, "there is always the chance that you could lose your house on the Square, lose a foothold in society."

Is there? thinks Tracey.

"Most importantly," continues Alan, "we will give you a new blueprint for living. We'll work out your finances. How to pay off that unsecured debt. And you'll have a spot on the show. You know you talked to me about the abyss? Well, as soon as you see a plan, you will see light at the end of the tunnel. That's the idea anyway."

Everyone laughs.

"We've got some scenes already sketched out," says Alan, steepling his fingers.

"The overall idea is that you, the Lottery winner, come to us with a financial problem, we do a bit of backgrounding, set our minds to erasing that problem, we bring in a few graphics, do a bit of number crunching, the problem is fixed, you sail off into the sunny uplands of credit."

Is it really as easy as all that? Tracey somehow doubts it. She doesn't want to be a problem, but money, for Tracey, never seems to be sunny anywhere, let alone on the uplands of credit. It was only uncomplicated once, and that was the night when they learned they had won the Lottery.

She doesn't want Alan to think she's wavering, however. Even if it does diddly squat to my finances, it'll be fun to be on telly, she thinks. The girls will be impressed. Larry will be impressed. As for Jane, Patrick, all that lot on the Square... She opens her eyes very wide and looks straight at Alan.

"Oh, God, could you really do that?"

"I don't see why not. Do you?"

"But I sell cosmetics. That's the income stream I have. Unless everyone really really wants to increase their orders, there's not much... "

Alan waves his hands excitedly.

"Don't worry. We'll give you a day by day plan. It'll all be great. And it will all look great on screen."

The wonderful make-believe that is television. Oh well.

Tracey smiles, nods at him.

Alan nods. The Team nods. Everyone sits nodding at everyone else for a few seconds. Any minute now, the Munchkin will start nodding, thinks Tracey.

Over lunch (Tracey: macaroni cheese, Alan: a green salad), Alan looks at her steadily. "I am going to make this work with you. I am going to turn you around."

"Are you?" she laughs nervously.

"I am. I'm going to make you see what life might be like if you aren't bouncing from one credit card to the next."

"That would be nice," she says sadly.

"It's entirely possible, and with someone who has been so publicly wealthy as you, utterly doable," he says, diving into his salad and waving a tomato at her. He smiles encouragingly. Then, he starts confiding in her. Tracey was not expecting this. She eats her macaroni cheese as he talks.

"It's like this. I enjoy focusing my team and my talents. And my story. How I was once – looking over the abyss, as you might say. Actually, I was in the abyss. I was mired in debt, and I pulled myself out. I think that is a message worth delivering to as many people as possible. That it is possible." He sighs.

Tracey looks at his neatly combed hair, his button-down shirt, the care with which the tie is married to the suit.

"Oh, of course, everything is fine, but you wouldn't believe it. Some people find it hard to talk about their finances to me. You are unusually open, Tracey, with your life."

"Am I?" she smiles. It feels like a compliment, although she's not quite sure.

"People, I think, ordinary people, they get a bit starstruck around me," continues Alan loftily.

"What sort of people?"

"All sorts of people."

He looks at Tracey.

"Do you think I am gay? You didn't think I was gay, did you?"

"No, no, why on earth would you think that?" she lies.

"Oh, no reason, no reason. I mean, it's not that I don't like gay people. I think gay people are great. Some of my best friends are gay," smiles Alan.

There is a pause.

"But I'm not."

"So what's the problem?" says Tracey. She likes these sort of conversations. Sympathy. She's good at sympathy. Or was it empathy?

"You're probably just working a bit too hard. Burning the candle, you know."

"Well, perhaps. It is a tough call, sometimes. You know, driving the whole enterprise. And it would be nice to have someone to chat to about it. All around me, I just have my Team. It's about finding someone who can understand me. Someone who I can relax with. Who might be able to forget that I am, you know, Alan Makin, and just treat me as if I was just plain old Alan. Someone who could, well, just hear what's burbling along in this old head of mine. A bit like I'm hearing how your finances are burbling along!"

"Don't tell me you think I'm that sort of woman."

I've never had anyone say this to me before, thinks Tracey. She feels a bit light-headed.

"Well, I don't know. But you might be! The way you stood up at the event, spoke out like that."

She smiles, blushes.

"It was remarkable. Standing up to me, a television personality up there on stage. I like you. I like your forthright manner. You're open and honest. I think our film about you is going to be excellent. I like your company, very much, and I think our viewers will, too."

"I'm terribly flattered that you, well, that you want to sort out my finances on your show."

"You seem like a very special person, Tracey."

Why is he doing this, she wonders. I bet he's gone on like this to plenty of women after those live shows. I bet he's had women longing for him to sort out their affairs. He's probably had affairs with some of them. Does he want to have an affair with me? thinks Tracey, with a thrill. She knows it's foolish, but she is flattered nonetheless.

"Thank you Alan."

"You do."

"Thank you."

"You know, you really don't look like a Tracey."

"So, how do you envisage my appearance on the show?"

"Right, of course. Let's talk about work. We will come to your house. Where do you live? Oh yes, how could I forget? The Square."

"It's only about ten minutes away."

"Yes, yes."

He coughs, adjusts the cufflinks professionally. Tracey is bewildered. It's as if the entire previous ten minutes haven't happened.

"So, we come to your house. Do a bit of filming. Understand your lifestyle. You know, are you a TV dinner family or a roast chicken family? Do you grow your own herbs? Are you... married?"

For some reason, Tracey feels reluctant to admit it.

"Yes, yes I am," she acknowledges.

"Perhaps we could meet your husband, your... children? How many do you have?"

"Two. Girls."

"Little princesses are they?"

"Well. One is sweet, but a sometimes devious eight year old. The other is a sixteen year old gym fanatic sworn to chastity and ankle-length robes."

Alan pauses, attempts to envisage this working well on his show.

"Really? How... surprising. Very interesting. Fascinating. Sworn to chastity? Well, maybe not do the children then. Might not go down too well on Daytime. How's your husband?"

"Loud."

"Hmm. Maybe have a rain check on that too. Perhaps it will be best if it's just you and me. You know. Intense, focused." He leans forward as if to personify these qualities. "On the sofa together. You know, sorting out your money problems. Of course, a lot of this will be done afterwards. In post production. In a studio. You know, graphics. Swoosh! The Lottery win. Bang! It all gets spent. Spend spend spend. That sort of thing."

Alan makes a waving gesture with his hand, as if to illustrate the screen cluttered with hosts of glowing mathematical figures, percentages, interest rates, all the panoply of financial advice he is going to gift Tracey with.

"Er, Alan."

"Yes?"

"Forgot to ask you before. Will there be something of a fee for this?"

There is a pause. Alan bursts out laughing. He almost spits on Tracey's plate, he is laughing so hard.

"Oh. Okay. Just thought I'd ask. Because, you know, finances are, well, quite tight. Which is why I'm in this predicament in the first place."

She giggles, embarrassed.

Alan looks at Tracey.

Tracey looks at Alan. She feels herself blushing.

Alan looks away quickly.

"If I siphoned off a nice fee for you, it would mean the rest of the budget would suffer."

"But my time... I'll have to give up some work in order to take part. I might have to think about it, Alan."

He looks at her archly, smiles in a deadly manner.

"No, no. Actually, I think, no actually, I'm sure, really sure that we can come to some sort of... arrangement."

He sighs, and shifts in his chair.

What does he mean?

"What do you mean? What sort of arrangement? Don't tell me you want some nail varnish?" She smiles nicely at him, puts a hand out on his arm. Maybe he would, she doesn't know. Perhaps the man likes to have his hands done nicely. She once did sell some clear nail varnish to a chap. About five years ago, but still.

"Well, Tracey. Funny you should say that, as a matter of fact."

All at once, he jerks his arm out, looks at his watch.

"I have to go, shortly. But can I just say, as I have said, I think we will have a very fulfilling project together. And over and above the demands of our proposed film, there might be a bit of advice from your area that I could use. In confidence. And we could... invent a payment for your consultation which could represent a fee for appearing on the programme. I think that is known in managment circles as win-win."

She opens her mouth. He puts his hand up to arrest anything she might say. Almost unconsciously, she takes a quick look at his nails.

"Look, I know what you are thinking. I'm not asking for anything you would not be able to explain to your family. And Tracey, I'll pay you for your time."

What? Is this man out of his head? He's going to pay me to talk to him?

"Alan, you can trust me with this. I'm not one to blab about my clients, or whatever you want to call yourself. But I'm not a therapist, you know. I sell nail varnish to people, and advise them on what sort of lip colour to buy and how to use it. I'm not sure I'm going to be much good at this."

He smiles.

"Oh, but I think you are Tracey. You really are. You may not know it, but you have a very understanding nature. I know you will understand me. I'd like to just have some advice. And you know," he says, sighing, repeating his promise, "I'll pay you to do it. So you won't get paid for the telly stuff, but you will for the… other things. Simply so it can come out of a different accounting pot. How about that?"

She forces herself to laugh, simply to show him she is on top of this new situation. She wouldn't mind it either.

"Oh, this sounds crazy. Alright then, how much?"

"I will give you what I charge my top clients. Which is £200 an hour."

Tracey nearly chokes.

"Alan. That is quite a lot of money. My God. That would be amazing. Really?"

Oh my God. What a mad world we live in. Why, she could make a quick £600 simply out of having lunch with the man. Which is more or less what she takes home in a fortnight. For lunch. With Alan. He is quite oily, now she thinks about it. Never mind. She'll manage it for the money. And the chance to appear on TV.

"Comes out of a different budget."

"Yes, alright. I'll do it. I'd love to."

She shakes her head, laughing.

"Alan… will it be talking only?"

"Talking only. And maybe some eating."

"No nudity? I'm only joking Alan, but I have to ask."

I'm not joking, and damn right I'm asking.

He throws his head back with laughter.

"It's not about THAT, silly."

Tracey goes very red.

"Sorry."

"It's very simple, when you hear what I need to know and what I think we should talk about."

What is he on about? Maybe he is a religious fanatic, thinks Tracey. Christ, I hope not.

"Alright. As long as you are sure I can help, I will. Will I ever have to feed the Munchkin?"

"Never."

"Alright, it's a deal."

She looks at Alan, smiling.

Alan looks at his watch again, beside the immaculate cuffs.

"Must dash. Helen will call you to set up the first research meeting. Don't get up. You stay here and have a cup of coffee. I'll get this."

After Alan leaves, waving through the window, Tracey sits on her own, in a daze. She eventually gets up, brushing crumbs down off her pink woollen suit.

Chapter Fifteen
Belle

It's like being at primary school again, thinks Belle as she kneels beside the trestle table in Philip's studio, stapling chicken wire onto a piece of hardboard. And where the fuck is Jas, Little Jas? She can hear him talking to Philip, laughing. Getting on with the boss, while she does all the hard work. It's the morning, so Philip is still in his white robe. She rests stiffly back on her haunches, looks at her work from the level of the trestle.

It looks nothing like Berlin, or a marathon course, or anything. It reminds her of a small model she once made of the surface of the Moon, after watching it done on *Blue Peter*.

"Jas!" she calls. "Can you come over here please? Can you advise me where I need to go now?"

"Where are you?" calls Jas.

"In the studio. Obviously."

"No, where are you in Berlin?"

"Wedding."

Silly name for a suburb.

"Right over."

He walks over to her, squats down.

"Is this okay? Looks like the Moon, frankly."

He laughs. "It's good. Very good. It'll all take shape in a

few days. Wait and see."

He elbows her.

"Philip wants to get his photographer in on Thursday, so this can go out to prospective clients. Honestly. This is going to be big."

He really hopes so. Philip hasn't said much to him about Belle, but having her working for him has sped up the process a lot. Jas thinks he will probably end up earning quite a lot more than he usually does. After all, he's the senior assistant now that Belle has come in at the bottom.

"Yoo-hoo!"

They both turn around. It's Gilda in the doorway. She's wearing a draped satin white Seventies trouser suit with stars on the shoulder pads and big Jackie O sunglasses. Her nipples jut through the satin top. She is clearly not wearing a bra.

"Elevenses?"

"Don't mind if I do. Bels?"

"Sure." She gets up, wipes her hands down her jeans, stretches her legs.

"Follow me follow," trills Gilda. "Down to the Hollow."

Belle walks slowly after Jas into the kitchen. She's been working with Jas for three days, and this is the first time she's been invited down here. Maybe they wanted to see whether I came back, she thinks.

She walks into the kitchen, takes in the fairy lights, the artfully scuffed lino on the floor, the mannequins standing in the corners wearing Spanish matador outfits. The kitchen table is designed around a roulette wheel and a long cloth from a casino, which has been treated with some sort of spray and is slightly shiny, rather than soft and fluffy. Rouge, Noir. Pair, Impair. I will have to tell the Populars about every single atom of everything in this room, thinks Belle. She notices an upright piano alongside the wall.

Gilda is airily organising coffee in an old steel percolator. Jas is smoking. He is allowed to smoke at Philip's.

"An original from the Fifties. Estudio Alessi," says Gilda,

waving the percolator.

"Oh," says Belle, sensing she has to say a bit more. "Lovely."

Where are the famous porn pictures, is what she actually wants to ask.

"Look around, darling," says Gilda, as if she was a mind reader.

Belle does as she is told, and suddenly, there they are. Black and white photographs, about six or seven of them, showing Gilda in sets of very complicated, rather dated looking underwear. She is only topless in two of them. These show her holding up rather pendulous, teardrop-shaped breasts with very large, dark areoles around the nipples. Blimey, thinks Belle, she's got big tits.

"Do you like them?" says Gilda chattily, pouring coffee, as if she was talking about food, or the weather.

"Er, yes," blurts out Belle. "They're… good."

"They're done by George Rasper. Do you know George?" says Gilda. "You know, the famous *Sunday Times* photographer. He wanted to capture the spirit of Twenties strip tease," Gilda says. "After Jonty Coward, the famous photographer. Did all the flappers, all the Bright Young Things. Do you know about Jonty?"

All these people. She has no idea to whom Gilda is referring. Belle looks at Jas, who merely smiles at her, stubs his cigarette on a heritage Quaglino's ashtray and raises his eyebrows.

"No, er, no, I haven't," she murmurs. "But I'm sure these capture the spirit… I mean, in black and white and everything."

She looks back at the pictures. Gilda is throwing her head back in one, and bringing up a feather boa between her legs. Belle wishes she could get her phone out and take a photo. Maybe when Gilda's on the loo, she thinks, she will.

Gilda marches up to the pictures and surveys them, as if for the first time.

"The only thing about it is that my tits are a bit TOO big, I think. Too big for the period, frankly. Pity. We should have had the session before I had my op."

Is there nothing that this woman won't talk about, thinks Belle. Her candour makes Belle feel embarrassed on her behalf.

She can't think of what to say, so she simply smiles and sips her coffee, which has been handed to her in a china cup shaped like a bucket. Belle suddenly has the image of Gilda and Philip wandering around the house, ordering every single element of it from some outlandish catalogue, in order to fulfil their need to be seen as arty throughout every single moment of the day and at every single opportunity to consume within that day. She wonders if there is anything normal here, like a vaccuum cleaner, or a loo brush. Probably not.

She has already ventured into the ground floor toilet decorated with the moulds of Gilda's genitalia scattered across the walls. Found it impossible to piss in it, sadly. She had had to hold it in until she got home, running across the Square, grateful to be back in a place with holiday snaps on the wall and normal things such as a straightforward fridge containing Onken yoghurt, and a toilet decorated with a picture of a blue cat.

She takes another sip from the cup, looks down, and suddenly screams, dropping the cup. It bounces away on the lino, flinging the residue of the coffee as it goes.

"Oh my God, Jas!"

"What, what?"

"There is a snail in my coffee cup!"

Gilda hoots with laughter.

"Oh, darlinka! Everyone falls for it!" She picks up a teatowel, mops up the spilt coffee and picks up the cup. Well, at least there's a bloody ordinary teatowel in this freak show of a house, thinks Belle.

Gilda holds the now empty cup over to Belle. Peering in, she can see there is a large and wholly realistic china snail cemented to the bottom of the cup.

"The more you drink, the more of the snail is revealed. It's sitting in the bottom of a bucket, you see. I think it's killing. Don't you think it's killing?"

"Yes," mumbles Belle. "Sorry."

"Not at all," says Gilda, eyes sparkling.

Cow. She planned that to happen. Give the new girl the joke cup, thinks Belle. Well, just you wait, Russian porn queen.

Jas walks over to her.

"Sorry, Belle. Shall we?" He points upstairs. "I think we have to get on with the Reichstag." He turns to his hostess, who is leaning against the roulette table in her silk suit, smiling.

"Thanks Gilda. The German Parliament calls."

As they walk upstairs, Philip is standing somewhat testily in the hall. He is dressed for the day in a blue boiler suit and spotted bow tie.

"Ah, Jas and, er… "

"Belle," says Belle.

"Yes, sorry. You two. I have to go out now. Magnus. Please make sure you continue with Berlin. I have the photographer coming tomorrow, now. So a state of readiness is all. As Alexander Fleming probably never said."

"What is he on about?" says Belle after Philip leaves the house with a flourish.

"This place is a loony bin."

"Just nod your head and smile," says Jas. "That's what I do. And get on with it. Last night, after you left, I finished the Brandenburg Gate. Take a look."

Chapter Sixteen
Roberta

Roberta rings the door bell, stands on the step, shivers in her coat although she is not particularly cold. Come on, come on. After a significant pause, the door opens, slowly. By nobody, it seems like.

She looks down to see the small personage of George standing, arms folded, waiting.

"Oh, sorry, there you are!"

"My mother is out." He beckons her in theatrically. "This is all the better."

"Oh, why is that?"

"Because then we don't need to practise. Or at least, not all the time. We can talk about my film for the Talent Show. I think that's what my mother wants us to do anyway."

Indeed, Jane had shouted up to George as she had left.

"I'm going to get some flowers. Dad will be back in five minutes. After your lesson, get Roberta to work out something with you for the Show, darling!"

"Sorry, I can't make you a cup of tea either. I'm 'not allowed' to," he says, giving quote marks around the despised command.

They walk into the music room.

"Here is Water." He proffers a rather smeared glass, half full.

131

"Oh, thanks, lovely," says Roberta, taking it and sipping a tiny amount. The glass is wet to the touch, which makes her feel slightly queasy.

"But George, we still need to do a little bit of music anyway, unfortunately. We must think about your Grade Two which is coming up." Roberta remembered that meeting with Jane in the road, which had been very strange. Jane had seemed very hurried, and unusually flighty. She didn't want Jane to start thinking that George wasn't progressing with his piano. He had got to get his Grade Two, that was clear.

"Thought you might say that," murmurs George.

He sits down with a thump on the music stool.

"Hanon?"

She puts the wet glass carefully down on some papers, so as not to mark the Blüthner.

He sighs, reaches up for the beige book, cracks it open and begins. Arrangement No. 1. The page is heavy with dense notes, each packed into military order along the staves.

"Do each one five times, George, please."

He does as she asks. Each time he repeats a phrase, it is as if a comb is running through the notes, teasing out the tangles, smoothing out the shape of the small exercise.

"Better."

I could listen to Hanon all day, she thinks. All day long. Listening to Hanon. It entertains your brain without fully engaging it, a bit like watching patterns of bricks, or running your eye up the long wires on a suspension bridge. It allows you to do something while thinking of something else, which Roberta has always appreciated. Although it probably belies a lack of focus, she thinks.

I bet successful people never release their brain fully in this way. They are always focusing on their ambition far in the horizon. She had once seen a Golden Eagle up close. It looked straight past her, focusing on the distance. That is how successful people are, she thinks. That is how her clients are. They are so busy looking to the future that they never focus on the present in front of them, the busy notes of Hanon climbing up and climbing down the scale. She might not be successful, thinks Roberta, but at least she knows what it is like to be consumed with music.

George turns and looks at her inquisitively.

"Go on," she nods her head at him. He continues. He is the most appealing child, she thinks with a rush.

Hanon is anything but artistic, at least not in the way most people normally think of artistic things, which is romantic and chaotic, ponders Roberta. But it is beautiful. This music is beautiful because it is fixed, disciplined, necessary. Every exercise is rationally and unemotionally considered. Hanon is like fundamental architecture. That is because it supports playing. Learning how to play it is like learning how to drive a car, or touch typing. It grants you the prowess to move on.

Eventually, George comes to the end of the next page.

"Now we have to do your pieces."

"But, Roberta... what about my film soundtrack?"

She holds a hand up. Grade Two must be conquered.

"Later. Let's get on with your piece."

He begins the short Mozart.

A commotion in the hall. Patrick's friendly face appears around the door.

"Hullo, Roberta. All ensconced I see. Good, good. George? Sounding good, old chap. Sorry I was late." He looks at his son inquisitively.

"Mater?"

"Out," says George. "Something about flowers."

A pause. "Oh. Oh, yes, I think she's getting flowers for tomorrow. Supper party tomorrow night, Roberta. All normal existence must stop because we shall all focus on canapés and how to fold napkins into swans."

He makes a face at Roberta. This mad old social whirl we engage ourselves with.

Roberta smiles at him, arranges her features neutrally and turns back to George. She is not going to join in,

133

conspiratorially, with the criticism of a dinner party – or, as Patrick insists on calling it, a supper party. She is paid to be here. But honestly. Mater.

"Go from the end of that bar."

Patrick backs off and closes the door, humming as if to show how at ease he is in his own house.

George plays the end of the piece, twice.

He turns to Roberta expectantly. She looks at her watch.

"Alright. Now we can talk about your soundtrack."

"Oh, brilliant. Right."

There is a silence.

"It's got to be three minutes long."

"Okay."

"And it needs to start off very dramatically. Sort of dah dah dah DAH."

Beethoven's Fifth. She smiles.

"Are you bringing along an entire orchestra, then?"

"Of course not. But haven't you always said that the piano contains the potential of an entire orchestra within it?"

He's too clever for me.

"Alright, a very dramatic start. Good. People will like that. Then what?"

"Then, then it has to go very very quiet. Weeny, weeny, like mice. And a bit dreamy."

Weeny dreamy mice?

"Sort of lovey dovey."

Lovey dovey weeny dreamy mice?

Roberta starts to get a bit nervous about what her pupil is going to produce in front of, let's face it, potentially most of her clients in the Square.

"And then LOUD again."

Well, maybe it will be alright, she thinks, dubiously.

"Sounds interesting. Shall we try working out a little sequence? Shall I write down some notes for you?"

She picks up his manuscript book where she writes down his weekly duties, and blindly rootles in her bag for a pencil.

134

"What's the film beside it going to show, then?"

"Well, I think it is going to be ordinary, and then dramatic, possibly with Darth Vader. And then ordinary again."

"Okay... Sounds good to me."

"I'm not so sure."

"Well, I think it will work."

"Yes. Mother doesn't. Roberta my dear, I hope you don't mind me saying so but you are a bit different from Mother."

That makes her laugh.

"Come on then, what about some big chords for the begining?"

He places his fingers on the keys, arms straight, and then presses them all down together, in the style of a maestro.

"Like this, I thought."

"I think you are in B flat. That's good."

She writes down the chords, simply.

"I'll play those a few times, maybe eight. Then it all gets twinkly. Like this."

George puts his face down, very close to the keyboard and plays three consecutive notes in a quavering staccato.

This is beginning to sound like some sort of piece which might have been composed by Dadaists, thinks Roberta. She has visions of chairs scraping and people leaving. Not really, nobody would be so cruel, but she sees she needs to take this piece in hand.

"Are you going to think about a melody?"

"What?"

"You know, a tune. You could incorporate Twinkle Twinkle Little Star, or something."

"Roberta, my dear."

"Well, if it's good enough for Mozart, it's probably good enough for you."

"This is a soundtrack. It's BOUND to sound strange. It has to go alongside the action on the film. But maybe you're right. Oh, I don't know."

He sniffs, looks straight ahead at the piano. Takes his

hands away from the keys. His face is suddenly very red.

"I've got a brilliant idea," says Roberta, who cannot bear tears from her pupils.

"What?" he says in a small choking voice.

"Why don't you set it to Hanon? It's completely neutral. You could set anything to Hanon. But it goes on and on, like a river. You know, you can have lots of action on the screen and dear old Hanon will just chug away in the background. And you can make some bits loud and some bits soft. Plus, it's something you know how to play, which is always a help for nerves. And also, it sounds properly classical."

"So my parents will like it."

"Well, let's just call that a serendipitous side effect."

He starts to smile, rubs his hands together.

"And now, for the world premiere… "

Roberta stands up. She'd like to give George, this strange little solitary boy, a hug. Or rumple his hair. She can't do that. Instead she picks up Hanon.

"I'll look at what we might choose and bring my suggestions back next week. Fortissimo, piano, forte."

"Yes. The thing is, Roberta," he says happily.

"What?"

"When everyone thinks I am practising, actually I will be preparing for my film score!"

Chapter Seventeen
The Dinner Party

She had written the menu for the supper party out a week ago, after the guest list was settled. It was her turn to deliver the long-formatted procedure. Three courses, sometimes four with cheese. Chocolates. Champagne as the sharpener.

"Do you remember when we always had a G&T before dinner?" Patrick sometimes says, longingly. "Oh for the days of the aperitif. When fortified wine was seen as a treat."

Nobody calls it dinner any more either. It's a supper party, lavish but in casual clothing.

As if they are all going to watch the sun set from the terraces at the Petit Trianon, having bedded down the cattle.

As the guests sit around the table, still in that strict Fifties gender formation always described as Boy, Girl (unless there is a gay couple present), the hostess takes a deep breath. The starter is crucial, for it is the starter which shall indicate the style of the evening. The evening shall either be Showing Off supper, in which case the visitors will be humbled by a spectacular dish revelling in an unfamiliar cuisine, or its counterpart, Nursery supper, in which the host deliberately humbles herself with school dinner standards.

Both are acceptable, depending on the day of the week, weather, and whether a child has insisted on being present.

Nobody likes children being there. Children at night are even more awkward than gay couples or someone with a gluten allergy. Gay couples are at least deeply fashionable, and can be very funny indeed. Allergies are annoying but are usually ironed out earlier. Children are just irritating.

"I think we will have squid, for starters," says Jane.

Patrick eyes her from the bed. This event is simply an invented hurdle, an adult challenge for people who don't have many challenges left. Unlike George, Patrick thinks, whose life is a stream of Grades and exams and achievements. Patrick considers his life to be a straight line of, well, living, interrupted occasionally by small hurdles such as holidays, the occasional illness, and dinner parties.

He doesn't even count having sex as part of the continuum, because it is not. He remembers a period when Jane never wore anything to bed. She would just wriggle in beside him, slightly slippery, her skin briefly chilled from the air in the bedroom, but containing a deep watery heat from her bath. Then, of course, they would fuck. Nowadays however, she gets dressed for bed, pulling a long dress or pyjamas over her naked body. That's it. As the material goes on, he sees the familiar soft contours disappear, breasts, belly, triangle, knees. It goes from chin to calf. There is no subsequent fucking.

This evening is no different. Chastely enrobed thus, Jane continues to discuss squid.

Which, as Patrick must acknowledge, is hardly an aphrodisiac.

"… spiked with chilli and served in kiwi fruit, on a bed of cous cous? It's a dish from Tangiers. I read about it in the *Observer* last week. Looks like a nightmare to prepare, but if I do it the day before… "

"What next?" asks Patrick lazily.

Jane has worked out the main course already. Lamb baked in individual tiny pumpkins. Followed by cheeses, specially delivered from somewhere in the middle of France, a place which Jane has heard is frightfully dull, but has amazing dairy. And then, as a deliberate nod to the nursery option, but with irony, a pavlova featuring Greek cherries and curdled Chantilly cream.

She sighs. The menu will take Jane a full three days to assemble and cost several hundred pounds in terms of raw ingredients, Champagne, wine, bottled water both fizzy and still, a range of cut flowers and a few downloaded tracks of something obscure and Seventies to waft around in the air.

The whole thing must be casual. Any artifice must be lightly draped across the night in an effect of naturalness. This is the style of supper parties on the Square, and Jane is the mistress of the oxymoron.

"Who's coming again?" says Patrick.

"I have told you this before. Beth and James, you know, the couple from work. Tracey and Larry. You and me. And Jay and Harriet."

He snorts, remembering the previous event at the Residents' Association meeting.

"Have you reinforced the chairs?"

"Patrick!"

"It was bloody funny though. Seeing that chair completely knackered and Harriet on the floor."

"Also I've done something rather brilliant."

"Oh, yes?"

"I am installing Anya, that au pair of Tracey and Larry's. I'm putting her in the kitchen to do the washing up. I've got her for a bargain price."

Patrick raises his eyebrows by response. He knows Anya. He thinks she is rather beautiful, in a wild Slavonic way. He has never spoken to her. She is the sort of au pair he would never have trusted himself to hire, in the days before George's school hours were so long there was no point in hiring anyone to look after him.

He turns over, away from his wife in bed and envisages Anya in the kitchen.

Two days later, the supper party is upon them.

As far as Anya is concerned, she is quite happy to be in the kitchen area of the knock-through for £10 an hour. She'd be happy to be anywhere for £10 an hour, frankly. She can hear the Seventies music upstairs, which she likes. She knows that at a key moment, the conversation and footsteps will move from the upstairs living room down to the basement dining 'zone'.

The candlelit dining table is prepared. Anya thinks it looks a bit like an altar; a high rectangle, swaddled in white linen and gleaming with silver, glass and flowers. She hears the guests clatter downstairs towards the dining table. Here we go, she thinks.

She considers heating up the cold, big plates ready for the main course. Certainly at home, her parents always liked hot plates for the meat dish.

Jane comes in suddenly, ready to carry out the squid and cous cous. Anya suggests that the main course plates be heated up. To her surprise this goes down very badly.

"Oh, no! Anya, not at all! Nobody has hot plates any more!" Jane cries.

"The whole point is that food must be served at room temperature."

Anya apologises for the idea.

Jane's face is rather flushed. She is wearing a pleated dress of silvery linen which has a high ruff at the collar. It has no sleeves, so it can show off her thin, long arms. The pleated skirt brushes the top of her knees. She is wearing sheer glossy tights and very high heels with a Mary Jane strap. Crystal earrings swing from her lobes. A small headband decorated with flowers goes around her hair.

She looks artfully decorated, almost in concert with the table.

Squaring her shoulders, she takes the wide china plate and walks with a tiny spring in her step towards the table. Good, Patrick has done the placements. Boy, Girl, Boy, Girl.

"So, everyone. Squid and kiwi." She pauses for the cries of acclaim around the table. Yes, tonight is going to be showy.

"Where does it come from?" she says, pleased to be asked. "Oh, somewhere in Morocco I think. Tangier? Casablanca? Yes, it's quite novel but apparently the flavours 'meld' together. Well, according to the *Observer*, they do!"

She serves her friends, who sit waiting to be fed. Jay, she serves last, a small smile playing around her features. She's not seen him since the dreary meeting in the park, but tonight is different. Tonight she is on show.

"Wine?" says Patrick, standing, grasping the crystal decanter, sloshing the light red liquid into the glasses.

"Apparently red is what must be drunk with this dish. According to the *Observer*." He rolls his eyes theatrically. "Only reason we get a newspaper these days! Supper party tips!"

Everyone laughs.

Unseen, George tiptoes past the table, making his way towards the kitchen where Anya is sitting, reading.

"Hello Anya," he says.

"Good evening George," says Anya, who has a soft spot for him.

"Aren't you meant to be in bed?"

"I suppose I'm 'meant' to have done a lot of things," says George, quote marks hanging in the air. "I'm 'meant' to have played the piano, for one thing, to the guests tonight. But I 'was not to be found' at the right time. What's this?" He pokes at the lamb in little pumpkin shells which is resting at room temperature.

"Don't touch that! For God's sake. Your mother will go crazy. Doesn't she think you are meant to be in bed?"

George looks at her. "Do you mean, does she think I am in bed? Or does she mean to put me into bed? Or would she be glad to know I am in bed?"

Anya smiles at her small inquisitor.

"All of them. Take this," giving him a chocolate truffle

141

dusted with cinnamon. It and several others have been positioned on a beautiful Moroccan 'heritage' plate made by Berber herdsmen, which will be produced after the ironic pavolva. He tastes it gingerly. "Ugh. That is vile."

"Alright, have this," says Anya, giving him a HobNob.

"Yum. Can I have two?"

"Go on then. Now go to bed."

He walks upstairs to the sitting room, and sits down quietly behind the sofa. George slips his Nintendo DS out of his pocket, and settles down for a long gaming session, munching his biscuits, discreetly out of vision. He slides the device onto mute.

Downstairs, Jane is watching her guests eat her food. As always, she is eating very little herself.

"This is amazing Jane," says Tracey, waving her fork in the air. "Have you done it before?"

She smiles, pleased that someone has asked the right question. "No, actually, no. I haven't. I like a challenge!"

"Gosh, you are brave," says Tracey. "I would never do something new at a dinner party."

Jane looks at Tracey. Still calls them dinner parties, how gauche.

Plus, she always has second helpings. It's been years since Jane has allowed herself a second helping. She gave up second helpings as a New Year resolution about five years ago, and never looked back.

Jane has a fear of getting fat not dissimilar to a fear of getting cancer.

She studies Tracey. When did she last see her? Oh, yes. Before going off to meet that finance guy from the TV.

"So, I've been meaning to ask you, how did you get on with your meeting with the television finance guru?"

Jane hopes, fervently, that the meeting was cancelled, that the plan isn't getting off the ground, that the project has been abandoned. She smiles kindly at Tracey.

Tracey looks at her blankly.

"Don't you remember? I saw you in the morning when you were trotting off to meet him? You were all dressed up in your suit!"

There is something not quite sisterly about Jane, Tracey decides.

"Oh, yes, yes of course. Well, I was off for a meeting with Alan Makin."

"Oh, Tracey, I've been meaning to ask you, how did it go?" says Harriet across the table. Harriet is wearing a very tight pink cashmere jumper which is stretched tightly over her breasts. It makes them appear rather like one of those security wrapped suitcases. She looks rather hot. She beams at Tracey.

"We went to hear the amazing Makin the week before," says Harriet to the assembled table, "and Tracey caught his eye. What was he like?"

"Good. It was quite interesting actually."

"Tracey's going to be a television star," says Larry. He nods across the table to his wife. "Tell them about it."

Jane looks at Tracey very intently.

"Oh, it's nothing really. He is doing a financial overhaul on me, for the programme, but it probably won't come to much, if anything at all."

"Really? You're going to be on television?"

She is so very disappointed about this, but she covers it up beautifully.

"Wow. Well done you! Sounds like it's quite a big deal. When's it going to be on?"

"Oh, that's nice of you, Jane, but really, it's not a big deal. Actually, he's really sweet."

"He is? What, Alan Makin?"

"Yes."

"Sweet? Really?"

"Yes, honestly. Once he gets away from all the celeb stuff. He has an office... I think he works very hard."

"Oh, that's disappointing," says Jane. "I was hoping to

143

hear he had a life of razzle dazzle."

"Well, he does have an iguana in a case in his office."

"No!"

"Honestly, he does. It eats crickets all day."

"Tell them about the deal you've struck, darling."

"Oh, Larry, please. It's meant to be very hush hush."

"Yeah yeah. This IS hush hush."

Jane looks more intently than ever at Tracey. Her eyes are like those of a little beady robin.

"Well, er, since Larry has put me totally in it, thanks sweetie, the thing is that I'm doing a bit of, how shall I put it, counselling for Alan. He's giving me financial advice, and I am giving him time to chat. That's what he needs, he says. Me time."

"That's not all," says Larry jovially. "He's paying her for it!"

There is a silence around the dinner table. The Seventies music plays on quietly. A distant rattle from the kitchen is the only indication of human life there.

Jane's eyes are so bright they look like they might self-immolate. Tracey looks down at her plate. She can't help smiling.

"What, paying you? Actual cash?"

"Mm. Yes. Think so."

"That IS astonishing."

"Why?" pipes up Larry. "Tracey does have a qualification in counselling, actually."

"Well, Tracey, you are a dark horse."

Jane doesn't much care for dark horses. She likes people to reveal who they are and what they are doing up front, so she can assess them, quickly, against herself and her achievements.

"So, how many times a week are you seeing him?"

"Oh, we haven't really arranged it yet," says Tracey.

There is a pause.

"Did I tell you that our son got into Burlington?" says her

friend from the City suddenly.

The focus wheels and the conversation changes, like a dance movement, to talk about prep schools. Alan Makin, his iguana, his money and his arrangement with Tracey are forgotten in the grateful desire from everyone to discuss something about which they each hold a reasonably similar opinion, namely schooling, which is shaded only by whether they individually feel that Latin is considered obligatory, or not.

Jane walks into the kitchen to collect the lamb and pumpkin.

"All ready here," says Anya, giving her the dish on a tray.

Suddenly, she finds the evening a bit less glittering than before. She's not sure why. It's the combination of Tracey being noticed by a television star, and earning money from it. That was annoying. First, she wins the Lottery. Now, she's going to be on television. How did someone who has never actually achieved anything, certainly not in the way that Jane has done, manage to be so lucky, she wonders crossly. Also there is the phenomenon of her husband, Larry, backing her up so comprehensively. Patrick is never so loyal, she thinks. It eats at her stomach. The smell of the food is actually somewhat nauseating.

She returns to the table with the tray, coolly acknowledging the cries of appreciation it provokes. She glances at Jay through the steam rising from the dish. He smiles at her. She looks down at the food she has produced, demure.

She hopes he will acknowledge her earrings, the flowers in her hair, the ruffles around her neck, her slim, slim arms. She looks up at him again. He is still looking at her. She knows he finds her beautiful and she's glad she has invited him.

Over the cheese course, Patrick is talking to Harriet about the problems of choosing what to put on the board. "It's as Charles de Gaulle once said, you know."

"No, tell me."

"'How can anyone govern a nation that has 246 different types of cheese!'"

145

"Priceless."

"It's probably all that anyone will ever remember he said."

They fall silent, imagining the horror of being remembered for a quip about cheese when in life you were famous for the act of rallying an entire nation, on your own, to resist Nazi rule.

Harriet heaps a biscuit with Brie, puts it into her mouth. This causes a few crumbs to land on the cashmere swaddled shelf of her bosom.

"More wine?" says Patrick, gallantly, as she tidies it up.

Jane eyes Jay. Indicates with her brows that she is going upstairs. She glances at the others around the table. The City couple seem to be getting quietly but progressively hammered on Patrick's best red Rioja. Tracey and Larry are chatting to them about budgerigars. That's a subject produced specially for a night like this, thinks Jane sourly. She looks at Jay again. Invisibly to anyone else, he nods approval to her and she leaves the room.

"Harriet, let me get you your fags," he says. "Are they in your bag?"

"Oh, darling, don't worry."

"No problem. I'm going up to the bathroom anyway. How about an inter-course gasper."

"Patrick, are you sure that's okay? Sorry. You know I am the last smoker on the planet."

"Of course Harriet. We love your addiction. Makes us all feel better about our own various foibles."

Jay stands, edges around the chair, carefully pushes it in, moves around the table.

Upstairs, Jane is already waiting for him in the sitting room, standing by the mantelpiece under the mirror, with her back to the door, glimmering in her silver pleats. He crosses the room swiftly, turns her by her shoulders, kisses her urgently, fumbles at her breasts, pressing his palms against them. The Seventies music continues quietly. Jay starts swaying to the disco beat.

"Could it be that... it's just an illusion... " he murmurs.

"God, Jay, be quiet," she laughs at him.

"Could it be that… in all this confusion… "

"Shut UP."

"Haai laaa haaaaiiii! Bur bur!" he says, clicking his fingers.

"Did I never tell you about my disco past?"

"Kiss me," she says, slightly drunkenly. She exudes the aroma of lamb. So amused is Jay by his disco moment that he decides to overlook this, and give her what she wants.

He'd quite like it too, come to think of it.

The pair are reflected in the large mirror hanging over the mantelpiece. They are now properly kissing.

"Oh, God," says Jane, pausing for breath, thinking about Tracey as a television personality and dismissing it in favour of thinking about herself, "I could have you right now, on the floor."

He looks at her for a moment, pondering the option.

"Really?"

The conversation chat from the supper party downstairs sounds very lively. Nobody appears to be climbing the stairs.

Could he? Can he? He thinks he could.

"Alright then. You asked for it, gorgeous."

"What?" She beams up at him, delighted. She knows she will love to carry this triumph within herself downstairs, the secret knowledge of such a transgression.

He beckons her to him, turns her by her shoulders to face the sofa, pushes her head down and hoists her skirt above her head. To his amazement, she is wearing pull-up stockings without underwear. This unexpected arrangement gives him a vast erection.

"Blimey, Jane."

She says something, but he has no idea what, since her face has disappeared into a cushion.

He drops his trousers, grasps her buttocks and slides his cock into her. A muffled cry comes in response from the cushion.

Jay finds the whole scene so outrageously exciting that he comes after about twenty seconds. He finishes, and slaps her on the arse a number of times.

Everyone is still chatting merrily downstairs.

"Come on, stand up darling."

"Alright, alright," she says, trembling slightly, turning round, standing, adjusting her skirt.

"Christ," he says, pushing her hair away from her flushed face.

"My God. An inter-course fuck. Inter-course intercourse. Have you ever done that before?"

"Hell, no! Could it be that it's just an illusion?" he says, clicking his fingers, moving backwards out of the room, laughing.

"One important thing. Have you got Harriet's fags?"

"Oh, fuck, no."

He returns to the sitting room.

Jane smoothes her dress, goes downstairs, walks triumphantly into the kitchen to collect the pavlova.

A few seconds later, Jay bounces downstairs, joins the table.

"Here you are, darling."

He tosses over a packet of Silk Cut.

Upstairs, reflected in the mirror, a pair of pyjamaed legs wiggles. It is George, behind the sofa.

"Ouch! Pins and needles."

Chapter Eighteen
Tracey

Roberta is at Tracey's door. It's time for Belle's lesson. She feels like clicking her heels triumphantly on the doorstep, like Dorothy. Since she had the conversation with Tracey, things have gone very well with this household. Her position is secure, Belle is back on the books, and Tracey is even considering lessons for Grace.

The door is opened by Anya, who merely raises her beautifully arched eyebrows in acknowledgement of her arrival.

"Good evening Anya," says Roberta.

Anya smiles in response.

"Good night."

"No, Anya. Good night is when you say good bye. Good evening is when you say hello, in the night."

Anya nods, briefly, storing the information.

"She's ready for you. But I think there might be a problem."

Oh no.

Roberta walks past her, into the house. Belle comes walking heavily downstairs.

"Hello Roberta."

"Hello Belle. How are you today? I hear there's a problem of sorts?"

"Nothing major. Only that we have to be quiet, apparently."

Roberta cocks her head quizzically and follows Belle into the dining room, essentially a darkened junk room with a piano in it. She turns the light on and gestures at the piano stool. Roberta notices that Belle is wearing a long robe with a tasselled hood attached to it. She looks like something out of *The Hobbit*, thinks Roberta. Belle sits on the stool.

"So, Belle. What's the story?"

"Oh God. Well. You know my mum is involved with that TV guy?"

"Er, no?"

Belle sighs. "You know, the man who does *Makin's Makeovers* on telly. Alan Makin, whatever."

"Yes. Well, no, but go on. And?"

"Well, he's come round. Tonight. He's upstairs!"

Belle points dramatically to the ceiling.

"So we have to be quiet. Mum's earning a lot of money doing this TV show with him."

"How interesting." Hence the sudden arrival of money. Roberta feels slightly disappointed that it is probably the presence of Alan Makin, not her phone call regarding Belle's future, which seems to have brought about a change in Tracey. Well, maybe they both came at the same moment.

She looks for Belle's book. But there is another, much more difficult book, open and ready on the piano desk. Beethoven Bagatelles. She turns round with a smile.

"Have you been trying these, Belle? These are terrific. I'm impressed!"

Belle pulls a face.

"Of course I haven't. They belong to Anya. You know, our au pair."

"She plays does she?"

Belle shrugs.

"I never hear her. I think she practises when we are out. Obviously she's much better than I am."

Roberta puts the Beethoven away, reaches for the Chopin.

"Shall we? I think we might use the metronome today. And in acknowledgement to the counselling session, we should put the practise pedal on, I think."

Belle nods her head, tosses the giant hood back behind her shoulders, puts her foot on the pedal and begins the prelude.

"Belle, could you possibly roll your sleeves back? Or take off your... robe? I think it's getting in the way, a bit."

The girl complies, standing up and wriggling out of the giant striped coat, under which she is wearing a long sleeved sweatshirt and tight running trousers.

"Belle, do you ever let your skin see the light?" asks Roberta, smiling.

Belle shrugs, turns to the Chopin, starts the piece again. The metronome ticks methodically.

Upstairs, Tracey and Alan are sitting on the sofa.

"That's Belle," says Tracey. "She always has half an hour piano on Thursday nights. Hope that's okay?" She looks anxiously at Alan. It's the first time they've met at her house.

He smiles at her, pats her hand.

"Oh, gosh, it's fine. Love the piano. And your talented children. Wow! She can play, can't she. Rather quiet isn't it? Anyway, not a problem."

They are meeting at Tracey's house because Alan says that he needs to see how she lives. *You are being depicted as one of the Squeezed Middle, you see,* he had written in an email to her earlier in the week. *So I need to come and see if your house is going to give the right sort of... tone. Alright?*

She had agreed to it. He had arrived, wiping his feet on the door mat, his coat slung casually across his arm.

"Hmm. Perfectly middle class," he had said, walking through the hall, noting the carefully arranged paintings, the flowers, the newly purchased pinboard with rows of keys, a pamphlet showing times of Pilates classes at the private gym, a map from the Paris Metro and other impressive detritus, casually parked behind parking vouchers.

"I thought we would sit down upstairs, because Belle is

151

having her lesson," she had said.

"Might have to tone this down a bit, you know," he says, referring to the pinboard. "If people think you are au fait with public transport in Paris, they won't feel very sorry for you... "

Alan Makin, TV star and household name bounds into the living room. Tracey stares at him, blinking, trying to reconcile the fact that this person from the television is actually standing in her home.

"Shall we?"

"So, what sort of week have you had, Alan?" asks Tracey.

"Oh, fine. Middling." This was not quite the case. Several of his key team had announced they were bored with doing financial makeovers and had handed in their notice.

"Been a bit of a personnel shift, actually. Various people have, shall we say, left the ship. Sort of thing that happens now and then."

"Has all your team gone?"

"Not quite. But a significant minority," sighs Alan. "They've all gone off to L.E," he says with undisguised loathing.

This television acronym is new to Tracey. She looks at him blankly.

"Light Entertainment. They'll be back for the autumn run. But at the moment, most of them have gone off to make a Talent Show, leaving a skeleton staff for the rest of this run," he says sadly. "Talent shows!"

"We're having one here in the Square."

"There you are! Sprouting up everywhere."

"Well, ours isn't being televised, at least."

Tracey pauses tactfully.

"How is the Munchkin?"

"Munchkin, oh he's with me now. We have a cartoon animation team in the room who needed the space he used to have. Apparently he gave some of the team the creeps. For some reason. So he's come to live with me. His box is in my bedroom."

Blimey. He really does love that animal.

"So are we still on for my bit on your show?" she says tentatively.

"Certainly are, my dear. Scripts have all been agreed. Next week, we'll do the filming, I think."

She nods.

There is a pause. They both listen to the scale of F Major seeping up from downstairs. Belle plays it as if she is typing.

"Now, Tracey, what we have to do is minimise your personal crisis, while making the status quo still seem incredibly disastrous to you and your family."

"How are we going to do that, then?"

"Simple. We will show how difficult things are, what things you can't afford, then we have a big graphic sequence in which I show how your money, your remaining money from your... win... can be turned around, the Makin Way. I think it's going to work. And we'll focus it here, on your home. So viewers can really understand who you are."

"Really? I always think my house is a bit chaotic."

"No, well, maybe. But coming over here, to the actual location. The Square, I mean. When you turn into it. That's what is so important."

The truth is that when he had arrived, Alan Makin had driven his car into the Square, switched it off and for a moment or two, had just sat in it at the wheel, mesmerised. All those identical houses. All those neat front doors. It all just seemed so... right, so ideal. He felt as if he had gone back to his childhood.

"You know, it reminds me of *Mary Poppins*. Or that moment in *Oliver!* Where they all start singing with barrows and flowers and leaping over doorsteps."

"Oh, God. Establishment, you mean." Well, that was what she had bought into.

"Perhaps. Perhaps it's something more. Maybe it's the way we should all live. Next to each other. In and out of each other's domains. Friendly. Neighbourly."

He thinks of his neighbours in his central London flat. Realises that the only living thing he really knows there, now, is the Munchkin.

"Mmm," says Tracey. "My neighbours don't say that when barbeque smoke is blowing over our wall into their garden."

"So, Tracey, what I need is all your paperwork. Bank statements, accounts for the last few years. And we need a simple explanation about exactly how you earn your income, and how much is earned. And what selling cosmetics comprises of. At which point I have to call in your favour to me. Can I do that, Tracey?"

He turns to her and smiles, in a manner Tracey recognises from countless chat shows on the sofa. She looks at him, considering him.

"Right away. I'm all ears."

He looks at her.

"I would like your advice. And even though I said it wasn't about lipgloss, it is."

Tracey looks at him.

"Lipgloss?"

"It's more about foundation, actually. I want you to give me some help with makeup, simply. The minute you explained what your work was, I thought, ooh, there IS a way in which you could help me."

She looks at him, amazed and slightly disappointed.

"I'm a redhead, right?"

She swallows, and nods. What a comedown. She thought he had the hots for her.

"Well, I would say strawberry blond, but go on."

"And my skin is very fair. My eyebrows, non existent. What I want is just a few tips, products, help with stuff which is going to bring... a bit of colour into my cheeks. And my hands, I'd like them to be... looked at. You with me?"

She nods again.

"I can't obviously go into Boots and test the samples. Or a nail bar," he continues. "But I want to try things out, so the internet is hopeless. I'm not asking for false eyelashes, dear. I don't want the full… "

Tracey so nearly says Monty. She almost has the word coming out of her mouth, and then shuts it in time. She senses this is not the time for ribaldry. Maybe there will be a time, but not now.

"… works," continues Alan. "But I would just be keen to know how to subtly apply it. I thought it would be easier to ask you. Than the girls in the makeup department."

She is still open mouthed, not knowing what to say. She fears he is bullshitting her.

He looks at her archly.

"Told you there would be no nudity."

She blushes again. What an idiot.

"Alan, I am sorry about that. I would be… I would be… honoured." It's not quite the right word, but it will do.

She hears a door bang downstairs.

"Muuuum, Roberta is leaving," yells Belle.

"Alright, thank you darling. Thank you, Roberta," bawls Tracey in response. "See you next week."

She hears the front door slam and turns back to Alan Makin whom she now regards with, if anything, a little more respect.

"Was this why you thought I could be on your TV show, then?" she says, laughing a little, slightly disappointed.

"That? No. Of course not. You are there for a different reason. Tracey, firstly everyone will be fascinated, because of the Lottery. Secondly, you are the ideal example of someone who spends before they earn. It's a national disease and you are simply a very sweet exponent of it. So, no, don't worry. You'll earn your place on my show alright."

He pauses, looks at the ceiling, then looks at her, laughing now.

"But I will pay you to show me how to pluck my eyebrows properly. And equip me with the latest in products."

"Of course. No problem, I'd be delighted. This is my field,

155

after all. I'm an expert in eyebrow plucking. And glueing in false eyelashes, you name it. But... why all the chat before about how understanding I am?"

He shrugs. "I think you are rather understanding, actually. But I needed to see if you were trustworthy without letting you understand why I needed your help."

God, she is so stupid. She thought he was trying to get into her knickers.

"Sorry, I feel idiotic. Of course, no problem, no problem." She smiles brightly at him, feeling blinkered and mentally dull.

"I've lived here for too long," she says, gesturing out of the perfectly proportioned window to the manicured lawn outside.

"I wouldn't be so sure," says Alan Makin. He stands and walks over to the windows, looks out at the scene before him, of entirely well designed, pleasurable entitlement.

"But we are going to need to make this house look a bit more rundown, frankly. As if you are suffering."

"As if we are suffering?" says Belle. She has just come upstairs and stands in her hooded gown, looking at Alan Makin with a furious expression.

"Ah, Belle darling, this is Alan Makin, the famous TV financial makeover presenter," says Tracey, stumbling over such an awkward introduction.

"Yeah I KNOW," says Belle. She turns on her heel.

Alan and Tracey look at each other. They hear Belle's departing footsteps.

"Belle thinks this whole show is ridiculous," says Tracey apologetically.

"She's a good pianist, though," says Alan. His show isn't designed for teenagers. He has no interest in them or their values.

"Yes, she's going to play something for our Talent Show. Oh, Alan," says Tracey suddenly, clapping her hands together.

"What?"

"Can I ask you something?"

"Oh, what's that? Is it something to do with getting an interest only mortgage, because if so, Tracey, I have seen some perfect products on the market for you… "

She laughs, loving this. She, Tracey, joshing around with a television presenter. In her house.

"No, God! No! It's a much better idea than that. But you'll need to check your diary first. Promise me you'll say yes if you check your diary, and find that you are free."

"Okay."

"Go on then."

"What?"

"Check your diary!"

Alan reaches into his pocket and brings out an unnecessarily large, bright yellow smart phone. He taps a succession of numbers into it.

"Three weeks on Sunday. Are you free?"

Is he free? Of course he is. If he's not doing a presentation, he's free. There is not much else in Alan's life bar the Munchkin and work.

"Yup."

"Well, Alan. I know your team have all gone off to F.E, no, that's Further Education, where did you say they had all gone?"

"L.E. Light Entertainment."

"And doing Talent Shows?"

"Yeee-ees?"

"And you know I said we were having our own Talent Show here on the Square?"

"Yes? I am supremely untalented. If it's not the analysis of a balance sheet, my dear, I am hopeless."

"No, it's not that. It's… could you present it for us, here on the Square?"

"Me? Present your Talent Show?"

Tracey suddenly realises she might have made an awful faux pas. Did television people just accept things like this?

157

Was there some sort of protocol in asking them? Should she have spoken to an intermediary?

"Oh, God, would you have to talk to your agent?"

He smiles, pats her on the knee.

"Well, normally, yes, but you know I like your Square. Makes me feel as if I am in a Hollywood set from something shot in the Fifties. Or, as I said, *Mary Poppins*. I'd be delighted to present your show, dear Tracey. Delighted. As long as I am given carte blanche."

"No problem," says Tracey, beaming, feeling that reeling in a proper celebrity means her presence on the Square has suddenly been wholly justified.

Chapter Nineteen
Belle

"And she was just so rude to him," says Tracey to Larry. They are lying in bed, awake.

"Well, that's normal," says Larry, yawning. "Come and give me a hug."

"No, I mean really rude. Almost walked out on him. Couldn't care less, couldn't give a damn that this was a STAR. A star of daytime television, sitting in our lounge." She pauses. "Sorry, sitting room."

"He won't mind. I'm sure he's been exposed to worse things in his life. Television is a nasty old world, I imagine," says Larry, who knows nothing about the world of television but is willing to hazard a guess that it's chock-a-block with utter arseholes.

"I think it's all this work she's doing over the road, you know, with that weirdo Philip Burrell. It has made her extremely, well, she speaks in riddles."

It was true. Since her exposure to Philip, Gilda and their world of the high aesthetic and joke mugs, Belle had regarded her home with increasing volumes of distaste.

"Have you heard of George Rasper?" she announced one evening over supper. "The photographer?"

Tracey, busy turning out the contents of jacket potatoes and

159

adding grated cheese to them, only half-heard the question.

"What?"

"George Rasper, the very famous photographer? Don't you know his work?"

"No, darling, why?"

"Oh, nothing."

Five minutes later, Belle tries again.

"Have you ever, ever heard of Jonty Coward?"

"No, darling. Why? Who is he?"

"Another photographer. God, nobody knows anything in this house."

Tracey turns from the potato, catches Grace's eye, shrugs.

"Are these friends of Philip Burrell's?"

"Well, not exactly Mum. I mean, Jonty Coward was alive during the First World War, so I doubt it."

"Well, I said I didn't know who he was," says Tracey patiently. "How is it going with Jas? How are the models progressing?"

"Don't talk to me about it. You don't know anything."

Actually, Belle was rather proud of her work. She was now on her third marathon piece. They had completed Berlin, which had been gently put into the back of a van and driven off to Philip's London gallery where according to Jas, it had gone down very well. They had also finished Loch Ness, which had been a private commission from an Edinburgh-based millionaire. Now they were onto Tokyo.

Belle didn't talk much, if at all, to Philip Burrell, but from overhearing brief conversations he had with Jas, it seemed as if Philip was planning to launch all of the marathons at once at a big opening show in his gallery. His dealer, Magnus, had been over to check on the work, and he seemed happy. Magnus was another weirdo, thought Belle. Cold fish in a suit.

The only time she had actually spoken more than standard greetings to Philip was one morning when they were finishing the Loch Ness model. He was still in his robe, and came unexpectedly into the studio while Jas was down in the kitchen having a cigarette and chatting to Gilda. Belle had been struggling with a Scottish hillock and had remained upstairs to see if she could get it right.

"So where do you live then?" asked Philip, after standing watching her for a few minutes. He had a sort of commanding attitude which made her jump.

"Over there. Across the road," she said directly, pointing vaguely in the direction of her home. "No. 17."

"Oh," said Philip, nodding.

"Yes," said Belle.

"Isn't that the house of the family who won the Lottery?"

Belle sighed.

"Yes. That's us."

"That must have been a shock."

"Yes."

"Arriving here, I mean. Where did you live before?"

"Down the road from Jas."

Philip looks at Belle with actual interest for the first time.

"So your mum is the one with the short skirts and the flash car?" He loves being direct with people, making them squirm with discomfort. It's one of his deliberately honed characteristics.

Belle sits back on her haunches, puts down her scalpel. She toys with the idea of telling him to fuck off, then remembers the weekly £100.

"Sometimes," she allows herself to say.

Jas walks in. "Hi, Philip, alright?"

"Yes, yes. Just talking to Belle. About her mama and the family's fascinating… provenance. Do you know I have never actually seen a Lottery winner outside the pages of a tabloid newspaper? Toodle pip."

He walks out of the studio, the belt of his robe swishing behind his calves.

"That man is a total wanker," hisses Belle to Jas.

Jas snorts with laughter, pulls a huge roll of chicken wire

over and cuts a length from it.

"He's an artist. What do you expect? He likes making people feel uncomfortable. He's alright really."

It's Gilda who Belle feels more at home with in the Burrell household. She looks forward to seeing her each morning, wonders what crazy outfit she'll be wearing, and what mood she has decided to assume for the day. She wonders whether Gilda ever drops the act, but if she does, Belle never sees it. Seeing Gilda every morning in her satins, her frilly knickerbockers, her tutus and tulle and lace in all colours of the rainbow, (but mostly pink), has made Belle begin to reassess the potential of being female.

One day she even got dressed to go to Philip's studio in a dress with short sleeves.

Her father noticed it immediately.

"My God. Belle in a dress, showing a bit of skin! Steady on, girl."

"Dad," said Belle, shooting him a dirty look over the breakfast table. "It's SUNNY outside."

"Never mind," said Larry. "It's a turn up for the books, actually poppet, seeing you in something unrelated to a sleeping bag. Or a Hobbit outfit."

Belle got up from the table.

"I have to go over to Philip's. We're finishing Loch Ness."

"Is it bonny Scotland which has turned your mind to femininity, pumpkin?" insists her father. "Is it the company of arty folk, one of whom is a Russkie, which has made such a change in you? Being with Luvvies? Russkie Luvvies?"

"I've noticed it too," pipes in Grace. "You never used to wear that dress."

"Tell me, is the house as sexy as everyone says?" snorts Larry, putting down his cup of tea. It's a question he has been keen on asking for some days now, but has never found the right moment. "Is it full of naked pictures and bullwhips and things like that?"

"Yes it is actually. Well, there are some topless pictures

of Gilda. By that man who nobody here has even heard of, George Rasper. He's a very famous photographer, you know."

"Topless pictures," echoes Larry. He roars with laughter. "That is hilarious! What, in the downstairs rooms?"

"In the kitchen."

"Blimey. I don't quite know how I'd feel, looking at knockers over my soup."

"Dad!" from Grace.

There is a pause.

"That's silenced you," says Belle nastily.

"No, no, I was thinking."

"What?"

"Whether you with your new contacts and your obvious charm, dumpling, whether you might get your mad arty Luvvie friends to do something for the Talent Show."

Larry couldn't really give two hoots any more about the Talent Show, the idea which had once been his, but Jane, who had heard about Belle's new job, had rung him up and demanded his daughter ask if the Burrells might like to be involved.

"Do you think you might ask them if they'll do something?"

"I think it's highly unlikely they will, Dad."

She does think about reminding Gilda about it, however, later that day. But she never gets round to it.

Chapter Twenty
Jane

God, this Mozart is beautiful, thinks Jane. The music is so insistent on its dynamic perfection that she cannot actually do anything other than put down her mobile, on which she had been sending an order to Waitrose, and listen to it.

Anya is playing the Bluthner. She is playing Mozart on the Blüthner in Jane's music room. Jane is not quite sure how this state of affairs arose so quickly, but here it is, and she felt it necessary to make the best of it.

No sooner had Roberta got home after teaching Belle, than she had called the au pair.

"I saw your book of Bagatelles on the piano at Tracey and Larry's house," she said.

She felt warm towards Anya, felt they were on the same side. After all, they both serviced families in the Square. Anya acknowledged that the book of Bagatelles was indeed her property.

"Look, you know Jane and Patrick on the other side of the Square? You know, him, overweight and chatty, her, ferocious and over smart?"

Anya indicated she did know the family, that she had helped at a dinner party they had held last week.

"Well, they have the most beautiful piano. Did you know

that? Did you see it when you were there? No? A proper Blüthner. Concert Grand size. Anya, you have simply got to go and practise on it. I mean, Belle's upright is all very well, but you know, it's a Berry. So a bit honky tonk. Whereas, on a Blüthner grand, you can really let rip, and it will sound great. Amazing actually. Nobody plays it. The Blüthner. Not properly putting it through its paces. I mean, I teach their little son on it. That's all."

About a week had elapsed since this conversation, but Roberta had mentioned it to Patrick after George's lesson, and when he saw Anya lugging the shopping out of the car one day, he called over.

"Anya! Yoo hoo! Patrick here! Just been speaking to Roberta, you know, our dragon of a piano teacher," he says, hurrying up and slightly out of breath. He liked Anya. Over and above those amazing cheekbones.

He remembered how solicitous she had been at that disastrous Residents' meeting when poor old Harriet fell through the chair. Plus, she'd done a great job washing up the other day.

She had a sort of chilly sexiness which fascinated him.

"Actually, Roberta is a lovely girl."

Anya looks at him patiently.

"Sorry, woman. She's a very lovely woman." Patrick coughs. "Great teacher. Anyhoo, she tells me you're a bit of a whizz on the old ivories."

Anya looks at him, quizzically.

Patrick looks back at her. He notices the perfect arch of her eyebrows.

"Piano playing. You are a good piano player."

"Oh, yes. Yes. I have always… I love to play."

"Well, look, do come round and practise on our piano. I mean, I know Larry and Tracey have a decent old joanna, but… "

"Joanna?"

"Never mind. English slang. But I have a very large one.

Piano, I mean. A lovely one. We love people to come round and play it."

"Yes, Roberta told me you had a lovely grand piano."

"Well, please. Otherwise it just sits there as a shelf for photographs. Please do come over and play it."

She is doubtful, but the next afternoon she knocks quietly at the door. Patrick is delighted, in fact he is rather pleasantly amazed, that she has taken him at his word.

"Marvellous, marvellous. Good, you've brought some music. Good, good. Otherwise you'd be playing Boy George's stuff, which is about Grade Zero!"

She comes into the hall, and he closes the front door behind her. Then, he holds the door of the music room open for her. She walks past him. He is gratified to hear her intake of breath as she takes in the lovely concert grand, smells the polish on it mingled with the scent of flowers on the mantelpiece. The room is immaculate.

"Now, Anya. I'm just going to carry on working in my study. Make yourself at home. Stay for as long as you like."

"Thank you," says the Polish au pair.

"No, thank YOU," says Patrick, backing out.

After about three minutes, Anya begins to play. She does a couple of Bach preludes, then launches into the Mozart study.

Shortly after this episode, Jane opens the front door and walks in.

"Hello?" She opens the door to the music room. Anya immediately stops playing.

"Oh, Jane, good afternoon, Patrick said it was… "

She is interrupted by Patrick calling to them from the kitchen. He has heard his wife's entry. He's damned if she will stop this wonderful moment, the piano taking flight.

"Jane darling, do you remember we invited Anya to play the piano for a bit?"

Jane, finding herself in the unusual position of being in a domestic situation of which she is not in command, backs out of the room, smiling at Anya.

"Do go on."

As Anya continues her piece, Jane sits down in the hall, on the bottom step where she and Jay had been pulling each other's clothes off, that time when Patrick came home. God that was a terrible moment. She is cross with Patrick for letting the girl play the piano. Right, she thinks.

I will punish him by thinking about fucking Jay. It's a punishment only I will know about, but never mind.

So Jane lies back on the stairs and imagines Jay servicing her while Anya plays Mozart on the Blüthner. Would that ever be a possible scenario? Could it be? She thinks it would turn her on. She thinks it would absolutely not turn Jay on. He'd probably want to turn it into a threesome. *That* was quite likely to turn Jay on, actually. She dismisses the idea from her head.

The notes go on and on, fluid, like running water.

She thinks about Jay, his physical beauty. She loves to run her fingers through his full head of hair. Lucky man, still luxuriant in his fifties. She loves his sly sexy smiles to her. His brown eyes. She loves his face, his profile, the back of his head. She craves his unclothed body with an almost palpable hunger. She sometimes wonders whether having a sex drive like this is normal for a woman of her age. A mother. A wife. God. The music goes on. She still wants to punish her husband.

She imagines Jay pushing her legs apart. She fancies him so much. Silly word, fancies. Schoolgirlish. No, what she feels for Jay is pure physical desire. She thinks of his narrow shoulders between her legs. She gets warm.

Jane sits up. This is madness, she thinks. She forces herself to focus on the music. It was, she sourly admitted to herself, of a standard she had never heard before in a domestic house. How had this girl arrived, a fully formed concert pianist, in their midst? The same girl as was doing the washing up at their party the other night. God, that party.

After the fucking incident upstairs in the sitting room, which was a turn on, she admitted, it had sort of fizzled out,

Jane thought. Everyone went home well before midnight. Anya had been very helpful, but then she was being paid to be helpful. That was what au pairs did. They did the washing up. They didn't play music on this level. Frankly, Anya has probably never seen Imogen Cooper, or heard of her, thought Jane. Or Alfred Brendel. Or ever attended a concert with Lang Lang playing as she, Jane, had.

The notes continue to pour out, immaculate.

Would she ever manage to get George playing like this? Very unlikely. She didn't understand the boy's soul, she realised. And to play the piano like this, one needed soul. What was Anya's soul? Where was it? She hadn't really focused on her during the dinner party. She just relied on her as a body holding a dishcloth. She had not realised that those slim, capable fingers could cope with a crescendo trill as perfectly as they could peel potatoes.

What did Anya think, this monosyllabic au pair who mopped the floor and never seemed to wince at London's excesses? How did she manage to play so beautifully? Did they even have pianos in, where was it she came from now? Weird sounding Polish place which sounded like Whoosh. Only you spelt it with an L. Imagine coming from a place called Whoosh.

She bet Anya had never played on a grand piano. The au pair's exquisite touch left Jane feeling shallow and uncreative. It wasn't a feeling she enjoyed having. She tries to think of Jay's beautiful hair again. She certainly doesn't want to hear much more music. She walks upstairs to her bedroom, thinks she might lock herself in her bathroom.

Yet Patrick, standing mesmerised at his desk in his study, has other ideas.

He hears Anya finish, the soft bump of the piano stool on the carpeted floor as she stands up, the careful closing of the lid of the grand.

"Anya!" he calls up. She comes directly to his summons. She is used to English people now and the way they operate.

"That was absolutely marvellous. Did you enjoy it?"

She nods.

"Sounded out of this world. Like having Ashkenazy upstairs. You have heard of Ashkenazy, haven't you?"

She nods again, a slight smile flickering over her face. These people.

"I know Ashkenazy."

"Right, good. Well, look. Please come back. Any time. I'd love George to hear you play. Maybe you could play a duet with Roberta?"

"Yes, maybe." Anya feels slightly lightheaded after playing intently for forty minutes.

"Of course, of course. Well, you know. Come over any time, either with her, or singly, you know… on your own… "

He looks at her unlined face with its clear brown eyes deliniated by the strong eyebrows. Those cheekbones. She smiles, but her face remains closed to him. She glances at her watch, a sturdy instrument on a slender wrist.

"I must go and collect Grace from school. Thank you so much Patrick. I'll be back!"

"Hasta la vista bebe," he says in his best Arnie growl.

She looks at him, startled. He waves his hand at her. Of course. She probably wasn't even born when the Terminator films came out. Idiot.

"Film reference. Never mind."

"Goodbye Patrick, thank you so much."

"Come back next week."

She turns and walks upstairs. Seconds later, he hears the front door slam.

"Wasn't that marvellous, darling?" he shouts up to Jane who, he thought, was still upstairs dealing with Waitrose. "Like having your very own concert."

There is no response.

If only she could come and play to me every Thursday afternoon, thinks Patrick. Then, perhaps I should pay her. To come over and play for us.

Would she be cross if he suggested it? Offended? Probably not. Funny lot, these Eastern Europeans. Send all their money home. Then they go back themselves. No notion of building a base here, even though they are in the EEC and whatnot. Or are we now all in the European Union Community? Whatever.

Would Tracey and Larry be annoyed, though? Hmm. Cross that bridge when we come to it. Probably not. After all, they were okay about hiring her out to do the washing up, weren't they?

He makes up his mind to invite Anya over to play the Blüthner every Thursday afternoon. He'll pay her £20 to do it. Every week. Dammit, if Alan bloody Makin can pay old Tracey to chat to him, he'll pay Anya to play to him.

He wanders across the kitchen, humming his customary little tune, and gets a non-Diet Coke out of the fridge. Ha! Jane is absent. He rips open the can and slakes his throat with the liquid.

Upstairs, Jane locks the bathroom door and reaches into the cabinet.

Chapter Twenty-One
Harriet

Harriet looks out of the window of her bedroom onto the Square. It is raining. But on the day of the Talent Show, it will be hot. Of course. Late afternoon in high summer. The hammering heat of the sun would have ebbed away but the sky would be dark blue, almost vibrating with what had once rested there, and left its imprint.

All the chairs would be lined up in serried ranks.

And Jane would have got everyone else doing menial things, like taking tickets, while she paraded in front, the conductor.

She, Harriet, would of course still be indoors. Brushing her hair and smoothing down her dress. She would have lost half a stone by now, too. No, one whole stone. Can you lose a stone in three weeks? It's summer. You always lose more weight in the summer. All those salads.

Now, the dress. Which one would she be wearing? It would be black, no, navy. No, cream. Long sleeved, with cream ribbons at the wrists. Harriet considers she is too old for short sleeves of any description. Bingo wings look terrible when you are playing the violin. She would wear cream ribbons and a gardenia in her hair. She thinks on the image this conjurs in her head. Ribbons and flowers. In cream. It's all a bit bridal, frankly. She didn't want to look like a bride. Or, heaven help her, a bridesmaid. Scrap the cream.

She'd wear lilac, a shade that really suited her. When she had had that Colour Me consultation, the woman said lilac was very 'her'. She couldn't afford a new dress however. Well, not really. She'd have to buy it on her credit card. Or Jay might buy it for her. She believed she deserved it. It was for the performance, wasn't it?

Harriet envisaged herself walking very lightly, in her new lilac dress and stockinged feet, into the hall, picking up her violin in its case which was just waiting there, ready for her. Almost at the same time she would slide her feet into new shoes. A perfect pair of nude heels. Jay, thoughtful man, would have already put powder in the shoes so her feet wouldn't stick. Her feet were, like her hands, rather wide, and they sometimes had difficulty in sliding into shoes.

She would look at Jay, and Jay would look at her, in his nice suit, with tears in his eyes, and whisper 'You go for it, girl,' and then he would open the front door and she would see all the chairs filled with all her neighbours, sitting there waiting for her to entertain them with her singular talent.

And then Harriet would walk out into the Square, her dress glowing in the gathering twilight. Everyone would be there. And she would smile at Brian, her son, who would be sitting next to, who would Brian be sitting next to? Probably Tracey's daughter Belle. Belle would be swathed in some sort of awful voluminous wrap with a hood. Never mind. Brian would look up at his mother and smile at her, so proud. And everyone else would be smiling. She didn't know who. Just everyone.

She would smile back, and then walk purposefully past the chairs, up to the front where Jane would be standing waiting for her. At which point Harriet's dream fantasy spins down, like a record suddenly losing speed. Jane, with her size 8 figure, was precisely the person who Harriet did not want to see, seconds before playing a Bach partita. She really wasn't.

Harriet was very happy to go round to Jane's for a supper party, to pretend to be friends, to kiss on both cheeks and feign interest in her child's education, but Harriet knew, deep down, that Jane had a sincere loathing for her. She had no idea why. She likes Jay well enough, thought Harriet sulkily. Always giggling with him over something. Whenever Harriet asks Jay what they talk about, he always has quite a believable answer, but it is never fully solid.

No, she is not going to play in front of Jane, to reveal her naked soul with her violin. Who could the presenter be?

She suddenly thought that the presenter needs to be a celebrity. Of course. It must be Alan Makin! He was the only celebrity she had actually seen off the television. And anyway, he knows about the Square. Of course! Alan Makin would be brilliant.

The television genius who everyone thinks is having some sort of *thing* with Tracey, who swears they are just working together on her show, well Alan could come to the Square and preside over the Talent Show.

Now she has fixed that in her mind, it's inconceivable that it wouldn't happen, thinks Harriet. So, Alan would be there, microphone in hand, and he would say 'I think we would all like to welcome Harriet, who is going to play the third movement of Bach's partita for solo violin in A Minor for us all. Harriet, when you are ready.'

And Harriet, who never felt a scrap of nerves when she played in public, never had, even for her Grade Eight exam at school, would stand quite still on her nude heels and put her beloved violin under her chin, and tune it with her right hand, expertly balancing the wooden instrument as if it was held by some invisible string. And then, amid the evening twittering and fluting of the blackbirds in their gorgeous Square, and a far off car alarm, and the faces of her neighbours, incredulous and surprised, she would raise her bow and begin the Baroque masterpiece...

"Mum! I have been shouting for AGES," says Brian,

striding across the bedroom.

"What on earth?"

"Oh, goodness, sorry Brian," she replies, flustered. "I'm sorry. I was miles away."

"It's Tracey. She's downstairs. She was locked out and came over for the keys, but thought as you were in, she'd stay for a quick chat. I put her in the sitting room."

"Thanks, sweetie."

She hastens downstairs, full of her dream.

"Tracey, you are the perfect person. I've just had the most brilliant idea."

They kiss on both cheeks. Harriet sits down beside her friend, takes both her hands.

"You know the Talent Contest? You know, the thing we are supposedly raising funds for. That Jane is organising?"

"Er, yes. What about it?"

"Well I have had the most brilliant idea." Harriet plumps herself up on the sofa as if she is a soft furnishing, and looks directly at Tracey. She so hopes her friend will back her up. It's all part of gathering support.

"We will need a really brilliant presenter. I know Jane wants to do it herself, but I think we should go bigger than that, and get a celebrity. Do you think, could you possibly ask Alan to do it for us? Alan Makin. It would be so amazing. I mean, people would really turn up to see him. We might even make some money!"

Tracey smiles. It's all anyone can talk about with regard to her. People have stopped asking her about anything else.

"I've had exactly the same idea. Actually," she says, pausing for effect, "I asked him the other day when we were discussing scripts."

"Oh, did you?" gushes Harriet, astonished, slightly disappointed but also excited that they have had the same brilliant thought. She grips Tracey's hands even tighter. "Did you really? That is amazing. How amazing. Serendipity! What did he say?"

"He said he'd have to ask his agent. No, he said he'd love to," says Tracey, deadpanning her friend. Then she laughs. She glances down at her hands. On one wrist glints a new bracelet that she has bought with what she terms her 'Makin Money.'

"Oh Harriet, he is really quite sweet. Not the sort of showbiz celeb that you see on the TV. I think he is actually quite lonesome. He asks me all sorts of things in our little chats."

"Oh, God, yes, aren't you advising him or something? You're not using that as a cover for something, are you?"

Harriet feels a bit nosy, but they are in her house, she reasons, and she hopes Tracey won't mind. Everyone's been talking about it.

There is an awful silence in Harriet's sitting room.

"I mean, not that anyone has said anything, of course."

Tracey looks at Harriet. Harriet looks back at her. The plane trees outside in the Square wave gently.

"You're not sleeping with him, are you?"

"Oh God Harriet," Tracey laughs, a bit too ferociously.

"Of course I'm not! Of course I'm not! I think he's gay, not that that matters, and he says he isn't, but I think he's in some sort of closet. Must be! Honestly the best friend he has in the world I think is an iguana. Of course I'm not sleeping with him!"

She's overdoing it a bit, thinks Harriet.

"Sorry, sorry. But you are being paid to counsel him, are you not? Give him advice or something?"

"Not really, Harriet, that was really hyped up by Jane and co, I fear. Actually he, you know, he just wanted some makeup advice."

"What? Makeup advice? For him? You are joking, aren't you?"

Tracey rather wishes she hadn't revealed this. Alan might be cross with her. Well, she had been surprised too, after all.

"Oh, just basics. As a redhead, he looks a bit pale under

175

the studio lights. So he wanted some tips."

"But surely he has people to do that sort of thing for him?"

"Oh, I don't know. I think he does, but he wanted a second opinion," says Tracey. "He likes coming here, too. He loves the Square."

She would really like to change the conversation. She suddenly remembers a perfect way of doing this.

"You'll never guess."

"No, what?" says Harriet, who would much rather talk about Alan Makin and his iguanana. Everything else seems a bit pallid by contrast.

"You know our lovely au pair? The Eastern Bloc one?"

"Anya?" says Harriet, dismayed that the conversation is taking a turn onto domestic affairs. Still, she thinks brightly, that girl is very nice, very nice indeed. For a Pole. Harriet has never forgotten being scooped up by her from the floor of this very room after that awful moment when the chair collapsed.

"Yes, Anya. Never know if anyone else knows her name. Anyway guess what?"

"Well, what? Come on, spit it out."

"She's started playing the piano at Jane's." Tracey pauses dramatically.

"For Patrick!"

"What?"

"Yes. Apparently Roberta, you know, the piano teacher that everyone seems to have in their houses, organised it for Anya to go and play their grand piano. She's very good, has played since she was tiny. Obviously she had a mother FAR better at getting her to practise than me with Belle, since the things she plays are just out of this WORLD. It's like living with bloody Liberace. Anyway, so she was playing away the other day and Roberta heard her on our crappy old upright and made it so that she could go round to Patrick and Jane's."

"And? What?"

"Patrick heard her playing Mozart and thought it was so... what did he say to me... so 'transcendent'... that he is

PAYING her to play for him every week."

"Oh my God!" giggles Harriet. "Everyone seems to be paying everyone else around here to do things for them. I wish I had the money to pay a cleaner, frankly. Really wish that with all my heart. Jay won't hear of it. So, do tell. What does Queen Jane think of that, then?"

"She hates it!"

"Really?"

"Really!"

"How do you know?" asks Harriet.

"She told me so herself!" says Tracey. "Well, not in so many words, but she came across the street the other day and said 'do you know your au pair is playing our piano on a regular basis, and do you mind? Because after all you are paying her to work for you, aren't you?' Like it would get Anya into trouble."

"What did you say?"

"I said that Anya was free to do what she wanted between eleven and four. Anyone who has ever had an au pair, and let's face it, Jane has had about a thousand, knows that."

There is a pause. Something has just occurred to Harriet.

"Do you think Patrick fancies her?"

"I don't know. I really don't. Dear old Patrick."

The women sit together in a silent reverie thinking about Patrick, and what he must face, living with someone like Jane.

Tracey stands up. "Right, I must go. Thanks for the keys. Sorry to bother you."

"Not at all. Sorry about, you know, asking you about Alan. But, talking of Alan, which we weren't just then, but anyway. Do you think he really will present the Talent Show?"

"Who, Alan? Yes, of course he will. As I said, he loves the Square. Always going on about it."

It was true. Every time Alan Makin came into its charmed space, he felt cosseted and caressed by it. Every time he went home to his immaculate flat which was, he had to admit, in a spectacular, Grade One listed building, but on a main road in Highgate, he felt brutalised. He would even talk to the Munchkin about it.

"Would you like to live in the Square?" he asks the reptile.

The Munchkin looks back with a basilisk stare.

"I'll take that as a Yes," says Alan, dropping crickets into the vitrine.

Chapter Twenty-Two
Roberta

Roberta rings the door bell and hops up and down on the step. She looks at the familiar blank faces of the houses around her in the Square. She's very pleased with herself. Everything seems to be working out as she hoped it might. Not only had she received a delighted-sounding text from Anya, who has secured herself some sort of practising gig round here on the Blüthner involving cash, but Patrick personally called to thank her. He sounded absolutely delighted that someone at last was taking that piano seriously. She was very pleased to have pleased him. She liked Patrick with a strength of feeling which she didn't often have for her clients. At this moment, she loved him.

The door opens. Roberta masks a momentary flinch of disappointment that neither Patrick, nor her small pupil is standing in front of her. It's Jane. Her least favourite member of the household.

"Hello Jane," she says, smiling graciously.

"Hello, Roberta," says Jane, acknowledging automatically, then turning her back on the teacher as she greets her, in order to shout up the stairs at her child.

"George! Your lesson!"

There is silence from the top of the house.

Roberta puts her bag down.

There is no noise from upstairs.

"I'll go and get him," she says. "Do you mind?"

She has to say something. She is going to say it, because she knows it will annoy her client.

"So I hear Anya came round and played the Blüthner, how was that?"

Irritated that the piano teacher knows things about the house which happen when she is not there, Jane affects vague forgetfulness.

"Did she? I can't remember. Not sure. Think so, but I was out."

Roberta knows this is a lie. She knows that Jane was in the house when Anya turned up, she is certain she was, because Anya told her. She also knows that Anya has been asked to come round to the house regularly. She thinks this is probably not something to mention to Jane.

"Oh, maybe I got it wrong. I thought you might have heard her. I have to say, she's a very good pianist. Really excellent. Beautiful touch."

"Is she?" says Jane, absently. "Roberta, sorry to rush away but I really have got something rather crucial to do."

What, like getting online to Ocado, thinks Roberta. She can see how Anya's proficiency rattles her employer. Well, other people can be skilled too, you know. It's not just the owners of houses in the Square. It is people like Anya, and myself. People who have allotments and dull jobs, and make regular, ordinary shopping excursions to dull places like Tesco, not Waitrose. And I am not a 'lesson', either, she thinks sharply. I am a real person.

She walks upstairs.

"George, hello!" she calls. "It's Roberta. I'm coming to extract you from your room."

She's quite keen to see his room. She is fond of George and she would like to see him in his terrain, as it were, rather than in the very adult world downstairs.

She knocks at what she guesses is his door. This is not a hard thing to divine since it is largely obscured by a giant poster of Obi-Wan Kenobi brandishing a large laser.

"Enter!" a small voice calls imperiously from inside the room.

She pushes open the door. The tone inside George's bedroom is crepuscular since the curtains, which are decorated with a pattern of planets and comets, are closed.

The array of toys and pictures within are testimony to an entire life; George's life, so far. There are still framed nursery rhymes on the wall from his baby years, alongside the long rectangle and florid Latin motto of the Official Prep School Photograph. His entire Lego city is also there, balancing precariously on his desk.

"Good afternoon my dear," says George. He is crouching over a computer.

"I am just working on my Film. The Film for which I shall play a live accompaniment at the Talent Show. I have decided," he says, sitting back on his haunches, "to wear a Storm Trooper outfit for the night. My friend Finn has lent me his Storm Trooper. In return for a fortnight of my Lego spider from the Lord of the Rings Collection." George pauses and considers the deal. "I think he will, anyway."

"Blimey," says Roberta. "I bet you'll win the contest dressed like that. Storm Troopers usually win, don't they? Can I see what you've done so far with the film?"

"No Roberta, they do not usually win," says George. "They are the elite military soldiers of the Empire, under the rule of Darth Vader. They are the enemy."

But Roberta is not listening. She is watching George's short animated film on his computer. She is watching something which in a minute's time she will hope she does not understand, something which will cause anxiety to surge through her body to her fingertips.

On the screen, a small Lego figure in a black cape and helmet is moving rather jerkily around several tall thin connected houses, also constructed from Lego. First, he is outside. There is a small tree, and a dog.

"That is Darth Vader," says George from behind her shoulder.

Roberta nods, concentrating.

"He is visiting our Square. Here he is outside our house." He pauses. "You'll have to imagine me playing the piano here. You know, that first rather dull bit of Hanon that you always make me do."

Roberta smiles.

In the next shot, Darth Vader then appears to be inside a house. He moves towards a table around which people are sitting.

"A boring party. The sort of thing my parents are always having. People just sitting talking. For HOURS."

Darth Vader leaves the party. He now has a laser in his hand.

"What's happening now?"

"This is Darth Vader summoning the Death Star. I am playing shooting sounds now, like this, *Peow Peow*."

"Is the Death Star his ship?"

"My dear, have you never SEEN *Star Wars*?"

Humbled, Roberta continues to watch while George's tiny hero executes a number of aerial tumbles and moves, with the laser. He then appears to hide behind a sofa.

At this point, two other Lego figures enter the scene. One male, one female.

They move to one side of the room. They are closely bonded together.

"Who on earth is this? What's going on?" asks Roberta, with a slowly growing sense of dread.

"Oh, that's my mother and Jay, our neighbour," says George, casually. "I think he was giving her some sort of massage the other night. When they had a dinner party. I was still downstairs by mistake, behind the sofa. I was meant to be in bed, but I was still up. And I thought it was really funny, seeing them on the sofa, and how funny it would be if Darth Vader suddenly appeared and brandished his lightsabre at them. Do you know, after Jay, our neighbour, had finished hugging her, he smacked her! On the bum-bum! I have never seen a grown-up do THAT before."

"You are going to show this film at the Talent Show?"

"Yes. It's taken me DAYS. It's all start stop animation. Done on my bed. Look, here."

He shows Roberta the 'set' which is lying in pieces on the floor.

Through waves of piercing anxiety, Roberta realises that if this film is shown at the Talent evening there will probably be no more piano lessons, anywhere, on the Square, for quite some time. And that she will probably be held responsible for George broadcasting a short film of his mother's adultery with the neighbour. She is going to have to think about a strategy. She must consign this film to the oblivion of erasure. She is going to have to come up with something, quite fast, the Talent Show is ten days away.

"George, this is great. But we must go and have our lesson. And I think we need to chat about it. Shall we turn the computer off, for now?"

"Sure, sure. Do you like it so far? Do you like the animation? I've got quite a bit more to do, you know."

"It's great. But I think I may have some other ideas for you."

"But I don't want your ideas. I have my own ideas."

"Yes, I know. But I have some good ideas which might go with your ideas. The best ideas are joint ideas, has nobody ever told you that?"

Roberta swallows, hard.

The giant figure of Obi-Wan gently swings behind her as she carefully closes the door, and leads her small charge downstairs. She thinks of the computer upstairs, with its lethal cargo, and feels nauseated.

She settles him at the piano stool.

"Right, now. Let's play 'The Bells of St Paul's'."

"Really? My dear, have we not grown out of that piece?"

"No, I think it's a great piece for you. And I think it's a great piece for the show."

"What, the Talent Show?"

"Yes, I do. I've changed my mind about Hanon. I think it's just too dull."

"Hanon? Dull? But you always said it was an important structural thing to do and would help enormously with my fingering."

"Yes, yes. But honestly George, it's an exercise. It's like turning up as... as a Storm Trooper and simply walking up and down in your gear. Never turning the lightsabre on."

"Storm Troopers don't HAVE lightsabres. They have Elite Guns."

"Well, their Elite Guns, then," says Roberta, flustered.

"Alrighty," says George. It's a phrase he has picked up from Patrick. He thinks it makes him sound an awful lot older, like a boy almost in Year 5.

"Now, 'The Bells of St Paul's' is a great piece because it's all about these little boys, isn't it? Climbing over the walls and knocking all the apples down with their sticks?"

"Yee... eessss?" says George. The long drawn out affirmative has also been learned from Patrick.

"Well, I thought that would be such a lovely thing to put onto a film. You could make those Lego trees, and you could make little boys, and... " She looks at his face. It has gone very red again.

"But what about Finn and my Storm Trooper outfit?" he says miserably. "I really wanted to do something about *Star Wars*."

"Yes but you can't do it about *Star Wars* at HOME," says Roberta firmly. Then she has a sudden thought. "It's against copyright."

"What? Is it?"

"Yes," she says. "George Lucas won't allow any publication

of a fantasy world alongside the world of reality with his patented characters. I read it somewhere."

"But I am not publishing anything."

"Showing a film at the Talent Show accounts for publishing. I think George Lucas wants to keep everything intact, not allowing it to go out into the, the outer world. As it were. Now, if you were just to show the fantasy characters on their own, in their fantasy world, that would be fine. Alright, let's not play 'The Bells of St Paul's'. Let's do something completely new. Let's have a look in this book," says Roberta, flicking through *Easy Classics For Piano* as she speaks.

"Aha!" she says, triumphantly. "Here it is! The theme tune for *Star Wars*! Composed by… "

"John Williams," says George. He looks up hopefully. "Is it in there?"

"You bet it is. And I will help you learn it. Do you have a version of the Death Star in Lego?"

George looks at his teacher. "What about the copyright? Isn't that going to be disallowed because of copyright?"

Why do I have to have such a bright pupil, thinks Roberta.

"Oh, this piece is out of copyright because so many small boys want to play it. That's why it's in this book. Now let's have a look at it. Could you play this while you show one of your Lego *Star Wars*… ships flying around? Do you have any?"

A small smile plays around his red lips. "My dear," he says, "I have General Grievous' Starfighter, with 1,085 pieces."

He puts his fingers on the keys and plays the chord of C Major four times. Da da da DAH.

"And I have the Millennium Falcon. Version Six, 1,237 pieces. It took me eight months to build it."

"Well," says Roberta, "phew. Why don't we use them? And we can get some sort of backdrop with planets on it and get those things flying around. You can film it and then on the night, you can show the film, and play the John Williams masterwork. In your Storm Trooper outfit from Finn. Happy?"

To her delight, George nods his head. The way she put it, with the mention of his friend, and the uniform, meant that it was going to happen. It really was.

"I know," he says. "We shall use my curtains as the set."

Saved, thinks Roberta.

Chapter Twenty-Three
Tracey

Tracey pushes her way into the crowded West End jazz bar where a pianist is sitting hammering at an old Berry upright. Next to him, a man is brushing a drum with steel brushes. They are playing that old standard, 'Ain't Misbehaving'. Well, she wasn't. She was having fun, though. A week of filming, not a week of packaging up cosmetics and organising people to go and sell them for her. This is her treat to mark the end of the shoot, a drink with Alan at his favourite bar.

Where was he? She suddenly sees him by the long bar, an island in the middle of the room. He is sitting on a stool with two glasses of Champagne at his elbow. His suit is as immaculate as ever. She notices with pleasure that he is wearing a tiny touch of the mascara she had recommended. She slides onto the empty stool he has reserved, next to him.

"Bubble?" he says.

She breathes in the effervescent liquid.

"Oh Alan. I cannot tell you how glad I am to be here."

"Why is that?" asks Alan Makin.

"Because at home I am Public Enemy Number One. Thanks to you!"

The piano continues its honky tonk routine, and suddenly the Square didn't matter too much, to Tracey.

She laughs as she sips the cool drink.

"Oh, no, why?"

"It's all your fault, Alan."

"Really?"

"Yes. Really! Harriet, Harriet, my neighbour. You know, who I went to the marquee with on that first time? Well she also had the idea that you should present our little show. And anyway I told her I had already asked you, and you had said yes."

"Yes, so? And?"

"Well, I went and told Jane. And she was so cross!"

It had not been an easy encounter. Tracey had bumped into Jane in the afternoon as she was awkwardly shoehorning George out of the family car, on his way back from school.

"Oh, Jane, just the person," said Tracey to Jane's pert bottom.

"Hi," Jane had said, standing up immediately, turning round, smoothing down her dress, tucking her hair back behind her ears. She did not look overly pleased to see her neighbour. George scrambled out of the car behind her and began to walk along the kerb, loudly singing 'Frère Jacques'.

"Hi, hi. I wanted to ask you whether I might make a suggestion for the Talent Show?"

"Fire away."

"Well, you know I am doing this filming with Alan, you know, Alan Makin. It's going really really well."

"Great. I'm delighted for you. Really pleased."

"And the thing is that Alan really loves the Square. Loves everything in it. I've told him all about us, and our Association, and the Show, and the fundraising, so… "

"So?"

"I asked him if he wouldn't mind hosting the Talent Show."

There is a barely discernable pause, a beat of silence.

"Hosting it?"

Tracey suddenly sees the gulf between her idea, and Jane's

master plan. She feels she needs backup.

"It was Harriet's idea, actually. She thought we needed, she thought it would be sort of nice, to have a celebrity do it."

"Oh, did she? Rather than keep it all in the Square? My, celebrity culture really has taken hold of everyone, hasn't it!" said Jane, with a harsh giggle. "First the Lottery comes to call, *grace à vous*, then it's all about famous people."

"Is that okay?" says Tracey. She is not even going to acknowledge the Lottery dig.

"I mean, had you thought about a presenter?"

"Yes I had. I mean, I thought I was going to step into the role myself. Though only, and this is the honest truth, because I couldn't think of anyone else mad enough to do it. But if you and Harriet think we need a celebrity, that's fine. Just fine. Great."

"Oh, Jane are you sure? Are you really happy about it? I mean, do you want to do it?"

"Nah. No, I don't," said Jane, who had privately been working out her opening words and had already booked a hair appointment for the day before.

"No, that's fine. Have you actually asked him, though? Will we have to pay him? Have you even thought about that?"

"Oh, I have asked him already," says Tracey, with a thrill of correcting Jane running right through her, "and he says he'd love to. I don't think there will be any payment. No, I haven't exactly put it to him in those words, but I think that all should be fine. Do I need to give him a running order, or special words to say, or shall I leave it up to him?"

"Mummy, can we go now?" said George, who had returned to the car, and was pulling at her coat.

"Let's talk about that later," said Jane with a flinty smile. "Sorry, must dash."

And with that, she had disappeared into her house, leaving Tracey standing on the pavement.

"And that was that." Tracey looks at Alan, laughing. "As I said. Public Enemy Number One. Whoops!"

"Well, never mind," says Alan. "The political intrigue of a Garden Square in London. Fascinating."

"But you will still do it, won't you?"

"Of course I will," he reassures her. "And no, I don't need a fee, in case you are wondering. Is she performing in the show itself?"

"No. Her son is. I think he is playing the piano and showing a film, or something."

"What are you going to be doing?"

"Oh, God, I hadn't thought. I was going to leave it to Belle and Grace to cook something up. Maybe I'll do something with them."

She sighs, sips her Champagne again.

"You look great. That the new foundation?"

"Yep. And a tiny touch of the mascara."

"Thought so. It looks perfect. Just gives you the definition you need."

"You sound so professional when you talk about makeup," says Alan, smiling at her.

All at once, there is a commotion on the other side of the bar. A man in a green shirt is trying to catch Alan's attention.

"Hey, Alan! Alan Makin!" yells the man.

Alan and Tracey look up. Alan smiles at the man, acknowledges his presence graciously.

"Viewers," he says to Tracey, who sits back on her stool, overwhelmingly impressed. This happy state of affairs lasts about two seconds, before it is made manifestly clear that this is not a particularly grateful viewer.

"Alan Makin, I've seen you on television and you are nothing but a great big cunt!" shouts the man.

"Supporting those bankers, those wankers, I saw that show you did, what about their bonuses, eh?"

Alan's smile has vanished. His face is white. He puts the palms of his hands down on his trousers, and turns to Tracey.

"They either tell you how marvellous you are, or how hideous you are," he says, with a twisted grimace.

"God, Alan," says Tracey, shocked. "Really?"

"Hey! Alan Makin! Makin! You are a cunt, do you hear me!" shouts the green-shirted man again. People start moving awkwardly away from him. Alan is frozen to the spot on his bar stool opposite. The pianist gamely continues to play jazz. This time, the bar staff respond. One burly man from behind the bar lifts up the counter, and moves round expertly to the green-shirted man, taking him firmly by the elbow.

"Come on, mate."

"Bankers and their bonuses! They are all cunts, and you are the biggest one of them!" The piano has stopped playing. There is total silence in the jazz bar.

"Arsehole!" is the man's final volley. He is summarily ejected from the bar.

There is an uneasy silence around the bar. The pianist starts playing again.

Tracey picks up her Champagne flute and drains it.

"Shall we go?" asks Alan.

She nods silently, slides off the bar stool.

"Does that sort of thing really happen often?" she says as they walk silently away from the bar.

"Well, probably once or twice a year. It comes if you are regarded as In The Public Domain," says Alan, proudly.

They are weaving through the crowds on Shaftesbury Avenue, past people queueing outside the theatres, standing in the street waving for taxis, running for buses. Someone bumps into Tracey. Alan genteelly takes her arm, guides her up a small side street.

"Well, that sort of put a hole in our evening. But it was an early evening drink. You probably have to be home by now, don't you? What would you like to do? Do you think you ought to go home?"

"Oh, Alan, I feel it's not right to end our drink on such a nasty note. What would you like to do?" says Tracey. She feels very sorry for him.

"I don't know. But I do know actually, I need to be home

pretty soon," he says, snapping his wrist out and checking his watch.

"Oh, why? Have you got someone coming round?" she says. "I mean, sorry, obviously you probably have things to do," she smiles, remembering they were only ever meeting for an early evening drink.

He pats his briefcase.

"Crickets. Live. They'll only survive another forty minutes or so in here."

"Oh my God!"

"Don't worry. The container is quite, quite sealed. But I need to get them home."

"Are you feeding them to… "

"The Munchkin. You betcha. Want to come and help me?"

And so it is that Tracey, National Lottery winner, wife to Larry, mother to Belle and Grace, presence of light and laughter on the Square, goes back to Alan Makin's flat to feed live crickets to a reptile.

"Wow, this is swanky," she says as she gets out of the cab, surveys the balconied apartment block with its Caryatids, semi-nude women made of stone bearing the portico of the building. She takes in the spectacular views across the Heath and down to the City.

"Lubetkin," murmurs Alan.

"Oh," says Tracey, who has never heard the name before and wonders what it means.

"Based on Le Corbusier. Probably our most perfect example of international Modernism," he says in the lift.

"Our what?"

"Britain's. You know, Le Corbusier. The vertical city."

Thus thoroughly daunted by this introduction to pre-War Futurist architecture, Tracey humbly follows Alan as the lift doors open, seemingly straight into the hall of his apartment on the fourth floor of Highpoint Two.

She walks into a double-height living room. It is white, immaculate, pictureless. Gentle lights quietly illuminate a room furnished with low sofas and curved tables. Two giant windows on either side of the room reveal immaculate landscaped gardens, sloping down. The lights of London spread out before her, almost at her feet. There is a tree inside the room, by the window. An indoor tree, planted in a shiny steel pot. There is no mess, no trace of soil or leaves on the white vinyl floor. Tracey does not quite know how to respond.

"Alan, this is amazing."

He has his back to her, is sorting out something by the bar. Tracey glances across, sees an illuminated case beside him. The Munchkin. The reptile is sitting on his branch, as perfectly immobile as when she first encountered him all those weeks ago at Makin TV.

"That's it," says Alan, almost to himself. He slides open a panel in the vitrine, expertly tips something into it, slides the panel shut at speed.

The Munchkin blinks twice, is galvanised into action. Still squatting on his twig, he swivels his head, tongue lashes the desperately leaping crickets who are hopelessly trying to escape their certain fate, and crunches each in a matter of seconds.

"I don't think I can look," says Tracey weakly.

Alan comes up behind her with a glass of rosé and brings the wine across her body, gently brushing her breasts with his arm.

"Don't. Just look at London," he murmurs.

She takes the chilled wine, sips it, looks across the darkening Heath.

"Berthold Lubetkin," murmurs Alan Makin into her ear. "He did the penguin pool at London Zoo. Then he paid attention to us human beings. Rather well, don't you think?"

Tracey has no idea what or who he is talking about. She feels like she is standing in a museum. Or on the Moon.

After a minute or two looking out of the window, Alan decides against telling Tracey that Lubetkin, disciple of Tatlin, was also architect of Finsbury Health Centre. He wanders off and casually sits on one of the immaculate sofas. It is decorated by a row of plumped cushions all arranged like diamonds along it. Adjacent to the sofa, is a low table on which rests a perfect assemblage of glossy magazines, all current editions, and a vase of peonies, all in bloom.

Entranced by the united forces of wine, and perfect interior design, Tracey understands she is to join him beside this display. She knocks back the wine, deposits her glass on a mirrored plinth beside the indoor tree, and walks, slightly unsteadily, towards the sofa. She knows what will happen next. It is a play. That's all it is. But the danger of it, the thrill of being in the moment, leads her forward. How dull life would be if she never experienced this moment, she thinks. As if he, Alan Makin, really did want to talk to her about makeup. What a fool. She should have had confidence in her first instinct. She realises she has started to sweat.

Alan proceeds to suddenly, expertly and confidently unbutton her shirt, unclasp her bra and suck her nipples. The last cogent thought that speeds through Tracey's mind as she lies back on the sofa and allows her skirt to be slid down towards the floor, is to wonder how many cleaners Alan employs, and whether they turn up every day. She decides, as he removes her underwear, that they definitely do.

Chapter Twenty-Four
Jane

He realises that he actually finds her too thin. He can trace the bones of her back with a finger. Her nipples jut out from tiny breasts. He knows Harriet aches to look like this. He sees her agonies every day. Standing at the fridge, worrying about whether to risk mayonnaise. She longs to be thin. But this is not the desired shape for Jay. Jane is simply too thin.

Still, he's not going to make it spoil everything. He's certainly not going to dump her. He doesn't think he could, anyway. He is frightened about what it would do to her fragile, tense personality. And he loves the fact that she aches to have sex with him. She loves it. Any time, any place, anywhere. That is what really turns him on. It makes it hard to resist her. Knowing that she is always ready for it. Day or night. Morning or evening. Once they had sex on the way back from the school run. In the back of Jane's Citroën. She had collected him after dropping George off and they had set to, in the car park of the shopping centre. On a picnic rug on the back seat. He enjoys the fact that she is always in a good mood after sex with him, too. Today is a perfect example of this.

She arches her back, smiles at him from the wreckage of the hotel bed.

"Have you ever slept with another woman?" he suddenly asks her.

"Every man's fantasy," she retorts. "But no. Why do you ask?"

"Just wondered. Any reason?"

"Never had the opportunity. I'd quite like to have done, though. But I'm probably too old."

"Why?"

"Well, I wouldn't know how to go about it. I mean I can hardly go to a lesbian pick up joint, could I? And I wouldn't know the first thing about what to do with a woman in bed."

"It's easy," he says. "You just do what you like having done to you."

There is a pause.

"I think it would be delicious," she says.

"You would just lick her tits like this," he says, licking them.

"And then slide your hand between her legs," he continues.

"Yes, but what about the fucking?" She is breathing quite hard now, pulling him on top of her again. God, she was good. Never satisfied. "That's the bit I can't quite renounce, you see."

It was true. She was unable to actually envisage ending her affair with Jay. She had always thought it was temporary, something she could dump at a whim. It started off in the summer. She originally put it down to a holiday romance. Then, she categorised it as something to keep her interested over Christmas. Then, she filed it under the title Twelve Month Fling. Now, she knew there was no reason to build in its obsolescence.

It worked, that was the main thing. She couldn't end it. Why should she?

She walks home, swinging her arms happily, that familiar delicious ache in her groin.

Although Jay had annoyed her, actually, between the action.

"Do you think your husband fancies the au pair?" he had asked, after they had screwed again, after all that lesbian fantasy chat which had really turned her on. Yes, he had actually asked her that. Jane had explained about how Anya came over to play the Blüthner. She had laughed in his face, but now she considered it, it worried her. There was the piano playing, for a start. The girl was a marvel. Nobody could deny it.

Then there was her height. That was pretty awe-inspiring.

Furthermore, Anya had a sort of measured stillness about her which Jane could see might be magnetic. Sort of. If you overlooked the Eastern European accent, the inability to say V properly. And the fact she was an au pair, which was really only one notch above being an actual cleaning lady.

She arrives home, throws her bag on the hall table and wanders downstairs into the kitchen, to find George standing in the middle of the room, eating a Müller Corner.

"Hello darling," she says to her offspring. "Please don't snack between meals."

"Good day," offers George. "Don't disturb me at this moment. I am about to go and finish my animated film."

"For the Talent Show?"

"The very same."

"Well, you'd better get a move on. It's next week. And George, you'll never guess."

"What?"

"Alan Makin is presenting it. The whole thing."

"Oh my giddy aunt. I thought you were. Who is Alan Makin?"

"Oh, never mind. He's on TV sometimes."

George seems entirely unimpressed by this personnel change. He finishes his yogurt, licks the lid, positions the spoon in a glass and wanders out of the room. Jane hears his feet running upstairs.

It is Thursday afternoon. At five o'clock, the door bell rings. It's Anya, shyly smiling on the doorstep. It's as if she has materialised out of Jane's thoughts, thinks Jane nastily.

"Oh, Jane. I, I mean Patrick said… I could come… "

"No problem," says Jane shortly, suggesting that it is indeed the precise opposite. "Come in. You know where the piano is?"

"Oh, yes, thank you."

Well I'm not bloody offering her a coffee, thinks Jane on her way to the kitchen.

Anya walks into the music room and puts her manuscript on the Blüthner. She gazes around, takes in the perfect furnishings. The Toile de Jouy screen. The oil paintings. One picture is of a man who is wielding a rifle and a very dead mallard duck. He has the same choleric complexion as Patrick. She wonders if it is an ancestor.

She pulls out the stool, sits down, plays her customary Bach prelude from the '48', then rests her hands on the creamy keys.

She looks at the manuscript. Beethoven. Piano sonata No. 14. In C sharp Minor; 'quasi una Fantasia' is the description. 'A sonata, almost like a fantasy.' She starts the piece. It is, of course, the 'Moonlight Sonata'. As she starts, the lovely opening ascending triplets in the right hand in conjunction with the sonorous octaves in the left travel down into the granite boudoir which is Jane's kitchen, and jolt through Jane's entire body as if she has been electrocuted.

Jane is downstairs, eating a biscuit. She allows herself one biscuit a week. This is her biscuit moment. And Anya is not adding to it with her fucking Beethoven. She is spoiling it. Jane feels like crying. But it is so beautiful, the liquid notes falling, the sustain pedal holding the whole beautiful melody in the air long after the keys have been pressed. And although she is trying to resist it, she cannot help but be transported by the music.

The movement finishes and Anya moves onto the second, and the third sections of the Sonata, pieces whose complexity and speed leave the average piano student far behind and wander into the realm of the committed pianist.

As Anya commences the Presto Agitato, the frantic third movement, Jane hears Patrick's key in the door. Good, she thinks. He's missed out on the bloody 'Moonlight Sonata' bit.

Anya is bent over the piano, focusing furiously on the notes as they come rattling out of the instrument. Patrick pops his head round the door.

"Anya! How marvellous!"

The playing stops, the notes collide and tumble together, falling through the air and into silence.

"Patrick, I hope this is alright."

"It's marvellous. Just what I wanted. Do start again! I mean, pick up where I came in. Sorry."

"I'll start from the beginning, it's no problem. I needed to warm up a bit."

"Righty ho." He backs out of the room, whistling.

She turns several pages back, and recommences the piece with the Adagio Sostenuo, the famous Moonlight bit.

The music ripples through the house. Patrick comes into the kitchen.

"Jane. Isn't this just terrific. My word! The 'Moonlight Sonata'. Never knew someone who could play it!"

"It's not actually all that difficult." She can't help herself. "I mean, I'm not taking it away from Anya, but I knew someone in my form at school who could play this when we were about twelve. Gets harder. But this famous bit is a piece of cake."

"I'd like to hear George play it then," retorts Patrick. "I think she's great. And it's just so nice to hear our piano being played by a real artist."

There is a pause as they listen to the playing. She has to ask him.

"Do you fancy Anya, Patrick? I mean you seem very keen on her."

He looks at her, startled, a bun half way to his mouth.

"Fancy her? No! Of course not." He turns away, chewing

mischievously. "Although she is rather severely gorgeous in a Slavic sort of way. Those cheekbones!"

He considers the prospect. There is no point in hiding anything from Jane.

"Well, I sort of do fancy her, I suppose. In an abstract way."

Even though she has just made love to another man that morning, still has traces of his semen dried on her thighs, the idea of Patrick fancying someone else infuriates her.

"What? What the hell is an abstract way?"

"Well, you know, if you weren't here, and neither was anyone else, and we were in the Sahara desert together, I'd probably have a go."

"Have a go?" echoes Jane incredulously. "What the hell sort of language is that?"

She looks at her husband of twenty years in a different way, actually looks at him from a different angle completely. She strips away the domesticated familiarity with which he has been so thickly veneered, sees him as a male predator on the vulnerable Eastern European au pair upstairs… no, it's too ghastly.

"God's sake, Patrick," she says. "We are not in the Sahara desert, thankfully."

"Well I like her coming here to play," he says stoutly. "And as I am the one who is paying… "

"What?"

He had failed to tell her this bit of the arrangement.

"You are *what*?"

"Paying her. I said I'd give her twenty quid to come and tinkle the ivories. You know. Why not? Poor girl, she probably sends it back to her family in Warsaw or wherever she comes from."

"Whoosh."

"Whoosh? What are you talking about? What the hell is Whoosh?"

"It's where her family comes from, you dunderhead."

"Oh, sorry. Well, as I was saying. She probably sends it all back. She needs it. And we have enough to spare."

"Paying her. I cannot believe it," says Jane. Upstairs, Anya is onto the Presto third movement. The notes cascade in a frothing fountain.

Underneath the cadenza, Patrick dimly hears a tweeting sound. He glances up at the kitchen clock, a confection where the numbers go backwards and birdsong emanates from the device on the hour, every hour. At this point, a wren is busily chirping.

A minute later Anya reaches the triumphant finish of the piece. There is complete silence in the house.

Patrick stomps upstairs to the music room. He swings open the door. He is cross with his wife, and is determined to have his way.

"That was terrific. Terrific. I wonder, er, Anya."

"What?" asks Anya.

"Could you possibly play for us next Sunday at lunchtime? Jane's parents are coming over. Might be rather nice. You know, showing off a bit! Give 'em a bit of Beethoven before the beef. Chopin before the chicken. Mozart before the... " he breaks off, unable to fulfil the end of the rather strained pun.

"... Mutton?" says Anya, whose family eat rather a lot of it in Poland.

Patrick is delighted that she has joined in with the joke.

"That's it!" he says, fumbling in his corduroy trousers for a £20 note, and giving it to her with the confidence of a man who is used to paying people in petty cash.

"So, same again, only on Sunday. Midday?"

"I'll come over on my way back from church. Do you go to church?"

"Good God no," says Patrick, with feeling.

"Well, see you then. Lovely."

"Lovely," echoes Patrick.

She slams the door behind her, walks lightly down the

steps and into the sun-filled Square. She knows just how Sunday lunch will be. Too much food, too much wine. The heat and smell of roasting meat suppurating through the house. She imagines being back in Lodz for her parents' Sunday meal. She feels homesick when she thinks about it. Without question it would be wholly provided by food from the family smallholding on the opposite side of the road. Potatoes, beets and cabbage all grown by her mother. They might have some meat from the family pig which would have been slaughtered earlier that week. Or just thick Borscht soup and homemade bread, followed by jellied quince. Her father would drink beer. Everyone would have gone to church, caught up on local gossip and had a chance to see friends.

"Tell us, Anya," her mother's friends would say. "What is London really like? What is the family like who you look after? Are they nice to you? What do they eat?"

"They waste their food," she would tell them. "They complain about having no money, but then they throw everything away."

Anya throws nothing away. The fridge at Tracey's house is evidence to it. It is full of tiny jars of cooked broccoli, small portions of rice and hard boiled egg. Half an onion, carefully wrapped in tin foil. A bowl of soup. A glass half-full of milk. It's how she has been brought up. She hopes she might have influenced Belle and Grace not to waste all the food she cooks for them and puts on their plates, but she doubts it.

Chapter Twenty-Five
Belle

She shakes Philip Burrell's hand. He is standing before her, smiling, clasping her other hand tightly to his, trying not to look down her top. He has already paid her, several crisp notes stuffed into an envelope.

He is very pleased.

"Darling. It's marvellous. The whole thing."

Belle blushes, smiles. She puts the money quickly away in her bag.

"Thank you Philip. I've had a good time here. It's been great."

She means it. She's enjoyed working at Philip's studio more than she had anticipated, not just because there was a satisfaction in doing the work itself, but because she realised Philip and Gilda had offered her a different view.

Things that she had considered unsayable, undoable, were said and done at the Burrells', just as if it was completely normal. Normal to have mouldings of genitalia in the downstairs loo, and topless pictures in the kitchen, normal to talk about long, long drinking sessions, and hint at other, more dangerous activities.

Gilda had even once implied very strongly to Belle, over the Brie sandwich at lunch, that she had, a long time ago, seriously toyed with the notion of having sex with an animal. And made it seem like a totally rational choice.

That was what fascinated Belle. She also loved the way Gilda played with the female dress code. Sometimes she was girly, other times butch. Her hair seemed to undergo almost daily transformations. Almost unconsciously, Belle had been influenced by this. It was a liberation of sorts to get out of her chosen uniform, dive into her mother's or sister's wardrobe and treat each day as an experiment.

Today, she is wearing a frilled, low cut dress scattered with tiny embroidered cherries. It is down this low neckline that Philip longs to gaze.

He feels he has the right to, anyway, because he has just been profiled in *Frieze* magazine. And he has just sold his first marathon course, which went for £150,000 at Basle Miami. He's been told that will be reported in the *Evening Standard*, possibly with another, much more readable profile, certainly with a photograph of him on the gallery's yacht which they had hired for the event. Ha. Let those johnnies at the Tate suck on that.

"It was your Amsterdam model," Magnus had told him, about the sale. "They loved the fact that it involved the sports stadium."

Why the hell is that of any importance? Philip has no idea. Still. What matters is that he, Philip Burrell, has had an idea. Marathon courses. He must get Magnus to patent it. He'll sue anyone who copies him. Even without a patent, he'll sue them. He can afford it. He can afford anything.

Jas is hovering behind her, shoulders squared, smiling at Philip.

"So, what's next, Sir?" he says.

"A knighthood," says Philip. His jaw hardens. "That'll be the day."

"No, I mean what course shall we do next?"

Philip raises a hand.

"Let them wait. Let them wait. Anticipation is all. I'll see. In the meantime, yet more golf holes beckon for you, dear boy."

He ostentatiously draws a pocket watch out from his waistcoat and consults it.

"Goodbye," he announces. "Off to the gallery."

Jas wanders around the studio, tracing a finger along the table. He doesn't want to do golf holes for Philip any more. After the giant glories of building the London, Berlin, Loch Ness, Tokyo, Amsterdam and New York marathon courses, he thinks golf holes might seem a bit pathetic. He sees how it will all play out. Patrick will spend his days at the gallery with Magnus. Belle will be back in her posh house. He will be in the studio, doing golf holes again.

"Will you come back here and help me?"

"Sure," says Belle. "I liked it. I liked working here. Makes my house look catatonically dull."

"You know, after this, we could do all sorts of other things."

"Sure," repeats Belle.

"Belle!" comes a light voice from downstairs. "Yoo-hoo! Jas, has she gone?"

"Not yet," yells Jas.

It's Gilda. Belle smiles. She runs down the stairs to the kitchen.

"Oh, Gilda, I was just off."

Gilda is wearing an old pair of fishnets and leather shorts, a Breton top and chandelier earrings. A brunette bobbed wig finishes the look. Belle puts her arms around Gilda, feels her bony shoulderblades. She kisses her cheek.

"Love the wig."

"Thank you. Would you like some tea?"

"Lovely. As long as it's not in the Snail Horror Mug."

They sit convivially at the table, perched on ancient school chairs.

"I was thinking Belle, about the Talent Show in the Square. It is next Sunday, is it not?"

"Er, yes, I think it is," says Belle, hoping to be vague.

She has a sudden burning desire to protect Philip and Gilda. The earlier notion of offering guided tours around their house, so that people could point and laugh at Gilda's topless pictures, now offends her.

Philip, he's a vain old thing. Let him fight his corner. But Gilda has a childlike vulnerability which Belle is anxious to defend.

"Would you like us to take part, kitten? It's been so lovely to… get to know the neighbours, by which I mean you, of course. So lovely. Whom should we contact? I think Philip and I should paticipate. After all, we are the only working artists on the Square!"

Belle considers the situation. She doesn't want to deliver Gilda and Philip up like something on a plate, an exhibit. Mad Artist and his Soviet Wife.

"I could sing a song," says Gilda slowly. "A Russian folk song. Philip might accompany me. He's great on the harmonica, you know."

"Why don't I talk to my mother about it," says Belle. "She'll know. Actually, yes, she's working with the presenter, she'll have some great ideas about what you could do."

She glances at her phone, gulps the rest of the tea.

"Gilda, I have to go now. I'll bring my mother over and we can have a chat about it."

She runs up the stairs, remembers the time when this house seemed threatening, and perverse. How could she have ever thought that, considers Belle. I hope they forget about the Talent Show, is her second thought.

Gilda hears the front door close and wanders around her kitchen. She looks at her black and white photographs on the wall without really seeing them.

"Well I hope she doesn't just disappear back into her life of Ordinariness," she says out loud.

Jas pops his head around the door.

"Bye, Gilda. That's me done. I'll be back tomorrow morning."

She waves a hand. The tips of her fingers are decorated with golden nail varnish.

Alone in the house, Gilda walks over to the window, looks out at the Square. The giant plane tree is fully covered in bright green leaves. It looks almost overburdened with foliage. She turns, runs upstairs to her bedroom, pulls out a sheaf of paper from her dressing table.

It is a song book, entitled *More Than A Woman*. She stands, smiling in her room, flips through the pages, hums a little, her foot tapping.

Suddenly, she tosses the book onto the bed and goes to an adjoining room. Her dressing room. There are boxes of shoes, with photographs on the front to indicate what is inside. There are rails and rails of coats. One chest of drawers only contains matching sets of underwear. Another only contains stockings. She opens a giant wardrobe, rifles through the beaded, glittering, satin dresses which hang in separate plastic sheaths. Gilda had a five year tussle with moths and is not going to enter onto that battlefield again.

She suddenly finds what she is looking for, and pulls it out. A vast sequinned gown with puffed sleeves, and a wasp waist leading to a giant, long skirt with train. She carries it reverentially to the bed. The stiff, beaded sleeves wrap around her neck, like the arms of a sleepy child.

Chapter Twenty-Six
Sunday Lunch

When Anya arrives to play the Blüthner grand for Patrick and Jane's Sunday lunch party, the household is in a frantic state.

"I mean, they grew up with rationing, darling," says Jane to Patrick, having explained why she is not going to bother with summer pudding, will not bother with summer pudding, and was never going to bother with summer pudding. She has knocked out a crumble instead.

"They just don't have the tastebuds. Good old fashioned food is what they like. Nursery style. Believe me, it's what they want!"

Sunday lunch has none of the pleasures of a dinner party, thinks Jane as she opens the door quickly to baste the lamb, and flinches from the heat of the oven. She thinks about the demanding necessities of Sunday lunch, of the table, food, timing. Plus, the food needs to be ready at once. And there is never a starter. Also, it's only her parents-in-law. So it's not really worth having food for showing off; Badoit water, mange tout, home made ciabatta rolls, that sort of thing. No point at all. They won't appreciate it.

Patrick, who knows his parents rather enjoy the exciting fodder they are occasionally granted by Jane, and in particular are very fond of summer pudding, merely raises his eyebrows and walks into the music room where he comes across George.

His son looks instantly guilty.

"George."

"Yes?"

"What are you doing?"

"Nothing. Just waiting."

George smiles beatifically at his father and ostentatiously picks up a book. It is a copy of *The Boy Pharaoh*, by Noel Streatfeild. An appropriate choice, thinks Patrick.

The door bell rings.

"Answer it!" yells Jane from the steam-filled kitchen.

"Alright, alright," mutters Patrick.

He opens the door, expecting to be enfolded within the sudden enthusiasm of his parents, relieved to have arrived on time. He jumps. It's Anya on the doorstep, volumes of sheet music in her arms. Oh, God. He had forgotten that he'd arranged for her to come and play for them.

He suddenly panics that it's the wrong thing to do, that it's going to look odd, having someone paid to play for just four people. Five, if you count the Boy. But here she is. He can't disinvite her now.

"Ah, Anya, great, great. Top stuff. Come in. Come in," he says awkwardly.

She senses the moment is wrong.

"Have I come on the right day, Patrick?"

"Oh God yes. Yes! Perfect. Come in. Now, you know the piano is here," he says, idiotically opening the door to the room. She walks in calmly.

"How lovely. Hello George."

"Why are you here?"

"I am to play for your guests. Won't that be nice?"

"But it's only Granny and Grandpa. They aren't guests. They don't even like music!"

"George!" interjects Patrick. "Your grandmother loves music. Take no notice of him, Anya. May I get you a drink?"

he says courteously, his equilibrium regained.

"Oh, just a coffee," says Anya, unused to being treated like a guest.

"Let me help you."

Patrick descends into the kitchen where Jane is coping with industrial quantities of boiling oil and roast potatoes. Anya follows him.

"Was that your parents? Unlike them to be on time."

"No, it's Anya, actually. Wants a cup of coffee."

"Oh, God, the au pair. Playing to us. Have we really confirmed her?"

Anya suddenly appears at Patrick's elbow.

"Oh, Anya hell-*lo*, what a treat that you're coming to play. Makes me feel like we'll be having cocktails at the Ritz! Would you like some coffee?"

"I'll get it," says Anya, who knows where everything is after helping Jane at the dinner party. She reaches up for the canister of coffee beans.

"Oh no, not those, Anya, if you don't mind," says Jane, barging past her to the same cupboard.

"Would you mind having this instead?" she says, getting down a jar of Nescafé Gold.

Anya smiles graciously. "Of course not."

You give me instant coffee, she thinks. I am going to fuck your husband.

Unaware of his new status as future sexual partner, Patrick has filled the kettle and is now pacing the kitchen.

"When would you like to start, Anya?" he says.

"How about now, for about twenty minutes," says Jane, smiling so widely her cheeks hurt.

"My parents have got to turn up first, Jane."

"Have they? Oh, right. Yes, I suppose they have. Well at least it's a novelty. I suspect this will be the first time they have heard live music since you were in the school orchestra."

He ignores the slight, pours the water and gives the mug to Anya. She walks gravely upstairs and sits down at the

Blüthner. That woman is so rude. She starts with her jazz repertoire which she used to trot out every Saturday night in a wine bar in Lodz, before she left for Britain.

To Patrick's delight, she kicks off with 'In the Mood'. It instantly lifts Patrick's heart. How did she know his parents would feel intimidated and overawed by Bach or Beethoven? Burt Bacharach was much more their style. He runs upstairs to tell her.

"They'll love this, Anya." She looks up at him, eyebrows raised in question.

"My parents. This is great. Top stuff."

After about five minutes of 'In the Mood', slipping expertly into some Simon and Garfunkel, the door bell rings.

George advances on the door, throws it open with a flourish. There are kisses and exclamations about George's amazing height as Patrick's parents come into the house.

"Darling," says his mother Joy. "The Square is looking perfect this morning. Just beautiful. And George, he's so big these days!"

"I say!" says Norman, his father. "Who's this?"

"Oh, this is Anya," says Patrick, beaming.

Anya breaks off from a rendition of 'Feelin' Groovy' and stands up.

"Sit down, sit down," says Patrick. "She's a keyboard maestro, and only lives next door, so I thought she might play for us a bit before we eat."

Jane comes into the room, wiping her hands on the back of her jeans. No point in dressing up. It's only Sunday lunch. It's only my in-laws.

"Hello Joy, Norman, lovely to see you. Yes, Patrick's idea for us to have a bit of music. Otherwise this piano just sits here, you see."

"Ahem!" says George.

"Well of course there is you, George, but Anya is the person around here who plays it properly. We are all in awe of her," says Jane, in a wholly unawed way.

The family sit around bolt upright on the sofas, listening to the au pair play. Patrick's parents are politely holding glasses of gin and tonic from which they take an occasional sip. Patrick and Jane are drinking wine, quite quickly. George is drinking juice, loudly, with a straw.

After a while, Joy comments on this. "Gosh, that straw is noisy," she says, frowning at George. She believes fervently that children should be seen and not heard. Very spoilt these days, children. Think the whole world revolves around them. She taps her foot impatiently. Patrick sees the gesture, realises that his mother is probably starving.

He stands up. "Ah Anya, thank you. That was just wonderful."

"But I haven't finished yet, I've only just started my programme."

"Well, we've really enjoyed it! Honestly, it's been great."

He sees that he needs to get rid of her, shepherd his parents downstairs and give them some food.

"Let me play on. Or maybe play for you after your meal." She is anxious he gets his money's worth.

Patrick hovers, unsure what is now socially proper to do with Anya.

"Great! Great! Well, why not come down and eat with us?"

On the way downstairs, Jane murmurs to her husband in that truncated way that married couples specialise in.

"What the hell? I don't want lunch with an au pair!"

"Well I could hardly leave her upstairs. Could I? George," he says loudly. "Could you lay a place for Anya?"

Oh God, thinks Patrick. Now we are going to have to cope with Anya all through the meal. Oh well. She's probably experienced worse. And it will give him a chance to look at those wonderfully arched eyebrows a little longer.

He foresees the forthcoming conversation. He knows exactly how it will play out and prepares himself to witness one of those moments in which middle class English people try to find common ground with agrarian Eastern Europeans who were born during the Cold War.

It is as he predicted.

"So, tell me Annie, is Russian your second tongue?" asks Joy politely.

Anya's manners are perfect. "Yes it is. We were forced to learn Russian, of course. We had to go to Moscow on school trips. Red Square, body of Lenin, St Basil's Cathedral," she says, smiling, feigning boredom.

She knows English people rather enjoy hearing about the superiority of their culture over the Russian equivalent.

"But nobody wanted to speak it. Everyone wanted to learn English."

She shrugs.

"So as soon as I left university I came over here to perfect my grammar. And my accent."

"Ah, university. You have a degree? Where was that?" says Norman. He suggests the only Polish city he has heard of. "Warsaw?"

"No, Krakow."

There is a silence across the table. "Mint sauce?" says Jane.

"What did you read there?" persists Norman.

"History of Art," says Anya. "Krakow is the Polish centre of culture. You know our Black Madonna, that is in Krakow."

"Oh yes, yes, super," says Norman, who has never heard of either place or icon.

Jane has heard just about enough of Anya's intellectual credentials, piano playing and knowledge of medieval panel paintings. She thumps roast potatoes on each plate. She takes particular pleasure in giving Anya five. Well, let her get fat.

"George is playing the piano next week," says Patrick. "We are having a Talent Show in the Square, and he's performing. Playing a piece on the piano. That is if we can get the bugger out into the Square. If not, it will be a keyboard."

His mother looks at him inquiringly.

"Can't he just walk out?"

"The piano, Mother. Not George!"

"Oh, how wonderful, George," says Joy. "What will we hear?"

George squirms in his chair.

"I am wearing a Storm Trooper costume," he blurts out.

"Marvellous!" says Norman. "Is that the same as a Super Trooper?"

"No, Dad," says Patrick. "That is Abba. A Storm Trooper. This is about *Star Wars*."

"Well," says Norman, laughing genially. "Let's hope it doesn't cook up Stormy weather. Or maybe it's your performance, which will go down a Storm, eh?"

George looks at his grandfather with a serious face.

"No, I am going AS a Storm Trooper. From *Star Wars*?"

"Please don't talk like an Australian, George," says Jane. "Beans, Joy?"

"Well, what are you playing on the piano?" asks his grandmother. "Thank you, Jane."

"I am playing the theme tune to *Star Wars*. Well I was going to play Hanon. You know, Hanon," says George. His grandparents look at him blankly.

"Hanon. Very boring exercises. I was going to play Hanon against an animation of Darth Vader invading our house, but Roberta told me I couldn't."

"Oh, what a shame," says his grandmother, who met Roberta once, was corrected by her about the best time to prick out cabbages and has henceforth disliked her intensely. "Is that the woman with the allotment?"

"Yes. She is also George's piano teacher," says Jane brusquely. "Gravy?"

"Why did she stop you?" asks Joy. "Piano exercises might be boring but you know they are essential, Georgy."

"Oh, she felt my film was a bit dodgy. The film I made to go along with the Hanon. I did a computer animation with Lego. And it was all my idea. I showed Darth Vader arriving to see Mummy on the sofa having her bum-bum smacked by Jay the next door neighbour. And Darth Vader has his lightsabre to attack them, you see."

A terrible quiet falls over the dinner table.

Jane actually freezes, her fork half way to her mouth. Her parents-in-law both cough and look down with fascination at their plates, as if this is the first time they have noticed there is food on them.

"This is delicious lamb, Jane," says Norman.

"So Roberta said… " continues George, anxious to hold onto his audience.

"That's enough, George," says Patrick. He has gone a funny shade of red. He refuses to meet Jane's stricken look.

"Cranberry?" whispers Jane.

Patrick swallows hard. He turns to Anya. "Tell my parents, Anya what is the main difference between life here and life in Warsaw, sorry, in where is it you live? Whoosh?"

"Lodz. The main difference? People in my home city are less bothered about their houses. Whereas here, the house is treated almost as a real life person. Or a pet."

"Is that so?" says Jane, faintly. Her brain is drumming inside her head. It's like an onslaught of white noise in her brain. She feels rooted to her chair. How the hell did George come up with that story? She shoots him a death stare, but he is busy playing with his napkin ring. Eventually, he drops it on the floor.

Jane sees herself as if she is crouched on the ceiling, or in another room. How the hell is she going to explain herself to Patrick? She quickly runs through a variety of options.

The first option must be that George has made it up. What could the second option be? That she was doing some Pilates with Jay. During a dinner party. It's such a ludicrous idea she almost laughs aloud, even in her frantic state of mind.

George has made it up.

It's the only thing to do. She'll have to laugh it off. Pretend it's a flight of fancy. Or maybe not. Why not come clean, she thinks, crazily. Anya is telling her parents-in-law about Lech

Walesa and Solidarity. Her mother-in-law is telling Anya that they had a lit candle in their front room one Christmas because of him. Jane blesses the Eastern Block and the fact that the Eastern Bloc au pair is there, talking.

"I'll get pudding," she murmurs.

She stacks the dirty plates and carries them out, where she considers her position, frantically.

What if she just confesses all? Like a skier seeing the potential disaster before her on the piste, she sees the future. Or what might be the future. The house with a For Sale sign outside, crates with divided furniture in the hall. George taken out of school. Sent to board. Or… where? Where would he live? And with whom? Well that bit is simple. He'd much rather live with his father, she knows it. If it came down to it, in a court, he would always want to live with Patrick. Where would she live, then? She'd have to leave the Square. And would Jay leave Harriet to come with her? Would she even want him to? She peers into her future and runs away from it, fast.

She gets the coffee beans out and grinds them. Everyone will have coffee, real coffee. Even the au pair.

Patrick comes into the kitchen, leans on the stone counter, looks at his wife. His face is blazing.

"What the fuck," he says slowly, "is going on?"

She looks up at him earnestly, opens her eyes very wide, and lies to save her marriage and the status quo, lies as if she can't stop, blaming everything on her child.

"I have absolutely no idea. You know what a silly bloody fantasy world George lives in, darling. I have no idea what he is talking about. I can only think… "

"What?" says Patrick coldly.

"I can only think that he has seen some crazy film at school and put two and two together to make five. I've been talking about Jay a lot, yes, I have come to think of it, a lot recently, what with all the help he has been giving me with the Talent Show. It's been a lot of work, Patrick, and you have hardly focused on my obligations for it. So I have been talking a lot about Jay… I think that must be it. I don't know what he is talking about, I really don't. Of course not."

Patrick looks at her, gathers up the pudding bowls.

"Well. I'm bloody glad that George is not doing anything humiliating for the show. That's all I can say."

He walks back, prepared to deliver crumble to his parents.

Jane feels like weeping over the granite island.

Chapter Twenty-Seven
The Talent Show (i)

The day of the Talent Show dawns beautiful and cloudless. It is very early in the morning. The moving team has turned up on time, thank God, thinks Jane. The team is the vicar's sole contribution to the day. It has arrived with a set of low trolleys on wheels in order to move the Blüthner into the Square. They're used to moving pianos; there are a lot of pianos in churches.

"I know, it's mad," says Jane to them, giggling. She likes flirting with workmen, in a superior sort of style.

The vicar's team walks past her, purposefully, to the music room. The grand has been cleared of its array of gilt framed family photographs, the flotsam of a marriage. It is now closed, waiting ponderously to be moved.

The team contemplates the Blüthner. "Bit of a thing, a concert grand," says one of the men, after a moment or so of silence.

"And it will have to come back later on this evening, you know that don't you? Has Reverand Ian told you that, too?" says Jane.

"Yep," says the man testily. He is measuring the Blüthner. He then measures the door.

"When did this thing last come in here?"

"Oh, ages ago."

She dislikes his slighting tone. She can't actually remember when, or how the Blüthner got here. Perhaps when they first moved in; Patrick and her, just the two of them. She had wanted to learn how to play piano, and he insisted that he buy it for her. She remembers protesting, and him insisting. She thinks it was on their first wedding anniversary. A symbol of their marriage, perhaps. A thing of beauty, hardly ever used but impossible to shift. And yet when it was first put in this room, it seemed to symbolise all their ambitions for the future, for how they were going to be, here on the Square. She feels a fierce protective love for the instrument. Even though she barely played it.

"At that time, it was all a bit of a slum around here, you know. I think we were just about the only people to have a whole house. Flats everywhere else." Apart from Jay and Harriet in their house, of course, she thinks with a stab.

The moving men are wholly unconcerned with the history of the gentrification of the Square. They are only focused on one thing. Moving the Blüthner.

"How did you get it in here?" asks the man.

Jane shrugs. "Pass. Sorry. Coffee, anyone?"

She leaves them to it.

First, they try rolling it towards the door, slanting it diagonally. The instrument creaks ominously, then lurches. The men put it quickly back on its feet. The men stand around looking at it, as if it is about to utter a pronouncment. When it remains stubbornly silent, they try another ruse. They tilt the entire back of the piano up, so it looks like a crazy upright in a dream. That doesn't work either.

Jane comes back with the tray of coffee and some shortbread biscuits.

"Thanks. We'll have to take the window out," the main man tells her, through a mouthful of biscuit.

"What?"

"The window. We'll have to get it through the window."

"Have you seen the drop outside?" she replies.

The men shamble round, open the front door, survey the architecture of the bay window and the level of the ground beneath it. There is a significant drop beneath the window sill, made worse by a trench dug close to the wall.

"It was a damp course… " Jane can't bring herself to explain in detail why there is a trench beneath the window of the music room.

There is an awful pause.

"We'll need to put up some scaffolding, I think," says the foreman of the team. "I mean, that's what we would do normally. We can't carry it. Can't lift it. We'll have to put a platform out from the window."

"Why ever can't you lift it out?"

"Health and Safety."

Oh, for God's sake, thinks Jane. She looks at the men.

"You look healthy enough."

The men look flatly back at her, drinking her coffee.

"We can get some scaffolding in, if you really want this piano outside, and back inside, but that will cost you," pronounces the foreman.

"How much?"

"£750. Or £650 cash."

Forget it. Bugger off with your silly trolleys. The Blüthner will stay put. Like my marriage, she thinks. It is not something that can be pushed around.

"Forget it. So sorry. Can you thank the Reverend for the thought. Leave the coffees when you've finished. Thanks for trying."

She turns on her heel, resolute. She will find a solution. She is not going to allow the day to be thwarted. There is her son, and his piece. She is not going to let him be pushed aside. Shame we can't use the Blüthner, but there is another option. There is always another option. There must be.

She hears the team depart in their Transit, slamming the doors.

She walks into the music room, drumming her fingers on the polished mahogany lid of the grand which, now closed, seems to have retreated into itself like an invertebrate in a shell.

She will call Tracey, she decides. It's a bit early, but too bad. There is no point in emailing or texting either. It has to be a phone call. Old fashioned and direct. As Tracey's precious TV star is now presenting the whole thing, she can have joint responsibility. Jane enjoys doing this; thinking of something, then justifying it immediately via a little debate in her head. The discussion of whether to call Tracey thus resolved, she puts it into action.

Tracey is lying on a sofa in the living room in Highpoint. She has got up very early and has arrived at the flat in order to go through Alan's script with him.

Before this task, however, the pair have enjoyed each other in an energetic and loud manner on the breakfast bar above the Munchkin's vitrine. The reptile had remained entirely neutral to these carnal goings-on, clutching his twig, motionless.

It's alright, thinks Tracey. In Alan's flat, it's alright. This place is so strange, it really is as if normal rules don't apply. She can screw Alan Makin here.

"Alan, can I just ask you something?" she says presently.

"Of course, my cherubina," says Alan. He is as yet still undressed.

"Have you got your script in your head? Do you know what you are saying?"

"*Mais sans doute*," he responds. Clad only in a towel, he parades around the room.

He is in a great mood. He loves hosting these little local events. Of course he does them for nothing, makes nothing out of it but there is something so gratifying about the waves of adoration that he feels his presence provokes, he does them quite often.

"When shall we go to the Square?" she asks, as her phone rings.

"Oh, God, it's Jane. What the hell," she mutters, pressing the tiny button on the device. Alan decides to start performing post-coital Alexander Technique stretches against the plate glass windows. Tracey fervently hopes nobody in the landscaped gardens suddenly decides to look up at the building.

"Jane, hello, how are you?"

"Good. Sorry to bother you so early. But I have a problem. God. The Blüthner won't go through the door, can you bloody believe it? Can't be done. Only way is through the window. And I'd have to pay £750 if you please, to the bloody vicar and his merry men. For the removal of a window, and scaffolding! What a joke. So much for our fundraising. Do you have any suggestions for an alternative, Tracey? I mean, I don't suppose you want your upright piano outside, do you?"

Tracey considers the situation. She hasn't got the energy to consider how on earth the Berry could be moved from her basement. Yet she thinks, vaguely, that there might be an easier solution.

"We have an electronic keyboard you could use. I mean, Belle does."

"Do you? Do you?"

"Yes," says Tracey, looking away from Alan, who is now almost prancing towards her. His towel has dropped off. Blimey. She is going to laugh out loud. She buries her face in the sofa. She loves all this messing around. It makes her feel young, unmarried, excited.

"It's upstairs in her room," she squeaks.

"Sorry, Tracey, I can't hear you."

She waves frantically at Alan.

"In her room," she says, gasping. "I have no idea exactly where. Underneath a whole load of shoes, and other instruments, I believe. Belle is in, she'll show you."

"Oh God Tracey, that would be amazing. Could we use it? Does it run off batteries?"

"No. Look, pop over. I am at Alan's, just… just tidying up the script with him. But do have a look. There must be a point we could run it off. Belle will show you where it is. She won't mind playing it in the show, either," says Tracey, keen to remind Jane there were others who had talent, apart from 'Boy' George. "Actually she'd probably prefer the keyboard to your grand, no offence."

In her relief, Jane decides not to be offended. I bet Tracey doesn't know the Blüthner is currently worth around £40k, though, she thinks. Plus, it was bloody nice of her, Jane, to offer it in the first place. As she puts the phone down, it occurs to Jane that a subtle shift has taken place. Tracey seems to have acquired a sort of quiet power. She seems a lot more self assured. Must be the television work. Jane knows Makin's Makeovers, featuring Tracey herself, is due to go out in a week or so. She has already resolved to be out on the evening in question.

She texts Jay. *Bloody grand. Can't be used.*

Jay is watching Harriet deliberate over her breakfast, worrying over the calorific content of a single Weetabix.

"I feel so nervous," Harriet says to Jay as she eventually decides to have marmalade on toast, for energy. "I wonder whether it was really a good idea to say I'd participate. I mean, it's mostly children, isn't it? Do you think people will think I am showing off? Do you think it will bore them?"

Jay smiles at her. "I don't care if you are showing off. Why not? Not everyone can play a Bach partita at a moment's notice."

"Well, I don't know if I can," says Harriet dolefully. "I probably can, but the way I feel right now, I doubt whether I can even lift the bow. Who is texting you at this hour?"

"It's Jane."

"Oh?"

"Apparently her grand can't be moved. She says that Tracey has an electronic keyboard, wants us to get it. I wonder if Brian could hop over and pick it up."

"Why can't she?"

"Too busy with chairs, apparently."

Harriet reaches for her mobile phone. She taps in a number. Her son Brian is still upstairs in bed.

"Yeah?"

"It's Mummy. Can you come down, please? I need a favour."

There is no response.

"Brian?"

"On my way."

Fifteen minutes later, Brian is standing on Tracey's doorstep. He rings and rings. Eventually Belle, clad in a puce-coloured bath robe, appears at the door.

"Yep?"

"Your keyboard. We need it. For the show. Apparently. That alright?"

"Fine."

She motions him in, leads him upstairs to her bedroom.

"There."

He claws past several dozen shoeboxes, four bath sheets, a guitar and a Hello Kitty laundry bag, before locating and grasping the Roland keyboard.

"S'it. Cheers."

"Yep."

Brian leaps down the stairs two at a time. The door slams. The entire exchange must have taken no more than fifteen words.

Jay texts Jane. *We have the keyboard. All systems are go, Head Girl.*

She tosses her hair back with satisfaction. Quite a thing, having a problem to solve in a tight deadline. She's always been good at it. Just shows her touch hasn't faltered.

She texts him back. *Do you want to deliver it over to me? Five minutes.*

At this point, the furniture van from Rayners in Wandsworth draws up with a flourish. The van is packed with 200 gilt stackable chairs that Jane has ordered. She explains to the man where she would like the chairs arranged, then turns to see Jay, languid, elegant, in her hall, casually leaning against the keyboard.

"Wonderful. I love you. You look wonderful. You are wonderful. Thank you."

"Thank Tracey. And my son."

She hates Tracey. She hates his son. She doesn't want to include them.

"Yes, well I don't want to. I want to thank you. You will watch, tonight, won't you?"

"Jane, have you forgotten my wife is playing in this?"

In the pressure, she had. The reminder burns her heart. She hates his wife. Not personally. Well, actually she does hate her, personally.

"Oh, yes. Silly me."

"Come on. Chin up. It can't always be about you."

"No, I know. Well, at the moment, I feel it never is, with you."

"Oh, rubbish! You know you are irresistible."

Yet he hadn't been around much recently. Jane is too proud to point this out, but it's clear. They haven't had a hotel day for weeks.

"Look, thanks for bringing it round. That is really great. Saves the day. I must thank Tracey. I must organise a table for it, and of course the projector."

"Projector?"

"For George's film. The new, improved version." Had she mentioned to Jay that George had originally intended to project a Lego version which appeared to reference their inter-dinner fucking? She didn't think she had. She wasn't going to now. It would seem so gauche. Anyway, that incident is over and forgotten. She thinks even Patrick has forgotten it. She fervently hopes he has. He hasn't mentioned it, at least.

"It's to be projected onto a sheet. At least that's the plan. Larry's putting it up."

Indeed, in the Square, at that precise moment, Larry appears, bustling, holding a thick white bedspread tightly to his chest. He waves in a frenzied manner over to Jay, drops the heavy cloth, curses extravagantly, collects it up again, carries on walking. Behind him trails Belle, carrying a stepladder.

"Belle, thanks so much for the keyboard," yells Jane.

Belle nods her head in acknowledgement of her usefulness, although all she did was to point out to Brian where, in the detritus of her room, the device had been abandoned. She carries on walking beside her father.

"Got to put this up here, apparently! On a tree!" he shouts over to Jane.

"This is all coming together," she shouts back, happily.

"Oooh Come Together... over me," croons Alan Makin as he screws Tracey for the third time that morning, this time on the leather sofa.

Chapter Twenty-Eight
The Talent Show (ii)

Her fears that nobody would turn up have proved unfounded. She's standing at the gate of the park in the Square, taking tickets. Or rather, taking money and giving people raffle tickets. Everyone is effusive about the event, and lots of people have come. Well, about thirty have already arrived. More will come, she tells herself. She knows most of them vaguely. Nice people who live around the Square. Everyone comes in smiling.

"Thank you so much."

"Great, thanks so much."

"I know. It's going to be great."

"I can't wait either."

Behind her, the chairs are in rows on the grass. People are already sitting down on them. Others have brought rugs and are sitting, chatting, opening Thermos flasks of coffee, bottles of wine, cans of Coke. Most of them are only about twenty seconds away from their front door. However, some people are behaving as if they are on a far-flung camping trip, worrying about bottle openers and unwrapping sandwiches.

Oh well. Jane looks down at the spoils. She must have made about £350.

She looks at her watch. It is 5.56pm. In a rushed phone call with Tracey, she was informed that Alan would be appearing at 6.15, to open the show at 6.30.

"One... two... one... two," intones Patrick down the microphone over by the stage. His voice appears, disconnected, from a large speaker under a tree.

Anya moves quietly around him, checking that Belle's electronic keyboard is level, drawing up the piano stool so it is easy to sit upon. Jane looks at her with intense irritation. Still, it's good that she's helping Patrick with the PA system.

She shudders as she thinks about what might happen if the sound fails. Larry's bedspread hangs from a tree behind them. A heavy piece of cloth, it looks rather fragile and is attached to a rope only by three plastic clothes pegs.

Jane's phone trills.

It's Tracey.

"Alright, we're ready. Has everyone arrived?"

"Well, I don't know. There seems to be quite a few empty chairs, but it's only six. I'd give it a bit longer." People are still arriving. There must be about sixty now in the park.

"Oh... okay."

Tracey sounds nervous.

George. She'd forgotten about her son.

"Tracey, I have to go," she tells her.

"Look, can you carry on taking the money?" she says to the Single Mother, who has just turned up. "It's a fiver minimum for adults and a quid for kids. No exceptions. Remember we are fundraising. Try not to give people change if they give you a tenner."

She throws the box at the Single Mother and darts out of the park.

At home, George is standing at the foot of the stairs. He is entirely clad in white. Finn's Storm Trooper costume. He hums a little tune.

He is ready. He is composed. He is aboard the Death Star.

He raises an eyebrow as his mother comes bolting in.

"George, darling. Sorry I'm late. Are you ready?"

"I am," says her son sonorously.

"Have you got your music?"

He looks at her, composedly. "Roberta has."

As she steps from the bus, Roberta finds George's music in her bag. God, that was lucky, she thinks as she hurries towards the Square.

Behind the bedspread in the park, Patrick is looking for the extension cable in which to plug a small spotlight. Anya comes behind to help him search for it.

"I think it's here," says Patrick, pulling out a cable from behind a laurel bush.

"Can I help you?" says Anya, leaning down. She turns her head towards him. He looks at her beautiful face. I might as well, thinks Patrick.

"Er, Anya, can I just… "

He lurches forward, kisses Anya. Awkwardly. They stand up, behind the bedspread, kissing properly this time. Patrick puts his hand on her breast, finds the nipple. Thrillingly, he discovers this is as exciting as he had fantasised it would be.

As she kisses Patrick back, Anya is deeply satisfied. Another part of her mind is, however, slightly worried about George's music, which she had been going through with him yesterday.

Where had she left it? Oh well.

Patrick breaks away from her.

"God, Anya. Sorry."

"Sorry?"

"I mean," he shrugs, smiles at her helplessly.

"Do you actually know where the plug is?"

She laughs. "It's here," she says, moving her bag and revealing it to him.

He pops his head around the sheet.

"God. Quite a crowd here. Must be about seventy people. Shouldn't we have some form of music, sort of while we are waiting?"

Anya nods, walks round the keyboard and turns it on. It

229

whistles, then the noise subsides to a low hum. She draws up the stool, puts her hands on the board and starts to play, quietly. Gershwin.

Patrick shakes his head. It is perfect. The girl is a wonder to him. "Perfect." He looks down the aisle of chairs to see Tracey and Alan Makin hastening towards him.

Alan is dapper in a pinstriped suit. Tracey looks slightly flushed.

"Do you have a microphone?" asks Alan of Patrick. He hands him the single microphone, purloined from the Scouts, who use it for their Christmas show.

"Ahem!" says Alan Makin loudly, down the microphone. The low level burble of conversation ceases. Anya finishes her piece with a small arpeggio to the tonic note, stands, and bows. A faint ripple of applause marks her exit.

"Thank you… " says Alan, realising he has no idea of the name of Tracey's au pair. "Well, thank you. And welcome, one and all, to this, the very first Talent Show in the Square. We have a lot of wonderful acts tonight. Nobody is going to be judged, as such. Simply sit back and realise how very very talented you all are. All of you! Thank you!"

A larger burst of applause. Jane runs up to Alan and thrusts a running order into his hand. "You might need this, you know. It's the running order. You have to introduce everyone."

"Thank you," says Alan, with the practised air of someone who is always being given running orders by inferiors. Jane recognises this. She bristles, but she cannot have people being unannounced.

"And now will you all welcome, er, Harriet, who is to play for us a wonderful Bach partita."

He gazes down the aisle as Harriet wobbles unsteadily up towards the area where he is standing. She is wearing the lilac. She is also wearing a pair of very high heels, whose vertiginous nature she has not quite mastered. She has a lot of makeup on.

"Thank you Alan," she says, waving her bow at everyone. "Hello, the Square!"

It's not Glastonbury, thinks Jane sourly.

Harriet turns to Anya, who is standing beside the bedsheet. "Could you give me an A, please?"

Anya obliges, turning on the tuning device in the keyboard. Harriet fiddles with her violin for about three seconds, pauses, takes a deep breath, applies the bow and starts to play.

Everyone leans forward to listen as Bach's creamy composition rolls out around the park, the wrestling arpeggios and runs of notes held together by the contrapuntal beat which overarches the composition like some sort of godly heart. On and on she goes. Jane watches Jay smiling fondly at her. Her stomach twists.

He's so proud of her, she thinks with dreadful malice.

She's so average.

Alright, she can play the violin, but so what? She's fat. And old.

Beside Jay, Brian smiles proudly too. He nudges Belle, who is sitting next to him.

"She's brilliant, your mum," whispers Belle.

Brian responds by holding her hand.

The notes are running inexorably to their final position. Harriet is in the home strait. She knows it. The audience knows it. Alan knows it. He grasps the microphone, ready to leap in and thank her when he is distracted by a terrible commotion at the gate.

"Yeah but we want to take part, right? Is our money not good enough for youse then?"

Everyone abandons their focus on Harriet, and Bach, and turns round to see what is going on. A huge man with a bull terrier on a chain beside him is standing squarely in the gateway, and shouting at Jane.

Harriet continues with the coda.

"We've got talents, you know!" continues the man. "Ain't we, Jacky?"

"Yeah!" shouts a young woman.

The man shoulders his way past Jane, ignoring her completely.

"Come on everyone."

Jane hovers beside the gate, her arms flapping uselessly by her side, her mouth open in astonishment as she sees no-one other than the vicar himself, the vicar! Leading a group of people, no, she calls it a *posse* of... dreadful people, the people who live in the council estate nearby, walking as bold as brass into what she, this evening, has started to refer to as the 'auditorium'.

They are dressed in sleeveless vests, tracksuit bottoms and trainers. Some are wearing football shirts. The children have aggressively short hair. Most of them have earrings. And tattoos. And giant golden chains. There are at least three dogs.

Jane is caught between standing her ground scornfully and heartily wishing she could sink into the ground and disappear.

The vicar waves his fingers in a conciliatory gesture to the astonished gathering who have, by now, completely forgotten about Harriet and her Bach piece.

Belle, hating herself for doing it, and Brian, are sniggering into their hands.

"Wot you find so fuckin funny, then?" shouts the woman called Jacky as she walks past.

They immediately drop their smiles.

"Nothing," whispers Belle.

She turns round properly and sees Jas. Thank God.

"Jas!" shouts Belle.

He waves, pleased to see her.

"Oh, Belle, hi, there you are."

He hurries up, pushing a smaller boy in the back.

"Go on Javi, Mum says she'll catch up with you."

Javi wanders away, unconvinced.

"What the hell is going on?" says Belle. "They ruined Harriet's piece."

"S'alright," says Jas. "Once everyone has sat down, it's alright. Just making sure nothing's going to kick off. But I've got to go."

"What? Why? You've only just arrived!"

She is conscious of wanting to uncouple herself from Brian, who is sitting closely beside her. She turns her back on him to face Jas.

"Where are you going?"

"Got to collect Gilda, haven't I?"

Gilda. Oh, God. Belle had completely forgotten that Gilda was planning to do something at the Talent Show. What had she said she wanted to do, was it sing something? Russian folk? Belle couldn't remember, feels a stab of guilt that she had never discussed it, as she said she would, with her mother.

She looks helplessly at Jas' retreating back.

His mother, Brenda, comes running up through the lines of chairs.

"Sorry, sorry. Ooh, Belle, hello! So nice to see you." She grabs Javi, the younger child, by the hand and takes her place with the rest of the recently arrived group.

Harriet finishes her piece. The front row clap with their hands up by their faces, as if to make up for the fact that everyone else has forgotten about her.

"Good evening," intones the vicar. "So sorry we are so late. Gathered some people from my community project who would like to join in, hope that's alright."

"What community project might that be?" says Larry to Tracey.

"Who knows?" replies Tracey.

The council estate group sit squarely on the left hand side, dragging spare chairs around from the back so that they can be together, maintain their physical unity.

Alan Makin smiles at them in what he hopes is a welcoming manner.

Then one of the women shouts out.

"Ain't you that chap off the telly?! Nobody told us there's

celebrities here! Hello! Hey! You're much thinner than you look on the box! Are you doing autographs after?"

Alan's expression changes immediately. He cocks his head towards her, delighted.

"Yes I will be doing autographs," his voice booms over the park.

"Oh, Christ, sorry," he says, switching the microphone off. "Yes, I will be doing autographs." There is already a small commotion in front of Alan Makin of people doing selfies with him in the background. Alan respectfully puts the microphone down and stands smiling as people crowd around him, their smartphones raised in totemic acknowledgement.

Jane has had enough. She marches up to Alan. She knew this should have been a private affair.

"Alan, please. We are in a public space so we will have to put up with this. But please, can we get on with our event. Poor Harriet."

"Ah, yes, so sorry. Right. Where were we?"

"Harriet," says Jane, icily.

Alan Makin regains his position at the front of the dais.

"Whoop whoop!" shout the newcomers. "Can I be on your show?" yells someone.

Jane turns, notices Roberta slip into the park. She waves a sheet of music at her.

Jane points theatrically to the house, where George is waiting. Roberta slips away again.

"Thank you so much, er, Harriet, for that wonderful piece and welcome to everyone who has just arrived. Now, who is next?" He glances down at the sheet.

Next on Jane's programme is a modern dance piece by the Dance Ensemble from Grace's school, The Prep. Oh, God. Alan Makin knows nothing about The Prep but correctly suspects that the troupe might be given short shrift by the newly augmented audience.

"Well, alright. Has anyone here got a piece?" he says, appealing to the new group who are sitting right beneath him.

What, thinks Jane, the hell is going on? She marches up to Alan.

"What are you doing?" she hisses. "There is a programme!"

Alan is aware of the entire crowd becoming restive. He carefully switches the microphone off.

"Look here, you stupid, stupid woman, these people want to take part! Can't you see it?" he says to Jane. Jane gasps at him. But she leaves the podium.

"I had to be uncompromising to her," he will explain later to Tracey.

Anyway, even if he had been paying attention to the small troupe of dancers from The Prep who were at that precise moment, shivering in their leotards behind the sheet, it would have been no good.

The large man who seemed to be the leader of the group has risen to his feet.

"Yeah, we've got stuff. We've got talent too, you know. Come on, Kylie," he says, grasping the hand of a small girl dressed entirely in white.

Jane rolls her eyes theatrically.

"It's hopeless," she says sadly to Patrick, flopping down into her chair. She is furious at the way Alan Makin has talked to her, and a tiny bit ashamed. She should have invited those dreadful people, but she just couldn't bear to. "It's hopeless."

She thinks about George and his piano piece with a sort of low level horror. Several women near her turn and smile sympathetically. Most, however, are loving the excitement and the combined frisson of jeopardy, class war and a possible fight.

"Most exciting thing that's happened here for about a decade," says Larry, to no-one in particular.

Kylie, a small child with furiously braided hair and a lot of blue eyeliner, takes the microphone.

"Mah baybeee luurves me!" she sings, both in key and a perfect mid Atlantic accent, into the microphone. "He lurrves me true!"

"Is this appropriate for a prepubescent child?!" sniffs Jane to Patrick, who is grinning and sitting forward in his chair.

"This is marvellous," whispers Patrick back to her.

"Have you gone mad?" she says.

Kylie comes to the end of her piece. Her compatriots all stand up and cheer her madly. Brenda is grinning and waving at her.

"Well done babe!" she shouts.

"Thank you Kylie," says Alan Makin grandly. "That was excellent."

He gestures to the dancers. "And now, from The Prep, a piece of modern dance."

Twelve girls in bare feet and lime-coloured leotards, each bearing wispy pieces of net, launch themselves out from behind the sheet to some music by Béla Bartók.

The middle class residents of the Square all sit watching the display and nodding their heads encouragingly. They would like to tap their feet, but the music doesn't seem to have any reasonable sense of beat, so they just sit there, smiling and nodding.

After this, several non-problematic pieces are rolled out. A child does a bit of unconvincing magic; Grace sings a Robbie Williams standard, with recorded backing. Another person from the council estate group gets up and sings 'When I Need You', by Leo Sayer. The Single Mother shows how her dog, a large and friendly Labrador, can walk on its back legs. Everyone laughs.

Kylie's father and some of his friends start smoking.

To Jane's astonishment, the vicar takes one off him.

"May I?" says the vicar, reaching for a Benson & Hedges.

"Gwan then Rev," says Kylie's father genially. "Have a Bennie."

Jane hears a commotion behind her, turns, and opens her mouth. No sound comes out of it.

The figures of Philip Burrell and Gilda are slowly walking up the path, accompanied by Jas, who is waving at Alan Makin.

"I think we have a last minute entry," says Alan, who is enjoying himself hugely by now.

Jas detaches himself from Philip and Gilda, and walks up to Alan. He whispers in his ear.

The audience is transfixed by the figures of Philip, who is wearing a white boiler suit imprinted with the outline of a naked man, and Gilda, who is in her long gown with a train, caked in beads, sequins and glitter. On her head is a small crown.

Alan coughs.

"I would now like to introduce tonight's surprise guests, our resident artists, Philip Burrell and Gilda."

"Piss artists!" someone shouts from the audience.

"Sssh," hisses someone else.

"Gilda is going to sing 'It Don't Mean A Thing If It Ain't Got That Swing'," says Alan Makin, somewhat incredulously.

Belle ducks her head down and giggles. What happened to the Russian folk, she thinks.

"Which, as everyone probably knows, is by Irving Mills. Music by Duke Ellington and… er, Philip Burrell."

He hands Gilda the microphone. She takes it in a jewelled hand and coughs loudly.

Philip, in the meantime, gets out his harmonica.

"No," whispers Jane, shaking her head. "No, no. Please no."

Patrick is enjoying himself hugely.

"Is this the sex-mad couple? I have to say, they certainly look as if they have talent. This is totally fucking brilliant."

Foot tapping, Philip Burrell starts to play.

"What good is me-lo-dy," starts Gilda, a mite huskily. "What good is mu-sic… if it ain't po-ses-sin' something sweet?"

Philip attacks the harmonica with gusto. Amazingly, he manages to hit the correct notes.

"It don't mean a thing if it ain't got that swing," croons Gilda, swaying in her beaded carapace.

"Doo wha doowha, doowah, doowha… "

The audience starts laughing, then clapping.

"That's more like it," shouts one of the men with the dogs, who, it turns out, is Jas' uncle. Jas smiles, relaxes, gives a thumbs-up to Belle.

"Fucking hell!" says Larry to Tracey. "They're not bad."

The presence of Philip and Gilda, who lack allegiances both with the residents of the Square and the outsiders from the estate, seems to provide something which everyone can enjoy.

Gilda comes to her final, triumphant 'Doowah'. Philip gives a trill on the harmonica. Everyone applauds, loudly.

Gilda bows deeply from the waist, throwing her head forward. Her crown bounces off her head, but Jas is there, gallantly picking it up and giving it to her once she regains her vertical position, somewhat dizzily.

She takes Philip's arm, waves to her audience, walks regally with her lover back down the path and out of the park.

"Thank you, er, Gilda and Philip," says Alan Makin faintly.

There is a commotion on the podium. What next, thinks Jane.

She doesn't know if she can take many more surprises.

It's Larry, setting up the projector. Oh, God. George. She has forgotten about her own son's performance. He is there, walking solemnly beside Roberta through the park, spectral in his Storm Trooper uniform.

"And now," says Alan Makin.

"In the spirit of George Lucas, I bring you the Square's very own George."

How could she have forgotten about him, thinks Jane. Thank God for Roberta. George marches up the aisle between the chairs in his outfit. He bears his gun aloft. He has his helmet jammed down over his head.

Jane's friends clap softly.

"I fear the worst," says Jane.

"Nah," says Patrick. "He'll be fine."

As soon as he reaches the dais and clambers awkwardly on it, he turns around.

"May the force be with you," a muffled voice comes out from under the helmet. The residents of the Square clap in a patronising manner.

However, Kylie's father and friends go mad with enthusiastic cheering.

"Oh what the fuck!" shouts Jacky.

"Whoop whoop!" shouts the person who had shouted the same thing earlier.

George removes his helmet, which has the effect of making his hair rise above his head in a crested tuft. He sits down at the keyboard.

He looks over at Larry. Larry raises his hand in a salute, and starts the projector.

By now, it is dark enough for the images to show up clearly on the sheet.

He starts to play.

Behind the sheet, Anya and Roberta are hugging each other and clenching their fists, willing for him to get through the piece without a major disaster.

As soon as he begins the familiar tune, everyone cheers loudly.

Darth Vader, in Lego, is there, flying above George's solar system curtains and wielding his lightsabre. The Death Star appears, and rather oddly, vanishes. A small Lego milk float appears for a brief moment, replaced by a hand bearing the Millennium Falcon which does a few circuits of the curtain/ galactic backdrop. Everyone cheers even more, then whistles and boos as General Grievous' own personal ship appears above it.

Larry turns to Tracey.

"This is clearly full of meaning for the child. Meanwhile I have not got the faintest idea what is going on."

Tracey puts a hand fondly on his knee. "Just enjoy it," she says.

The music comes to a short, assertive climax.

"My idea," whispers Roberta to Anya. "Short and sweet."

Darth Vader swoops once more across the screen, followed by a train of other figurines from the movie. Chewbacca, Han Solo, Princess Leia and after a pause, Yoda.

George triumphantly finishes the piece. His small hands play the final chord.

He stands, puts his helmet back on, regrasps his gun, and bows low.

The audience are all on their feet, cheering loudly.

"Fucking masterstroke," says Patrick, running to the front. He leaps onto the dais, embraces George, who stands stiffly to attention.

"Well done old sport," he whispers in his ear.

"Dad! You are so embarrassing!"

"Well done lad," says Patrick, taking no notice of his son's attempt to push him away. "Erasing the class war with *Star Wars*. Bloody brilliant."

George acknowledges this mysterious motto with a nod, jumps off the dais, walks down through the cheering audience. Roberta skips round the sheet, grabs the music from the keyboard and follows him away and out of the park.

"Encore! Encore!" shouts the crowd to George's retreating back.

Patrick finds himself still upon the dais with Alan Makin.

"Back off," whispers Alan. "I need to wrap this up."

Humbled, Patrick walks around the sheet where he finds Anya, laughing.

"Your son is marvellous," she tells him.

Emboldened by this, he enfolds her in his arms and kisses her, properly this time.

"And now," says Alan Makin. "That is the end of our fundraising Talent Show. Thank you, all of you, for coming. I really mean it. I will be here for a short while," he says, nodding to his fan base, "to sign autographs. I have also brought copies of my latest book, so if any of you are keen…

it's quite a good read, I think."

Behind the sheet, Patrick and Anya are clenched together. He decides to venture towards unclipping her bra.

"That man Alan Makin has no shame," pouts Jane to Harriet.

"Where is Patrick?" she says, to nobody in particular.

Patrick's whereabouts are soon made very public. As Alan steps off the dais to sell books to his fan base, Larry, mindful of the fact he must not forget to take back the bedsheet, leaps onto it.

Without any warning, he unties the rope holding the sheet in place. The sheet falls to the ground, revealing to the entire audience the sight of Patrick wildly kissing Anya. The only noise in the Square is a few seconds later, when people start wildly reaching, scrabbling for their phones in order to capture the moment.

"Not only that," as Belle, still gasping with excitement, later tells Roberta, "but he had his hand right up her shirt!"

Chapter Twenty-Nine
Tracey

In the Square, banks of irises are nodding gracefully, their violet sheen offsetting the sward of emerald grass behind them. A flamingo willow provides splashes of creamy ivory. Scarlet roses stud the earthy beds. The park keeper bends down, picks up the last remaining empty crisp packet, surveys the flattened grass, straightens his shoulders.

The chairs were all taken away early that morning by a van from Rayners. The small podium had also been removed. In short, there is nothing left standing of the Talent Show in the Square.

In Jane's room, the curtains are still closed. Jane is still in bed.

"And I may remain here all day," she shouts towards the door, a half sob catching in her throat.

"Would you like a cup of tea?" asks Patrick gently.

"Fuck you."

After a while, Patrick calls George down for breakfast. They begin to eat Weetabix together. A spirit of male cameraderie is palpable in the room. This has been largely brought on by Jane's refusal to talk to anyone since last night. Having run back to the house in a fit of hysterical sobbing, she is now disdainfully ignoring all living creatures in it.

The impact of the end of the Talent Show on the Square has been significant. In response, a respectful community silence has been draped over Jane and Patrick's house. Nobody has dared to call, ring or email. This has been a group, yet somewhat unconscious, decision. The other way of looking at it is that nobody dares.

"Alright, old sport?" says Patrick, to George. "Any, er, plans?"

The boy nods brightly.

"Yes. I am going to take apart General Grievous' ship today and rebuild it."

"Ah," says Patrick knowledgeably. "General Grievous. Good name. Is he a Jedi?"

"No," says George.

"Isn't he linked to… Yoda?" offers Patrick, hoping to impress the child with another name from the film.

"No," says George happily. "But Yoda IS a Jedi, at least."

"Oh. Well, it's Sunday, isn't it? Nice to have a day full of nothing. Do you have any prep, sport?"

"No," says George.

Patrick, at a loss for other avenues into George's diary, gives up the attempt at conversation, and resorts to the *Daily Mail*. He whistles a little. He feels the brooding presence of his wife dripping through the house like malicious oil.

Over at Larry and Tracey's house, there is a similar hush, although Larry persists on breaking it. Essentially he is far too amused to stop talking about it all.

"It was just that the timing was so perfect," he says again, to break a conversational lull. "Couldn't have been better if it was on stage. Which, in a way, it was. Masterful."

"Dad," says Belle wearily. "We know you think the timing was perfect. You keep telling us that it was. It may have been perfect for YOU. It was not perfect for most of the other people concerned, frankly."

"Just the way that they didn't actually realise the curtain had fallen down, for a good few crucial seconds," he chortles.

"That was the killer. Good old Patrick. Tongue right down her throat! Hand up her wotsit."

"Dad!" says Belle, desperately. "Will you kindly shut UP. The way you go on about it, it's weird."

"Shut up everyone," hisses Grace. "Here comes Anya."

"Morning," says Anya, coming into the kitchen.

"Morning," the girls chime in unison.

"Good morning Anya," says Larry, beaming as if his face is about to be bisected.

"How are we feeling today?"

"Fine," says Anya neutrally.

"Did we enjoy the event last night?"

"Yes, it was good," says Anya. She is not going to rise to this.

After she and Patrick had been so dramatically revealed by the dropping curtain, she had turned, picked up her bag, unplugged the keyboard and shouldered it. Then she had left the dais, carrying the keyboard. It was such a long piece of equipment that nobody could see her face or, more importantly, catch her eye.

She had simply walked back to Tracey and Larry's house, carrying the equipment. Then she had not come out of the house again.

The phone rings.

"Who can that be?" says Belle. "Nobody ever uses the landline. Hope Grannie is okay."

"It's probably some electricity salesman," observes Larry, barrelling over. He picks up the reciever.

"Hello," says a commanding voice. "Have you fired her yet?"

"Ah, good morning Jane," says Larry, signalling furiously for the girls and Anya to leave the kitchen, or at least, stop talking. Anya melts away.

Grace and Belle turn into one giant ear.

"What was that?" asks Larry, although he has heard her perfectly.

"I asked if you have you fired her yet. Have you fired her… your… au pair?"

She cannot name her. She spits the offensive word out.

"Jane, Jane," says Larry in what he hopes is a placatory tone.

"Don't Jane Jane me," retorts his neighbour icily. "Have you fired her yet?"

Larry takes a deep breath. "No. And I don't intend to."

There is a dreadful silence on the other end of the line.

"It's a free world and she is a grown woman. I'll take a look if you like, but I don't recall anything in her contract which says she must not kiss her neighbour… deeply," he adds, mischeviously.

There is more silence on the line.

"Well thank you very much," says Jane, eventually. "I am so grateful for your neighbourly support. How on earth do you think I can carry on in the Square, holding my head up when everyone has seen your… bloody au pair, of all people, snogging my husband? Have you thought about that?"

"I'm sure everyone has forgotten it already," lies Larry. "Give it a week, Jane. Jane? Damn."

He replaces the reciever in its cradle and wanders to the kitchen door.

"Tracey, do come down here," he shouts.

"You should know that Jane has just called. She probably wanted you, but she got me instead. Then she slammed the phone down on me. She is in a frightful bait."

He turns back into the kitchen, smiles at his daughters.

"This is the most excitement I can remember having since we won you know what. Marvellous stuff."

Tracey appears in the doorway, humming happily.

"What? Do you know, I've just been counting the money we took last night, Larry. Lucky I was still at the door when all the… fracas happened, otherwise who knows what would happen to the cash box. Jane just abandoned it, you know. Rushed off! Anyway, we've made nearly a grand, that's good isn't it?"

"It's marvellous," says Larry, pulling his wife close to him and embracing her.

"You are a clever bird. And well done for snaring old Makin. Those chavs just loved him, didn't they? And he loved them. Must have sold about twenty bloody books, the opportunist."

"Don't call them chavs."

"They are chavs."

"They are not. One of them is an old swimming friend of Belle's. You know, Jas. Introduced her to Philip and that mad old Gilda. But you're right. Alan was perfect."

"Celebrity. Bring a famous person on, everyone is happy. The ideal social glue."

"If you say so."

"I do say so. Apart from all the… stuff with Anya, last night looked like it might be heading for a very nasty face-off between Béla Bartók and a Staffordshire Bull Terrier. Very nasty indeed."

Tracey wags a finger in his face.

"Don't forget Gilda. It don't mean a thing if it ain't got that swing."

"How could I? Bonkers. But apart from Patrick and our lovely au pair, tongues at dawn, it was the combined forces of Alan Makin and *Star Wars* which did it for me."

Tracey giggles, remembering George's Storm Trooper outfit.

"I love that child."

"George?" says Larry, pouring more coffee from the Bodum Cafetiere. "He is a true original."

He drinks his coffee, musing on George's household.

"Poor old Patrick, though. He's probably had such a thorough bollocking he won't be able to sit down for weeks."

He shakes his head, smiling.

"Don't be so gleeful," says Tracey. "It wasn't a very edifying sight, frankly. Was it? I for one was just relieved that George had been taken away by Roberta."

"Was he?"

Tracey nods. "Yes, she had whisked him off. I think he was about to faint from lack of air in that *Star Wars* suit."

Larry laughs. "The whole evening was entirely surreal. A night of 'talent', headed by a B-lister from daytime television, nearly sabotaged by locals, with an injection of madness from a former Communist in an evening dress, saved by a child in a *Star Wars* outfit, only to climax with a bit of extra marital carnal activity in front of everyone. In our front garden. As it were. Extraordinary." He pauses, considering everything. "Jane will come round."

"Yes. I suppose so. But the joke is that Jane is hardly a saint herself."

"What?"

"Oh, come on Larry. You must know."

"What?"

She puts a hand fondly on his hairy forearm.

"Jane has been screwing Jay for bloody years."

Larry chokes on his coffee.

"Bloody hell Trace," he splutters.

Tracey gets up, goes over to the sink.

She looks out at the Square, considers its controlled beauty, its uniform regime of proportion and line. Does its severe architecture keep everyone in line, or is it simply all for show? She thinks that it is probably the latter.

"If all these front facades of the houses around here fell off, you know, as if they were suddenly blown off by a hurricane, or removed by a giant hand, you'd find that how people SEEM to live is completely different from how they ACTUALLY live."

Larry smiles.

"Trust a true makeup artist to observe that. How long has this been going on?"

"What, Jay and Jane? Oh, I don't know. I only found out about nine months ago."

"How?"

"Jane told me. I think in a weak moment. I was at the Royal College of Music with Belle before her Grade exam. And Jane was there with George for the same reason. They had gone off to the warm-up room and we, we were having one of those conversations married women sometimes have, you know, about sex. She obviously wanted to tell someone about it. Either because she wanted to confess to someone, or because she wanted to show off to someone. Or a bit of both."

They had been sitting in a sepulchral waiting room, adorned with plastic chairs and old copies of *Gramophone*. Belle was taking Grade Four, George Grade One. As they both learned with Roberta, their exams were in successive order. Roberta had taken them both to the warm-up rooms, to practise scales and arpeggios, and run through their pieces one last time, leaving Jane and Tracey to sit. Being a basement, there was no phone signal. So the two women were forced to chat to one another.

"So, how's things?" Tracey had asked Jane. Before she knew it, Jane had launched into a carelessly desperate confession about how things were with Patrick.

"And we just never do it, you see," Tracey remembers Jane saying. "So I started doing it with someone else. Almost had to."

Tracey remembers wanting to ask, and not wanting to know at the same moment.

Yet Jane, never acute about the nuances of adult curiosity, continued, carelessly.

"So I occasionally… get it together with, guess who?"

Tracey didn't want to guess. She really didn't. She had an ache in her stomach when she thought of Jane, lonely in her sexless marital bed.

"Oh, don't worry, Jane," she had told her, looking desirously at the door.

"No, guess," insisted her neighbour. "You know him quite well. Lives in the Square, actually."

Tracey looks helplessly at Jane. "I have no idea."

"Fat wife."

After a pause, Tracey hazards a guess.

"Not Jay?"

Tracey remembers Jane laughing slightly, and wiggling her feet as if amid a schoolgirl crush, and then nodding her head slowly with the satisfaction of a conquering queen. The ache in Tracey's stomach deepened.

"Yup. When we got together, I think he needed it almost as much as I did! Anyway, what we have is lovely. Really is. It's all about the sex. That's it. It's not as if I want a substitute for Patrick, nothing like that. Why would I want that? Oh, God, Tracey, I am sorry. For telling this to you. Please keep it to yourself. You will, won't you?"

Tracey agreed, and she had kept her word. She hadn't told anyone. For a few months after this, Jane would give her a knowing smile, or even a conspiratorial wink when Jay was in the room, but Tracey had steadily refused to acknowledge them. After a while, the nodding and winking stopped.

Tracey was so consistently discreet about the episode that Jane had begun to wonder whether she had actually invented the whole scenario thanks to nerves over George's exam. By the time she had the dinner party at which all were present, Jane had convinced herself that she had dreamt the confession.

She hadn't, of course. Tracey knew. At Jane and Patrick's dinner party, she had noted the moment when both had left the dining table. She had observed Jay's adrenalin-mottled cheeks. She had noted Jane's arch-coquettishness, when the pair returned from upstairs, ten minutes later. She remembers feeling almost jealous of Jane, the hostess. With sex, on tap.

Tracey remembers all this. She looks at Larry, smiles at him fondly. At least their bed is not a barren desert. And the thing with Alan... well, that can be finished now. In her head, she has parcelled it up with the television documentary. After the screening next week, she would have no need to see Alan

Makin ever again. Ever. It was a neat, civilised ending. Not messy. Tracey hated mess.

"So."

"Got to forgive Patrick everything then, don't we?" he snorts. "I'm certainly not going to fire Anya NOW. Not that I was ever tempted, but you know."

Again, she strokes his forearm. It is warm and familiar.

"I think we all just carry on, don't we? Try to forget about it."

"Don't you want to ask them both over for the screening party, anyway? When is that, actually?"

She is startled to have the screening mentioned by her husband. With a low visceral thrill, Tracey rethinks her resolution. She recalls how it feels to be screwed on Alan Makin's sofa. Maybe, she worries, she is just like Jane. Maybe she too needed that spice. And now Alan will be here, at their house, for the screening.

She has no worries about how he will be. She knows he will be discreet. It's how she will be that concerns her.

Larry is still laughing about the party.

"Who shall we invite, both of the dissembling couples? Anya and Patrick? Jay and Jane? Or some other combination? Hey, why don't we turn it into a Seventies wife-swapping night, since that is what our neighbourhood is beginning to resemble."

"Larry, stop it. Jane is clearly devastated."

That's what she likes about Larry, though, thinks Tracey.

Never takes anything too seriously. If nobody died, it's okay. That is her husband's motto.

She doesn't really know what goes on inside his head, even after years of marriage. He doesn't care to show her. "I can't stand people who 'let it all hang out'," she remembers him telling her when they were first married. Larry has surfed through life on jokes and backslaps, so far. It has been a strategy which has served him well. After all, he won the Lottery, didn't he? He sees no reason to stop it now.

All of which is good, thinks Tracey. She won't tell him about Alan. She won't tell anyone about Alan. She doesn't need a modern day confessional to a best friend. She envisages the remonstrations going on at Jane's house and puts the excitement of being undressed by Alan to the back of her mind. She vows that a similar event will never threaten her family life, on this side of the Square. She thinks she will arrange a neat ending.

Chapter Thirty
Jane

"I mean, if you look at it logically darling, you haven't got a leg to stand on," points out Jay. "Turn over." She obliges, kneeling. He parts her ass and starts fucking her from behind.

Oh God, I am lost, thinks Jane.

"Yes but I deserve being screwed by you, you see. Whereas Patrick… " She abandons her sentence, gives out a little sob. Her face is buried in the pillow. It is impossible to discuss the semantics of her husband snogging the au pair while her lover is entering her. Jay knows this.

Afterwards, he picks up the subject again playfully.

"… So you see, what is your objection? That it was done at all, or that it was done publicly?"

She turns over, smiles at him ruefully. She's irritated by her better mood. The sex has made her much more cheerful.

"I suppose if Patrick snogged the au pair and I never knew about it, then it doesn't really matter. Look at us. Nobody knows, so no harm done. No, it was the public thing of it. So bloody embarrassing. Oh my God. What an evening. I still keep having flashbacks, like it was an experience in the Gulf War. Maybe I am suffering from Post Traumatic Stress Disease."

"Stress Disorder."

"Whatever. Did you enjoy ANY of it?"

"Are you kidding?" says Jay, standing up and stretching. "I enjoyed ALL of it. It was hilarious. From start to finish. Brilliantly planned throughout. By you. I mean, you won't like knowing this but I felt bad for Harriet. However, she says she hardly noticed the invasion of the Sans-Culottes."

"Jay, please!"

"Well, it was an Off With Their Heads moment, wasn't it? Like something out of *Blackadder*."

"Hmm. I don't want to remember that bit. I don't want to remember any of it."

"Darling. It was a success. Did you raise a lot of money, though?"

"Yeah."

"Do you care about that?"

"What, getting new fences for the park? Nope."

"Do you think Tracey is screwing Alan Makin?"

Jane laughs at this.

"Oh for God's sake Jay. Of course she's not. She's much too prim for that. I mean, she wears tarty things, occasionally, but I think she's very buttoned up."

"You are the only real sexual adventurer on the Square, aren't you? Or at least, you hope you are."

It was true. She likes to think of herself as such. The only brave one. The one to go out and get what she deserved. The one in the vanguard, forging ahead. No, Tracey would never have the guts to shag Alan Makin. She hopes she won't, anyway. Jane wants to be the only naughty one in the Square.

She remembers, or thinks she remembers, that she had told Tracey about her affair, but it was so long ago. She's probably forgotten about it, thinks Jane. Especially now. How could Tracey believe that she, Jane, was capable of infidelity when everyone saw how upset she had been about the bloody au pair? Every time she thinks about that event she feels panic, rising in her body, choking her. A wave of rivalry consumes her with hot fire.

"Well, I hope he's feeling really shitty about things," says Jane.

"Who, Alan Makin?"

"No, of course not, you berk. My fucking husband. Oh Jay. Will you do something for me, now?"

"The usual?" says Jay, smiling. "My pleasure." He passes his tongue across his lips, and kneels down.

As it happens, Patrick is not feeling particularly bad about Jane, or his behaviour, or whether the Talent Show was or was not a disaster. All he cares about is what is going to happen between him and Anya in the next twenty minutes.

Anya has dared to come round to Patrick's house. In order to collect her music, which she had left in the seat of the Blüthner's music stool. She'd never play the grand again, of course. And she has taken precautions beforehand. With her phone. *Patrick, is Jane in?* she had texted him. *So sorry, but I need to collect my music.*

Coast clear. Führer out. Boy out. Come over, if you dare. Be my guest.

She gets the message, taps the phone on her hand, thinking.

"Tracey, I am just popping out for an hour or so, thank you, is that alright?" she shouts up the stairs.

Why does he use Hitler's nickname for his wife, thinks Anya as she walks around the Square. English people still think Hitler is a living presence, she ponders. And while not a benign one, certainly one you can make regular jokes about.

She had been watching repeats of *Dad's Army*. She was amazed by it. At home in Lodz, the war, which had essentially flattened most of the old city centre, had been so thoroughly traumatic that, even now, having a TV comedy show about it, and repeating it unchanged for several decades, would be unthinkable. A bit like having a slapstick show in Auschwitz. She shudders and rings the door bell.

"Ah, Anya!" says Patrick, surprised, as if they had not just had an exchange of messages indicating he would be seeing her in about two minutes hence.

She raises an eyebrow and steps over the threshold. The door closes behind her. There is an exciting tension about the moment. She has no time to do anything other than fleetingly note it, because immediately the latch snaps shut, and Patrick is kissing her wildly in the hall.

God, these English men, thinks Anya. Have they no sense of place, time, formality?

"Come to collect your music, have you? Think I believe that?"

He rubs his hands up and down her dress, pawing at her. She breaks away, gasping for air.

"Patrick, are you sure? I mean, this is your house."

"Quite sure," he says diving at her neck, running his hand through her hair.

He will take her, that is no question. But where will he take her? She wonders about this as he grabs her bra strap. In her experience, British men are very happy to bring a lover home, but they have a horror of defiling the marital bedroom with the au pair. In this, Patrick is nothing if not typical.

"Kitchen," he murmurs, propelling her towards the stairs.

And so, in full view of the offensive jar of instant coffee, Patrick screws Anya on the kitchen table. He does so with a sort of exerted desperation, wiping beads of sweat away from his face from time to time. He just about manages to get his trousers off but his socks are still on.

Afterwards, rearranging her skirt, she looks at him fondly.

"You can think about this at breakfast tomorrow. When you are sitting at this table eating your bacon and eggs."

"Oh, Christ!" says Patrick, smiling sheepishly. "Christ, Anya. That was wild."

He sits down on a chair. She swings her legs off the table, jumps down, pulling up her underwear.

"Come and sit on my knee."

She obliges, looking around the room as if she has never seen it before, never spent a dreary evening doing the washing up while the English laugh and chatter over a ludicrously

255

detailed meal.

It's much better this way, she thinks. Seeing it as a woman, not a drudge. But then it always is. Anya has quite an experienced line in sleeping with, if not her actual employer, then her employer's friends.

"Where is George?"

"Gardening with Roberta."

"How funny."

"I know… she asked him to help her on her allotment. Know what an allotment is?"

"Of course. Everyone has one at home in Lodz. Where is… Jane?"

"Out. Look, Anya… "

This was the other thing that Englishmen did. Got in a terrible twist about explaining why they couldn't marry the au pair. They'd love to, of course, dying to see her again, but you know. School fees. Mortgage. Life.

"I know. It's fine. I know. I'm going to be gone soon anyway."

"Are you?" he says, feigning disappointment.

"Don't pretend to be sad. I'm going back to Poland in a fortnight."

"Will you ever come back?"

"Maybe. Depends on my academic course."

"I'll miss you."

She laughs at this, jumps off his knee, kisses his forehead affectionately.

"No you won't. But it was nice, yes? And I have so loved playing on the grand piano. You are a good person, Patrick. I'll go and collect my music. I'll text you in a few days. Maybe come and play the lovely piano one last time."

"Do, do," says Patrick uncertainly. "When… the Führer is out."

She looks at him and laughs.

"Jolly good," says Patrick, to her departing back. "You are a lovely girl, Anya, do you know that? Skills and beauty.

What a combination."

Totally wasted on the Square, he says to himself, as he washes his hands at the kitchen sink.

Back at the Travelodge, Jane has managed to get the window open, and is now leaning dramatically out of it. The sex has made her feel good, but she still feels hot, inside, when she thinks about her husband being turned on by another woman.

"You know what I really feel like having is a bloody fag. Or taking drugs."

"Oh, come on Jane. Do buck up," says Jay, bustling around, snapping his jeans against his bare legs, and then putting them on.

"No need to start wanting to poison yourself just because your husband snogged the au pair. All husbands snog the au pair at one point in their married life."

There is a pause.

"Really? How very depressing that information is. Sort of like realising modern British life is indeed modelled on a Carry On film. Did you?" says Jane.

"What? Snog the au pair? No. Harriet insisted on having male au pairs for Brian. Said he needed a role model. Why I could not perform that role is a mystery to me. Anyway, on the subject of Brian."

Jay takes a deep breath. He has been a coward about telling her, and has been dreading doing this for weeks.

"Oh, yes?" says Jane, warily.

"I need to tell you that we're going off for a few days. Week or so."

"Who is We?"

"I just said. Me and Brian."

There is another pause.

"Off? What do you mean, off?"

"Away. Abroad."

"Oh."

This is something Jay has been planning for a while. He

has been putting off telling her, because he does not want to explain his motives. He wants to go away with his son. He wants to go on a cycling holiday with Brian, and now that the boy had finished his exams, there is no real reason why not to. Harriet was content to stay at home, and the summer stretched ahead.

"Darling, I don't see you on a bicycle for eight hours a day, with a backpack too," he had told his wife, who has more expensive tastes.

He had found a little company on the net who organised trips around France. You stayed in perfect little hotels on the A roads, dinner and bed and breakfast was all laid on, and you simply cycled from one hotel to the next. He couldn't wait to do it. He had got all the Michelin maps, showed them to Brian.

They had spent a few happy evenings, planning the route with all the maps opened up and laid out on the kitchen table. Oh, of course, he could have done it online, with a mileometer, but on the kitchen table with the jaunty red-backed maps, and a ruler so you got the distances, that was so much more fun.

"They throw the bikes in, even lay on a rescue service if you get a puncture," Jay enthuses to Jane.

Her stomach turns over.

"So you're leaving me here. Fuck's sake."

"Well, darling, it's only for three weeks. Twenty days, actually. Eighteen if you don't count the ferry days."

"Sounds like three weeks to me."

"Well, I needed to take old B away somewhere. He's been a trooper with the exams. And very good with his mother."

This was the wrong thing to say.

"Funnily enough, I don't care how bloody good Brian is with his mother. I dislike his mother. I hate her."

"Jane, please."

She is crying now, a single tear runs down her face. She throws herself down on the bed dramatically.

"And now everything is awful. Everyone will be laughing

at me because of that fucking au pair, and the Talent Show was a write off, and now you are buggering off to France on a bike."

"Cheer up."

"Why? What for? What the fuck do I have to cheer up about?"

"The au pair is going back to Poland." Oh, but his timing was good. Perfect actually. Fucking perfect.

She sits up, brushes the hair away from her damp eyes.

"What?"

"Tracey told me. I forgot to mention it."

"Forgot?"

"Well, sorry. I was too busy fucking you my darling, and caressing your beautiful body."

He pushes her back on the bed, removes her robe, embraces her. Her warm body relaxes against his. Gratifyingly, she feels he is getting an erection. He is proud of his stamina. He pretends to scratch his shoulder and sneaks a glance at his watch.

They probably have time to do it again.

"When?"

"When what? Oh, when is she leaving? I think next week some time. In a fortnight everyone will have forgotten about her, apart from you. Now just lie back while I give you something special. Again."

"Again," murmurs Jane, stretching her arms above her back, diving into the ecstasy.

Chapter Thirty-One
Roberta

He is breathing deeply and digging, his small hand grasping the trowel's wooden handle, pushing the instrument deep into the dark soil. He squats, perfectly balanced. His two feet, strapped into his new leather sandals, are flat on the ground. His knees are bent, his buttocks only about two inches off the ground. He leans forward and pulls something delicate up and out of the soil.

Then he stands up, by the simple method of merely straightening his legs. The delicate, rose-pink thing twists from his chubby fingers, spinning, reaching blindly upwards.

"Look, Roberta. A worm!"

"Yes. Very good." She walks over the soil to him.

"They are crucial to aerate the earth. And of course, they feed the birds. Drop him back. Then come and help me stake these beans."

"Him. How do you know it's a male worm?"

She laughs. "I don't, George. Actually I think worms are hermaphrodite."

"What does that mean?"

"It means they are both male and female at the same time."

He pauses, thinking about this.

"That would be good. If adult humans were both male and

female at the same time."

"Really? I think it might be a bit confusing, myself."

"I think it would make for many less arguments."

Roberta considers this last statement.

She is not really very sure just how much George knew, or saw, or understood about the Talent Show 'hiccup' in its closing moments. She didn't know if he saw his father kissing Anya. She didn't even know if he really understood what he had witnessed between his mother and that neighbour which he had translated into his little Lego play.

She suspected he grasped more than he was willing to confess, but felt the task of questioning him would be not only impossible but also undesirable.

Anyway, she wanted him to see her, Roberta, as a sort of respite against the cloying tensions of his house and the Square. Talking to her is as if he is talking to someone outside his world. Just digging in the allotment would provide some form of relief, she felt.

In this, as in most things concerning her pupils, Roberta is correct. George is fascinated by this new project, gardening.

"All these things. All this string, and this cutting and digging. When will we see the plants?"

"In about four months," says Roberta.

"What, after my birthday?"

"Yes, if your birthday is in less than four months' time."

There is a pause.

"Takes quite a long time, doesn't it?"

"It's a bit like the piano, George. You have to do all the preparation before you can play a really intricate piece. You have to do all those exercises you don't like very much."

"So digging things up is like Hanon?"

"Sort of."

They continue to work, chatting once every so often, then stopping and concentrating on the job in hand.

Eventually George sits back on his haunches again.

"Roberta?"

"Yes?"

"Do you think I could go home now?"

She stands up, discounts the slight twinge of irritation at being interrupted in the flow of her gardening. Then she brushes down her trousers.

"Of course. Come on. Let's have a glass of water and then I'll take you home."

George sits perkily on the back seat of the car.

"Next week I am going to my Cub Camp. We're all camping," he continues, "at the Scout HQ."

"Oh, really?" says Roberta politely.

"It's brilliant. There is a zip wire. And we will be cooking outside. I'm going to be sharing my tent with Finn."

George looks happily outside the car, envisaging the delights of Cub Camp to come.

Roberta drives on, thinking how very pleasant it must be to have a life as organised and structured as George's.

Presently, she is aware George is still talking. She tunes back into the conversation.

"And then I gave Finn back his Storm Trooper outfit, because Daddy says he'll buy me a Darth Vader one anyway."

"Oh, good," says his piano teacher, absently.

"It has that really nasty breathing when you tap a special button on the front."

"Does it? That's nice."

"I think Daddy wanted me to have it because I won. I did win, didn't I? At the Talent Show."

"You certainly did."

"It's a pity you can't play *Star Wars* for Grade Two."

"I think you can play other pieces by that composer, actually. But no, not *Star Wars*."

"I wish I lived on the Death Star."

"No you don't."

"Yes I do. Living in the Square is so boring. I want to move. Finn says that his mother says people on the Square are lucky. Finn says that everyone on the Square is rich. He says if I live there, it means I am rich. But we're not rich, are we Roberta?"

"Well, I suppose you are well-off."

"What does that mean, well-off?"

"Well, it means your parents don't have to worry about money, too much."

"Ha ha! My dear, they are worried all the time. Mummy is always saying how worried she is."

She pulls up outside the boy's house. It presents her with its usual bland facade of perfect proportion and muted tone, in step with all its neighbours. Some flattened earth in front of the front window, caused by the vicar's moving men in their attempt to get the Blüthner out, is all that indicates an event took place in the not too distant past.

Roberta rings the bell. The door opens. It's Patrick.

"Ah, Roberta," he says cheerfully.

"Thank you so much for having George. George!" turning to the child. "How was the allotment? How did the weeding go, old sport? Ready to do some for us now?"

"Very good," announces George. "I found a bisexual worm."

Patrick looks quizzically at Roberta.

"Don't worry," says Roberta. "He was very helpful."

"George, have you thanked Roberta?" says Patrick.

George is almost half way up the stairs.

"Thank you my dear," he calls imperiously. "I am now going to build my General Grievous ship."

"Roberta, thank you so much for getting George up to scratch for yesterday," says Patrick evenly. "He was great, wasn't he?"

"Yes, he was," says Roberta, equally neutrally. "I'll be back on Thursday for his lesson. We'll get back to his normal pieces."

Everyone will get back to normality, thinks Patrick as he closes the door behind her. He's rather sad about this, if he must be honest.

Screwing Anya on the kitchen table. What a thrill that was. Although, up against the sheer hassle of being discovered by Jane, he's not sure if it is worth repeating. Anything for a quiet life, he thinks. Is that dreadfully middle-aged, or just caring? He considers this as he steps down into the kitchen in his socks for a can of non-Diet Coke.

Chapter Thirty-Two
The Screening

It is there. The programme details. Printed in the *Radio Times*. 8pm, BBC1. *Money worries? Makin makes them history. Follow financial guru Alan Makin as he bowls his financial grey matter into the world of the squeezed middle, and solves former Lottery winner and makeup artist Tracey's overdraft in one deft stroke.*

Tracey reads the citation twice as she walks upstairs.

"Belle, have you seen this?" she says to her daughter, waving the magazine urgently at her.

Belle pulls back the towelling sleeves of her robe, grasps the *Radio Times* with what Tracey considers a signal lack of excitement.

"Oh. Yeah." She gives it back to her mother.

"Is that all? Belle, I am on television tonight."

"Yes, Mum. I know. No-one cares."

"That is a horrible thing to say."

"Sorry, I didn't mean it rudely."

"Well, how is that not a rude thing to say?"

"No, I just meant that television is a big deal for you and Dad. Obviously. It's not really that huge for... anyone of my generation. Not many people watch television any more."

"Well I am sorry, but who of your 'generation'," says

265

Tracey, giving Belle's word quotation marks in the air, "has appeared on BBC1 of late?"

"That's it. No-one. But no-one is too bothered about TV. They all want to have their own channels on YouTube," says Belle.

She sees the effect this has on her mother's face.

"Look, Mum, I'm sorry, that was the wrong thing to say. It's great you are on TV. I'll obviously be watching. Is anyone coming over to watch it with you and Dad?"

"Well, of course they are," says Tracey, exasperated. "We are having a screening party."

Belle is aware that some form of gesture needs to be made, in atonement.

"Can I help?"

Her mother provides her with the answer Belle had hoped for.

"No, I think Harriet is doing everything."

Yeah, I'm doing everything, thinks Harriet crossly in her kitchen as she butters a large baking dish and slings a spoonful of mince over the greased porcelain. Lasagna. Lasagna for twenty, which, in her book, is mass catering. Not knocking up a simple supper.

Still, she had said she would do this for Tracey. She slides another spoonful over the base.

"As I introduced you to Alan Makin in the first place, it's the least I can do," she had said. Yes, it would have been nice if Alan had landed on her, Harriet had thought. But that thought was followed swiftly by the knowledge that she'd have only worried about what to wear all the time, and about looking fat on television, so it was probably just as well. She had played the violin in front of Alan, hadn't she? So she had showed off her skills too, in a way. Pity the Talent Show hadn't been on television, but never mind. That was probably just as well, too. Given all that went on.

She sniggers at the thought of it.

"Hello darling, what are you laughing about?" says Jay,

coming into the kitchen after his shower.

"I was laughing at the thought of what would have happened if our Talent Show had been on television," says Harriet.

"God help us," says Jay with feeling.

He thinks about Jane.

"Well, I would have come out quite well, wouldn't I?" asks his wife.

"What? Oh, yes, of course you would. You would have been marvellous. Now, I must go and get dressed."

He turns, walks away from her in his towel.

"Jay?"

"What?"

"What are those long scratches down your back? You look as if you've fallen into a bramble bush, or had a fight with a cat."

"What? Oh. Oh, I just got a bit energetic with the, the loofah."

"The what?"

"You know, the sponge."

"Do we have such a thing in the house?"

Jay doesn't wait for any more. He disappears upstairs.

An hour later, the lasagna is ready. Harriet takes it from the oven, covers it with tin foil, and protecting her hands with two tea towels, carries it carefully over to Tracey and Larry's house.

"Oh phew. God, this thing is heavy," she says, as Tracey opens the front door.

"You are a marvel," says Tracey. Tracey looks no less marvellous herself. Her hair is piled onto her head in a volume of curls. Her makeup is so artfully blended that it seems as if she has nothing on her face but bare beauty. Her manicured hands are perfect. Her stockings shimmer. Her silk dress clings to her.

"That's a nice dress," says Harriet, feeling hot and sweaty from the lasagna.

"What, this? Do you know where it came from?"

"No," says Harriet, not wanting to know.

Tracey leans into her friend.

"Prada. Alan bought it for me," she whispers.

"God, Tracey," says Harriet.

"He insisted. Said I deserved it. It arrived yesterday in a box."

It is a beautiful dress. Harriet watches Tracey walk into the kitchen to sort out the drinks. The navy fabric swings around her body. It is made of heavy, printed silk. High at the front. Low at the back. Half length sleeves. This will just be the first triumph for her, thinks Harriet sourly. This show will be a springboard for Tracey to be on more shows. I know it will. She'll probably get her own makeup range now. I wonder if she'll ever remember me, the fat neighbour, who kicked it all off for her.

She sighs. Someone comes past her in the hall. It's Anya.

Good God, even she's dolled up to the nines, thinks Harriet.

"Harriet, good evening," says Anya.

"Oh, hello," says Harriet. "Are you watching the show tonight too?"

"Of course," says Anya.

"I thought you were off to Poland. When are you going?"

They can't wait to see the back of me here, thinks Anya. Even Harriet, whom she knew had a soft spot for her after that incident with the chair.

"Next week. Now, please do go into the lounge and have a drink."

Lounge. Oh well, she is from Poland, thinks Harriet.

In the living room the chairs are all arranged in a semicircle around the television. Larry is putting small dishes of olives on various tables.

"I know, I know. Don't say it. Looks like we are to have a seance," says Larry.

"With Alan Makin as our intermediary between the spirit

world and the Square."

His shoulders shake with mirth.

"Sit down, Harriet. Everyone will be coming in in just a minute. Thank you so much for cooking supper. Tracey is very nervous."

"She doesn't look it."

"That's all a front," says Larry confidently.

The door bell rings.

"Excuse me," says Larry, leaving the room.

"Help yourself to an olive."

Harriet starts eating, dolefully and mechanically putting olive after olive into her mouth, hardly biting the first before following it with the second.

She is pleased to hear Jay and Brian in the hall, followed by a chatter of other voices from others who have obviously arrived on the doorstep at the same time.

The living room door opens. Jay, Brian, and the Single Mother all come in, followed by Larry and Grace.

"Is Alan Makin himself turning up?" asks Jay jovially, to nobody in particular.

"Of course he is," says Tracey, coming in behind him with a tray of drinks.

"Bubble, anyone?"

At that precise moment, the door bell rings. Grace looks out of the window.

"It's Alan!" she says.

Tracey smiles. She feels triumphant to her fingertips.

"Well, go and let him in."

After a minute or so, Alan strides into the living room.

"Hello, hello everyone," he announces. He looks around at the room, in which there are only seven people.

"Where's the crew? Is this it?"

"Oh, no, not at all," says Tracey quickly as the door bell rings again.

It is the production crew, four or five muscular and monosyllabic men. They enter the living room as one body

269

and stand by the door, shunning all food and drinking Carlsberg out of the can.

Eventually there are about a dozen people in the room as the opening titles of *Makin's Makeovers* roll on the screen.

Astonishingly, Jane has arrived. She is last to turn up, with George at her side.

"Patrick can't make it, but I couldn't miss this for the world," she announces to the room. She has a lot of makeup on. "George was dying to see it, Tracey."

She gives Jay a bright, glassy eyed smile. He bobs his head, and then focuses resolutely on the screen.

Anya quietly slips out of the living room. She's not too bothered about the show, and she can watch it in her room anyway. But she is very keen to avoid a confrontation with Jane.

Tracey pops up on screen, smiling nervously.

"The pre-sequence sequence, folks," says Alan.

"I'll admit it, I had no idea what was in my bank account from day to day," announces televisual Tracey, walking towards the camera.

"God I sound stupid," mutters Tracey.

"Yes but your legs look great," says Larry, nudging her.

"Only 10% of what people say on television actually sinks into the viewer's mind," says Grace. "I read that somewhere."

Alan Makin coughs, loudly.

"Shhh," says Belle. She looks up at Brian, who winks at her.

"Do we know how many people across the UK are actually watching this?" says George, loudly. Alan does a loud intake of breath.

"Shhh!" hisses Belle.

"About four point five," says Alan.

"Four point five what?" asks George

"Million," says Alan.

"Will you all shut up? Sorry Alan, I don't mean you, but everyone else," says Tracey.

And so the programme begins.

Alan is perfect, easy, charming and full of solutions. Tracey is surprisingly entertaining, full of endearing problems but only too ready to be guided. Graphics fill the screen showing how her finances got into trouble, but how easily the problems can be solved.

"Yeah, if I start working twenty-seven-hour days," says Larry in a low voice.

"Dad!" says Belle. "Shut UP."

"Thought you only counted YouTube as important broadcasting," whispers Larry.

"Dad!" says Grace.

The door bell rings. Grace looks out of the window.

"Belle, it's Jas!"

"Who?" says Alan.

"Oh, one of the chavs from the other day," continues Grace. "He's been working with Belle and that weird Philip Burrell guy."

"What?" says Larry, leaping up out of his chair. "Don't tell me those wacky artists are here."

Alan glances out of the window.

"No, no. Just one person. Oh yes, that's Jasper. I remember now, I invited him round. He was very keen to see the show. After the Talent Show he came up. Wants to ask me about getting into television afterwards, you know."

Larry sits back down. "Well, if anything happens… "

"Don't talk rubbish, man. These people just need a chance. I do this sort of thing a lot, you know," says Alan, adjusting his collar.

"Jasper!" murmurs Larry, astonished. "What sort of name is that for someone from a council estate?"

"Shhhh!" says Belle. "I worked with him all over the Easter holidays. He works for Philip Burrell, you know. Jas. I was at Primary with him. You know. We made the marathon courses."

The bell rings again.

"Grace, be a dear and let him in."

271

After a few moments, Grace heralds the arrival of Jas. He walks in shyly.

"'Lo"

"Jas!" says Belle.

"Alan invited me," he says.

She smiles warmly at him. He is in her house. Without her even having done anything about it. She remembers how nice he had been to her at Philip's studio.

"Fantastic. How are the golf holes?"

"Good."

"Marathon courses?"

"Nah. Magnus thinks we might have 'saturated the market' with them," Jas says. "But Philip's onto something else now."

"What?"

"Olympic stadiums. Check them out. I've put some shots on Instagram."

Belle laughs. She is definitely going to kiss him. Screw the Populars and her vow for chastity. Screw being polite and wistful with Brian, too. She can't be doing with private school boys. She is going to fuck Jas. She knows it. She is going to lose her virginity to him. She will. These thoughts take about three nanoseconds to course through her head. She feels full of exultation.

The group murmurs a welcome. The programme continues to its entirely predictable conclusion.

"So from now on, my working week is sorted," chirps Tracey from the screen.

"I pay myself every week, I pay into my tax account every week and when the tax bill needs to be paid, ta-dah! The money is already there in my account. Thanks, Alan!" She bounces off screen with a jaunty wave.

Alan's face fills the screen as he gets into his car and drives away, the financial superhero coming to your street soon to sort out your money woes. The address for his website is frozen on the screen for a few seconds.

Everyone in the room laughs.

Tracey nudges Alan.

"Thanks Alan!"

Alan graciously nods his head, accepts the acknowledgement, relaxes in his chair as the credits roll.

The crew nods sagely as their names briefly appear on the screen. There is a ripple of applause as the last credit, for Makin Productions, flashes up.

"And now, *Family Guy*," says the continuity announcer.

"Oh pleeese Dad," says Grace. "Can we watch *Family Guy* now?"

"Are you stark staring mad?" says Larry. "We are having a party to celebrate your mum's programme. That does not involve sitting around watching *Family Guy*."

He snaps the television off.

"Only because it features a man like you," mutters Belle, getting up out of her chair and going to stand next to Jas.

"Hey," says Jas. "Your mum looked great."

"Mmm," says Belle noncommittally. "Tell you what. Shall we go upstairs? We can watch Netflix on my laptop."

Jas looks torn. Forget Netflix, he's not stupid. But Alan Makin and his promise of a chat is downstairs. He looks at Belle.

"Quickly," she whispers, touching his hand. That does it. Alan Makin can wait. He is going to take this girl's clothes off in her bedroom in the Square, from whose windows he can just about see his own flat.

"Excuse me," says Tracey loudly, as she walks past them with a tray.

"I shall replenish these, I think," she announces to nobody in particular. "Then we can all have Harriet's delicious lasagna."

As Belle and Jas walk upstairs, Tracey clicks down to the kitchen in her very high heels. A strand of hair has come adrift from its pin. It snakes softly down the back of her neck. She kicks open the kitchen door, walks in and puts the tray heavily down on the table. The programme is over. She must face the lasagna.

Someone comes into the kichen behind her. It's Alan.

"I honestly feel as if nothing nice is ever going to happen again," says Tracey, as the phone starts ringing.

"Rubbish," says Alan. "Listen to that. That is people ringing to tell you how great you were on the show. You were!"

"But it's been, oh I don't know, it's been... " she looks wildly around the four walls of her kitchen, all so carefully styled. The very fact of her expensive kitchen's existence used to give her so much delight. Now it seems pathetic, inadequate.

"Don't worry," says Alan. "You'll go on to do other things. And now with all your finances in great shape," he jokes.

"I suppose so," she says, dolefully, rinsing the glasses under the tap. Her notion of a quick exit from Alan Makin suddenly seems rather undesirable.

"What about... us?"

Alan puts a perfectly manicured hand onto the island. She looks at his nail varnish. It looks totally wrong in her kitchen.

"Tracey, you know. You are a lovely woman. You've been great. You are great. You were great on the show. You were also great for me, very very helpful. In key areas. And physically, wow."

He chucks her under the chin.

She looks up at him, choked by the almost parental gesture, forgetting about her wish for a civilised, neat ending, forgetting about her independence, wanting to continue being wanted by a celebrity. "And?"

"And all the other stuff. Wonderful. You are a wonderful woman," he repeats. "But look at what you have here. It's..." he spreads his hands wide.

Tracey looks at him. She suspects he has said this kind of thing before. She thinks of his glorious solitude in his designer flat. Lubetkin. The Munchkin.

She's grateful, in a way, for Alan's manner, but she would rather that she had instigated it, not him. She thinks he is thinking she is emotionally devastated rather than disappointed, and this irritates her.

"It's domesticated bliss, is what it is," she says sourly. "With lasagna for twenty people."

"Tracey. Come on. Tell you what, let's not finish on this sort of note. Are you free tomorrow?"

She looks up at him, hopefully. Anything not to completely leave the charmed world of production, the fantasy of the perfectly constructed and scripted television show, the notion that life too could be like this, if only one worked just a little bit harder.

"Yes. I am."

"Good. Come with me to London Zoo. I'm taking the Munchkin to his new home."

"What?"

He shrugs. "It's time. I'll tell you about it tomorrow. Ten o'clock. I'll pick you up."

They walk upstairs, back to the sitting room. Jane and George have gone. Everyone else, including Anya, is sitting around drinking beer and watching *Family Guy*. Grace is sitting on her hands, grinning with triumph. Belle and Jas are conspicuous by their absence.

Chapter Thirty-Three
Tracey

Tracey stretches her body in bed, contemplates the slumbering hillock beside her. Fifteen years. For fifteen years she has shared a bed with this one person. She contemplates the next fifteen years. Without any variation, she thinks. Apart from possibly the hillock growing larger.

Larry turns over, flings his arm out in order to embrace her. It catches her on the nose.

"Ow! Fifteen years in bed together, and you still do that most mornings," says Tracey loudly, her eyes streaming.

"What? Oh, sorry love."

He gives her a fond cuddle.

"Don't be dissatisfied. You were great last night. But telly isn't everything."

"I know. I'm alright really, darling."

On the landing, she bumps into Anya, who comes out of the bathroom brushing her teeth.

"Anya, you're up early."

"That's because I'm leaving, you know that. I must be at Gatwick by eleven. Didn't you get my message?"

"What? I thought you were going next week!"

Anya ducks back to the bathroom to rinse and dry her mouth. She returns out to Tracey.

"No, no, sorry, Tracey. I decided to get an earlier flight. They have seats." She shrugs. "My mother says she wants to have me home in Lodz early. My uncles are collecting me from Chopin airport. I did leave you a note in the kitchen."

Do they always do this in the middle class world, thinks Tracey crossly. The living conditions between employer and au pair are so intimate that they see you in your nightie, or find (and read) your bank statement. Yet when it suits them they pretend to be distant, and arrange things how they want it. As if you simply didn't count. Never mind the contract, the fondness for their small charges, the closeness you have shared. Tracey knows there is probably no point in railing against it, being formal, waving bits of paper about. It's just how it is. It is their final trump card against the English bourgeoisie. You need us, they say. We don't need you. You, the English employer, can be replaced at any time. There are lots of you out there.

"Oh, Anya. We will miss you. Have you said goodbye to the girls?"

"No, but I will. I'll get them up and have breakfast with them."

Of course you will. Eat our food, spend our money, snare the affection of our children and then go home.

"Well, let me know if you need any help."

She wanders back into her bedroom, sits on the bed. She feels rather shocked by Anya's announcement. At the same time, however, she starts to think about the girl in the past tense. She'll have to find a replacement. Maybe this time she'll get one who can drive. And cook decently. Tracey thinks she'd rather have a decent cook than someone who plays the piano, what a minefield that ended up being. Maybe it would be better to get a man. Eastern European, of course. An Eastern European male au pair. That would send shockwaves around here, she thinks. But at least a man wouldn't get off with one of the neighbours' husbands.

She pokes the semi-conscious Larry.

"Anya's off. Says she's booked on an earlier flight."

Larry mumbles incoherently.

"A week early. Never mind the inconvenience for us."

"Shame. Yes, I think I saw a note in the kitchen. I liked her. Good girl. And, of course, bad girl, ha ha."

"Yes, well I'm thinking of getting a male au pair next."

"Ha!" laughs Larry. "Are you bonkers? No way am I sharing a house with some Croatian bodybuilder. Or a Polish builder."

"Well, at least it would stop problems with the neighbours."

"Not necessarily. It might make them worse. A male au pair might end up in bed with our piano teacher. Or one of your friends. Or you."

He nudges Tracey.

"Would you like to be in bed with a Croatian bodybuilder?"

Tracey looks at him anxiously. Does he suspect anything, she wonders.

"Do we need one at all?" continues Larry. "A nanny, that is."

Tracey sighs, then jumps up off the bed, anxious to finish the conversation.

"Oh, Christ. I have to go. I'm going to London Zoo this morning. With Alan."

Ten minutes later, he is there, sitting in the car outside Tracey's house.

"The Munchkin? He's on the back seat. Get in, TV star," he says, patting the leather passenger seat. Tracey inhales the rich perfume of a recently valeted Mercedes.

"I got the Overnights," says Alan, smoothing his hair and smiling.

"What?"

"The ratings. Shows us, well, my company, how many people watched the show last night."

"And?"

"Really rather good. Better than average. Four million."

The car glides out of the Square.

"I thought you said it was four point five who normally watched."

"Yes, but the Overnights don't count Catch-up."

"What the hell is Catch-up?"

"iPlayer. Recordings. Sky Plus. Usually adds on a million or so. So it's good. Very good."

"Is it?" says Tracey dolefully.

"It's all good," says Alan firmly. "You'll be getting more TV work after this, I know it."

They pull into the car park opposite the Zoo.

Alan produces a piece of paper which indicates to the person in the car parking lodge that they don't need a ticket, since they are here on business.

He opens the back door, pulls out a large plastic travelling case. Tracey looks into it. In the middle of the case, the Munchkin is squatting balefully.

"Was it difficult to get him in?"

"Not really. I sort of got hold of his branch and tipped him off it."

"God. Weren't you worried about being bitten?"

"I moved very fast. And I wore gloves."

They arrive at the public entrance of the Zoo. The ticket booth is shuttered. Alan pulls out his phone, taps in a number, speaks brusquely to the person on the other end of the line.

"Yes, hello is that the Reptile House? It's Alan Makin with the iguana. We're outside the main gate on Prince Albert Road."

Presently, a side door opens and a young man wearing a ZSL jumper comes out.

"Morning!" says the young man breezily. "If you're quick, you'll see the camels walking through."

Alan and Tracey follow him inside the Zoo.

"Wait here," says the ZSL man.

After a few seconds, four Bactrian camels come swaying past them, led by a small woman, also in a ZSL shirt. The camels walk one behind the other with semi-closed eyes, a towering line of disdain and odour.

"We used to do the same with the elephants, before one trampled a colleague. Then they had to go to Whipsnade," observes the young man. "Oh, here come the llamas. Well, one of them."

The llama appears. It is like a smaller, furrier version of the camels. It is wearing a blue harness and is being led by a diminutive person.

"That's Perry," says the young man.

"That's George," says Tracey, astonished, as the small figure holding the halter proudly advances.

"George! What on earth are you doing, leading a llama around London Zoo?"

"Keeper For A Day," says George calmly as he passes the group. A London Zoo employee hurries up and walks beside him.

"Morning," says the employee. "Normally we don't let our Junior keepers lead the animals, but Perry is an exception."

Tracey is speechless.

"That child seems to get everywhere," she says.

"Shall we?" says Alan, lifting the box carefully. "It's a bit cold out here for him."

The heat hits them as they enter the Reptile House. Tracey walks past the adjoining glass fronted cells in which various lizards, caimans, snakes and salamanders crouch.

Cell after identically shaped cell, each animal living next door to the other. They are grouped into vague categories. But they have no way of knowing that they are there with their biological cousins. As far as they know it, they are alone.

One small green reptile is sitting on a large leaf. Above it hovers a disembodied human hand. The hand is holding a small can. It is watering the reptile with the can. The animal basks in the shower, luxuriating in the water, clinging onto the dripping leaf with extraordinarily long fingers, its snout turned upwards to the shower from the watering can. It has an air of utter bliss.

"That's to replicate the effect of living in a rain forest," says the ZSL man.

"Oh to be looked after like that," observes Alan.

You are, thinks Tracey sourly. What with your fan base and your ratings and your Overnights. They shower on your head in just the same way. And you cling onto the leaf of fame in similar fashion. Soaking it up.

Alan is shaking the hand of the Director of the Reptile House. The Director is grinning. He squats down and peers into the Munchkin's case.

"Morning, you," says the Director to the Munchkin.

"How did you get him in here?"

"I manoeuvered him in very gently," lies Alan.

"Because he looks rather agitated."

"Really?"

"They don't like being moved." The Director stands up briskly. "Never mind, can't be helped. We'll settle him in. Has he been fed recently?"

"I gave him some crickets last night," says Alan.

"Good, good," muses the Director. "We'll keep him backstage for a few weeks, let him settle in before bringing him out on show."

"Will you miss him?" whispers Tracey to Alan.

"Well, he was a good… project. But these things have a duration, don't they."

Tracey looks at the Munchkin inside the vitrine. Such a complex, beautiful animal. Cast away and dismissed as a project. For the first time, Tracey thinks she will welcome having a respite from Alan's life, perfect though it may be. She finds it altogether a bit mesmerisingly terrifying.

"So perhaps we could have you back here, when the iguana is ready to face his public, yes?" says the Director, shaking Alan's hand again. "Perhaps we could have a bit of a public do for the unveiling?"

"Yes, yes," says Alan. "As long as, you understand, my, er, previous charge of him is not handled, in a, how shall we say, unprofessional manner."

The Director understands perfectly. Alan Makin does not want to come across as someone who has willingly kept a large and rare animal, who was possibly illegally imported, in a small glass case in Highgate for a long time.

"You did the right thing," the Director of the Reptile House assures the TV presenter.

"Thank you. I know," says Alan.

"Does this happen a lot?" asks Tracey suddenly.

"Does what happen a lot?" says the Director. "Television stars arriving at the Reptile House? No."

"No," laughs Tracey. "People giving you their pets."

"Yes," says the Director, with a faint weariness. "But not often with iguanas. It's usually with terrapins. People buy them when they are tiny and then panic when they grow to the size of frying pans. Then they offer them to us. We usually can't take them, but we find sanctuaries for them. It's better that than the other solution."

"Which is what?" asks Tracey.

"Throwing them in the Thames."

Tracey gives a little shriek of horror.

"It happens," says the Director.

Tracey looks at him. He may be an expert in reptile behaviour but she figures he is also pretty knowledgable about the human side of it too.

They leave the dark concrete of the Reptile House, its scaly inhabitants moving quietly in the humming heat under their individual sunlamps.

"I haven't been here for years," observes Tracey as they walk into the fresh air. "Shall we have a quick tour?"

"As long as I don't step in any camel dung," says Alan fastidiously.

They turn left, past the pygmy hippos and Hugh Casson's brick Elephant House, now a showcase for tiny monkeys.

As they are standing observing a family of wild boar, a family of humans comes up to Tracey.

"Excuse me for asking," says the mother, "but weren't you on the telly last night?"

"Sorry?" says Tracey.

The mother repeats her question.

A warm glow of delight suffuses Tracey's entire body.

"Yes, yes, I was."

"You were great!" says the mother, beaming. "Can I take your photo? Actually, can I do a selfie?"

Tracey nods her head, beaming back. "'Course you can, yes, yes," she says, combing the hair out of her eyes selfconsciously.

The mother crowds up to Tracey, stretches her arm out, takes a selfie of her and Tracey together. Then, because she is of a certain age when these things still carry weight, she jumps as if she has just remembered something. "Tell you what, can I have your autograph?" She shoves a Visit London Zoo programme at Tracey, and rootles in her bag for a pen.

Tracey looks at Alan, smiling hopefully. Alan is smiling too. "Told You" he mouths, then turns to the woman.

"Yes, Tracey was the star turn in my report," he says loudly to the woman, who has found her pen and is proffering it to Tracey.

"Oh gosh it's YOU," says the woman. "Alan Makin!"

Tracey notices that Alan exhales quite deeply at this moment. A sigh of relief, she thinks. Maybe he was worried that he wasn't going to be recognised as well.

"Ooo can I just... take... this," says the woman, bringing the phone out once more, grabbing Alan by the elbow and squeezing close to him as she takes the shot, the proof that she is in finger distance to someone famous. Alan visibly relaxes, smiles, puts his head on one side. He is having a good time. He has got rid of the Munchkin and he is being feted. Tracey and Alan both sign the programme...

Tracey and Alan both sign the programme, Alan with his professional swirl. Tracey isn't quite sure how to do this, and so ends up simply writing her first name. Then she puts a smiley face below it.

"Thanks, thanks so much," says the mother.

"Not at all," says Alan. "Thanks for watching."

"There you are," he says to Tracey as the family depart. "That's going to happen to you much more, now."

It doesn't, though. They walk through the entire Zoo, up past the Children's Farm, the big cats and Bug World, then down past the parrots, the penguins and the shop and under the tunnel to the tapirs, zebra, giraffe and something called a bongo, which Tracey has never heard of before but learns from the information printed on a stand is a very shy relation of the zebra, which lives in the depths of the Congo rainforest, and was only discovered a few decades ago.

Nobody remarks on them. Nobody recognises them. The Zoo gradually fills up with shouting children and parents vainly trying to contain them. Nobody cares that Alan Makin and she are also visiting the Zoo, the day after their programme was watched by four million people. Five, if you count Catch-up.

Someone must recognise her. Tracey is conscious of laughing too loudly, of presenting her face to people too blatantly, of not behaving normally. She worries that she hasn't done her makeup well enough, that she's not wearing very fashionable clothes. She thinks about having a public persona. She wants, above all, more people to come up and praise her, and treat her as their friend and ask for her signature with the smiley face. Maybe the thrill of fame will replace the thrill of having sex in Alan's giant flat, and alleviate the regularity of life in the Square. Maybe, thinks Tracey quickly, she will be the most famous person in the Square. That would be something.

"That was nice," she ventures to Alan as they leave the Zoo past the giant Snowdon Aviary with its ibises and herons, and the small enclosures for the owls, who are all fast asleep, ignorant of the dead white mice, still bleeding, which the

284

keepers have tenderly left below their perches.

"What, the Zoo? I know, lovely. Such a London treasure."

"No, I meant the autograph. My autograph. The lady who came up and recognised me."

"Oh, I know. Did you like that? Well, I have to say, having had it both ways, that in my honest opinion, life is so much nicer when you are a bit famous. Not too famous, of course," says Alan hastily, to his protegee. "But being recognised is lovely. If you get too famous, then it becomes tiresome, as you have seen with me, haven't you? People do give me a hard time sometimes. It's tough. But getting a little bit of fame is just right. Lovely."

He is treating me a bit like the Munchkin, thinks Tracey as she climbs back into Alan's car. I am a project. Or at least, I have been. I've shown him the tricks of my trade, and he has shown me his. We have shared one amazing evening. That's the summary of it.

Tracey looks out of the window. She knows, despite herself, that this is a good ending. Much easier this way. And actually, she welcomes his cool stance. What if he got all emotional on her, demanded eternal loyalty and her to move in with him into the Lubetkin building? No, it's much better this way. Probably.

They drive back to the Square in silence. Its perfect symmetry enfolds them as Alan elegantly curves the car in front of Tracey's house.

"Well, thanks for coming to the Zoo with me. Thanks for doing that. I think it was the right thing. And it was a good thing. It was also so good to see you after the programme. As I said, it's all good."

Tracey nods.

"Look, I have to go now. Onto my next… "

"Project?" says Tracey, with a faint smile.

"Yes, well, project, programme, you know. Look, you are great. Were great. Thanks for everything. We will hook up again. Maybe after Christmas? And Tracey?"

"Yes?" she says dutifully, climbing out of the car, standing on the pavement beside her house.

"Look after those finances! And get a better autograph!"

From an upstairs window in the Square, someone is practising the piano. Out in the middle of the park, Gilda and Philip Burrell are performing Tai-Chi. Philip is in a pure white tracksuit. Gilda is wearing a Hello Kitty onesie and fairy wings. Tracey looks at them and envies their freedom and absolute determination to behave exactly as they feel, without the slightest indication that they know they are being observed and commented on by the neighbourhood. She even envies Gilda's experiences as a topless model.

Chapter Thirty-Four
Jane

It is pouring with rain as Roberta stands on the doorstep of Jane's house. Water sluices off the grey slate rooves of the houses in the Square. It pours from the drenched leaves of the London plane trees. It gushes down the drainpipes. Not one resident has ignored the need to keep their drainpipes in order. Not one drainpipe is leaking. The water is perfectly directed into the guttering, an immaculate piece of rain orchestration. Even the coving on the road works in symphony with the drainpipes, draining the drenched street straight into the kerbside where the water is caught and cascades into the drains.

By the time George manages to open the door, Roberta is soaked.

"Aha," says George with his usual sangfroid.

"Good afternoon, George," says Roberta. "My plants are going to love this, aren't they?"

Patrick appears in the hall. "Gosh, you are wet," he observes unnecessarily. "Stair rods, isn't it?"

"What are stair rods?" says George.

There is a pause as Patrick wrestles with the question.

"Er, I think they are bannisters. Or balustrades. Or are they those things which keep the carpet tight on the step?"

says Patrick as Roberta takes her coat off and hangs it up on the Alessi hat stand. "Don't know, old chap," he says, finally. "But when you say that they are falling from the sky, it's clearly raining. Hard."

"Shall we?" says Roberta to George, opening the door to the music room.

"I have a wonderful piece that I thought we might look at. Particularly today."

"I led a llama around London Zoo yesterday," says George excitedly.

"Did you?"

"I was Keeper For A Day."

"Really?"

"I was. And do you know who I saw there?"

"Who? Apart from animals, that is. David Attenborough?"

"No!" says George, laughing. "I saw Tracey and, you know, the presenter of the Talent Show. Andy Makin. They were there before the general public turned up."

"Alan. Alan Makin. Oh, really? What were they doing?"

"Well, when I saw them, I was with Perry. You know, the llama. But afterwards we had to do some tidying up in the Reptile House, and I heard the Director talking about Andy, sorry, Alan Makin and his reptile."

Alan Makin is a bit reptilian, thinks Roberta.

"It seems as if he has had a very big lizard, an iguana I think, in a teeny tiny case, and he gave it to London Zoo. The Director was very cross with Alan Makin after he left because he discovered all sorts of problems with the reptile, and said that Alan Makin hadn't been looking after him properly."

"That's a shame. Did you enjoy being Keeper For A Day?"

"Yes I did."

He settles down on the piano stool and looks up at his teacher expectantly.

She brings out a new book and opens it.

"The 'Raindrop Sonata'. By Chopin."

George points to the window, and smiles.

"Oh, that's clever of you, Roberta my dear."

She smiles at him.

On the other side of the Square, a front door slams. It's Anya, leaving in the rain, bound for the airport now called Chopin, in Warsaw.

"Now, George. Chopin made this tune up when he was very unhappy and all he could hear was the rain drumming on the roof of his house."

"Where was he staying?"

"He was staying with his partner who, who was also called George actually."

"Oh. Was he a gay?"

"No, George was a lady. She was his girlfriend."

"That's funny. Why would she have a boy's name?"

Roberta sighs. "Shall we just work out where the raindrops are drumming?"

Footsteps running down the stairs. Roberta ignores them as they go past the room and down into the kitchen, although she hears Jane's voice calling urgently.

"Patrick, Patrick, quick!"

She hears Patrick and Jane run past the door and back upstairs.

"All you do with your left hand is just beat out this tune, dum dum dum, like this, like the rain," says Roberta.

Upstairs, Jane is running from room to room. It seems that there is a lot of rain which has come through the roof, and is now falling in Jane and Patrick's bedroom.

"Look, look, it's coming right through the light fitting, Patrick have you turned the electricity off?" shrieks Jane.

"Well, it's clearly off," says Patrick testily. "I mean, the light is not on, is it?"

He places a series of buckets under the ceiling rose.

"Perhaps it's not rain."

"I am going upstairs," says Jane. "I'm dreading what I might find in George's room."

She runs out of George's room and into the spare room.

"The leak must be in the other part of the roof, it must be in the valley of the butterfly," shouts Jane down to Patrick.

"What are you talking about darling?"

"The butterfly! It's a butterfly roof!"

Patrick raises his eyebrows. Just like Jane to remember details like that. He vaguely recalls the nature of the roof, described to him in delicate detail by the surveyor when they bought the house. To give the outward appearance of a horizontal, classical line, the roof itself is an inverted peak hidden behind a flat parapet, like a pair of butterfly wings resting on the house. To the person on the street, who can only see the parapet, it looks as if there is no roof at all.

This aesthetic used to confuse George, who would insist on drawing his home, when he was young, with a typical peaked roof.

"Where has our roof gone?" he would ask. "Has it blown away?"

It is not the butterfly design. It is something far worse. It is the entire water tank. Perhaps encouraged by the downpour outside, the tank has burst open and its contents are cascading down the wall and into the house downstairs.

Jane starts screaming at Patrick.

"Buckets, buckets! And a plumber! The carpet is sodden. The bed is soaking. Oh my God."

Dum dum dum dum, continues the piano from downstairs. It is a tune that Jane knows.

"Oh, very funny. She's got the boy to play the sodding 'Raindrop Prelude' or Sonata or whatever during a Biblical downpour which will cost us thousands."

"What?" says Patrick, struggling upstairs with a ladder and another bucket.

"Roberta. And George. Playing the 'Raindrop Sonata'."

"I think that's quite witty," says Patrick.

Jane raises an eyebrow and sits down on a step outside her bedroom.

"Oh for fuck's sake. It is bloody cheeky, can't you see?

A woman who we PAY to educate our son, teasing us. I am firing her. But first, I am calling the plumber. Along with, probably, half of North London."

But as she brings out her phone, and looks at it, she sees a text from Jay. Her lover. Her neighbour. Her fantasy. *Darling, we are going today. Brian and I. Can I possibly kiss you before I take my thighs into hell and back?*

Oh, God. What a day to choose. Her stomach squirms. She taps a message back. *Fuck off. Our house is about to collapse. We have water everywhere.*

Patrick leaves the room with a brimming bucket.

Jane looks down at her phone, willing it to vibrate. After a minute, it does. *Oh darling. Please don't be cross. Come round.*

She immediately replies. *I must call the plumber. Can you wait?*

He waits. Brian waits. They wait, with their bikes and their Lycra cycling gear packed, and their special shoes and their Michelin maps.

Roberta finishes the lesson early, because she is worried about getting home.

The rain eases off, turns itself into a familiar drizzle.

The tank, however, has not stopped. The entire upstairs floor is now impossible. Huge dark streaks line the walls. The ceiling drips ominously. The carpet is a marsh. Water has even penetrated the hall downstairs.

Jane puts a cashmere jumper on and collects her family together. She is distracted, but not so much that she can't have a quick glance in the mirror, to check she looks elegantly dischevelled. Good, she thinks. She wants Jay to think she has been suffering, but not so much that she has lost control of her style.

"Darling? George," she cries. "Tonight, we have been invited round to Jay and Harriet's."

"Well, that's all very well but what about the plumber?" mutters Patrick.

"Someone is coming in two hours," says Jane dramatically.

"Goodbye, then," calls Roberta up from downstairs.

"What, what? Oh, bye Roberta. Sorry, I am a bit distracted," yells Jane.

"No worries. No lesson next week, then?"

"What?" Damn these teachers, thinks Jane, as she runs downstairs, sweating lightly. Always needing organising and somehow… servicing in some way or other.

"Not coming next week?" she says to Roberta. Well why the hell not? I suspect she's off to some bloody symposium on Chopin. Or a concert. Or a recital.

"Yes, isn't George away?"

"What?"

"George. I think he's at some form of Camp. Cub Camp?" Roberta offers gently.

Oh, Christ. The needs of her son. Bloody never ending. And now the piano teacher has remembered it and I have forgotten it. Showing me up again, bitch.

"Oh, yes, of course. Yes. Roberta, you have a better grasp of my diary than I do!" says Jane. "A fortnight's time then. Marvellous. Thanks a lot. Lovely to hear the Raindrop piece. Very appropriate. Let's hope we don't need to segue into Britten."

That'll show her.

"What, 'Noye's Fludde'?"

"Well done. Roberta, there are no flies on you. See you in two weeks. Goodbye."

Roberta walks off through the Square. She is glad to be away from Jane. She looks forward to having some time to herself. She thinks of all the things she can do in her allotment.

Jane notes the water tank has, at last, stopped. She shuts the door, leans against it. She can hear the ceiling upstairs drip fatly onto the carpet upstairs.

Suddenly, the face of her child appears at her elbow, a permanent reminder of her moral failings. She feels her life is a shambles.

This is not how adulthood was supposed to be, surely, with a child she does not understand, a husband who has transformed into someone she hardly knows, and a lover who reinforces the status quo.

Plus, a house which is falling apart, yet is so valuable she dare not sell it for fear of future profits squandered.

"Mother."

"What, what George? Can't you see I am rushing about?"

"No," says George, logically. "I can see that you are leaning against the door. Now, can I ask you something?"

"What?" says Jane warily. "Is this a good time for questions?"

"I am going to Cub Camp next week, you know."

"Yes, I have just remembered. Roberta reminded me."

"And, well. The thing is this. Mother, I need to practise putting up my tent."

Jane looks at her son.

"Do you have any idea of the things I have to organise at the moment? Do you? Do you?" she shouts at him.

"Mother, don't shout."

She gathers herself together.

"Sorry, sorry. Obviously you don't have any idea, but yes, go on."

"So I thought tonight might be a good night."

"What for?"

"You know, to see if the tent is waterproof. And to get to know how to put it up. Think how much fun it would be to hear the rain outside and we are all dry inside."

"Put up your tent? Tonight? In this house? All of us? Are you crazy?"

"Yes. I thought we all might put up the tent, and sleep in it. It's a three man tent. And I don't want to sleep in it all on my own anyway. At Cub Camp, I'll have Finn."

She looks at him, exasperated.

He steadily returns her gaze. Jane realises she envies him, his ability to be fundamentally in one situation at a time, not always torn, as she is, between one thing and the next. She is jealous of his sure footed position at the centre of his own small world, a world involving challenges and trials and goals which he is happy about attempting. She admires it, and wishes she could share his boundless optimism, in which every week is an excitement, and a gruesome but inexpensive experience such as Cub Camp a thing of joy.

"Please, mother. If we are going to Harriet's perhaps we could do it in her garden."

A wave of love comes over her for her son. Giving her approval is such a little thing.

And it would make her feel a bit less cross about Jay's cycling holiday. If he can do that for Brian, then surely she can do this for George. But there you are, she thinks. I am letting George do it, but for the wrong reasons. I am letting him do it because my lover is doing something similar with his own child. Does this make it a worthless gesture? She doesn't know. She wishes she was a better person. But then, she thinks, imagine what she would have had to jettison. All that sex.

"Mother," comes the small insistence at her elbow.

Forget it, thinks Jane. Just concentrate on being in the moment.

"Alright. It's mad, but we'll try and do it. As long as Harriet says it's alright."

Then if there is a disaster, we can always sleep over there, she thinks, although even Jane's formidable nature quails, slightly, at asking the wife of her lover for a favour.

George's face is a picture of incredulous joy. He really had not thought his mother capable of giving her blessing to this plan. He rushes upstairs to collect the tent.

"And torches. Mother, we will need torches."

And so it comes about that Jane, Patrick and George end up sleeping in George's Cub tent, not in their own garden, but in the garden of Harriet and Jay, their neighbours. Jane gets there first.

"Hello," she says to Jay on the doorstep of his house.

"Darling," says Jay. He glances anxiously over his shoulder to check his wife isn't in the vicinity, and then embraces her warmly, if swiftly.

"Come in. We must go, but come in."

Jane stomps in.

"Patrick and George are on their way. The house is a nightmare. We are going to have to leave the Square for at least a month. Where we will go, I do not know. Possibly my parents' in Guildford. George wants us all to camp in your garden tonight. I agreed, partially because I feel guilty that I never do anything for him. And you are taking your son off for three weeks."

"Eighteen days actually."

"Well. Anyway. Our house is really hopeless at the moment, and I don't dare to put the electricity back on. I know outside will be a sodden marshland, but do you think Harriet would mind?"

Jay looks at Jane, and suddenly bursts out laughing.

"My God! You! In a tent!"

She hates him.

"Yes, well I am not that hopeless, you know. I could say the same about you… on a bike."

They look at one another, middle-aged lovers impaled on a trident of guilt and desire and duty, forced into costly adventuring for the sake of their children and from a notion, imbued on them probably by post-War parents, that things done out of doors, without a computer screen in attendance, are virtuous necessities.

Jane closes her eyes wearily.

"Alright, if you must know, I am steeling myself. It's going to be ghastly."

She opens her eyes and looks at Jay.

"If I had looked at myself twenty years on, after I moved here, all fired up and full of ambition, and young, I would be horrified to see how little I have managed to achieve. When will it all work out? When will it be easy?"

Jay strokes her cheek briefly.

"It never will," he whispers. "That, my darling, is the joy of adulthood."

Brian appears in the hall.

"Dad," he says quietly.

"Sorry, sorry Jane, we must be on our way. Can't miss the Eurostar."

And they go, jaunty with their gleaming bicycles. Jane notices him looking around the front of the house, pointing out something to Brian.

She wonders vaguely why he is remarking on it to his son, passes through the house and sits down in the kitchen. Her lover's kitchen. God, what a mess she has made of everything.

Eventually, Harriet gives them all a cup of tea. Jane is looking at the kitchen clock, wondering how long putting up the tent is going to take, and whether Jay has caught the Eurostar. She envisages him settling down with his son, getting the maps out, perhaps having a small glass of red wine.

It is at this point that Harriet sits down, settling her ample frame on the bench opposite Jane, and delivers the coup de grâce.

"Well, we have news for you."

Oh yes, thinks Jane. What news could you possibly have that might suprise me, fat cow?

Harriet opens her mouth. "We have put our house on the market."

There is silence in the room. Patrick comes sauntering into the kitchen.

"Well, shall we sally forth into Flanders Fields?" he says, to nobody in particular.

Jane cannot speak. That is what he was doing at the front of the house, she realises. Showing Brian where the For Sale post was going to go, the little shit.

"Yes, Jay and I have decided it's probably quite a good

time," continues Harriet. "Market and all that. And with Brian needing university funds, it's probably the best thing to do."

"But where will you go?" manages Jane at last.

"I don't know. World's our oyster. Maybe stay in central London. Maybe... not."

"Are you really going to sell? Won't you miss the Square?"

Harriet laughs, long and loudly. "I don't think so. Oooh, no. Miss it? Ha, ha ha."

She knows, thinks Jane, recalibrating everything in her head. She knows Everything. No wonder Jay is on the Eurostar. Coward. She feels hot and sweaty.

"Estate agent says he has some considerable interest already," says Harriet merrily. "From a famous person as well. No idea who. But he thinks we might have an offer within the month. So, you'll have an exciting new neighbour. Once you come back."

Patrick glances at Jane. She looks utterly composed, smiling and nodding at Harriet. He is quite sure, however, that not very far beneath this polite surface, his wife is at sea. Red and white blotches have suddenly appeared on her neck.

"What fun. My, Harriet, you are a dark horse," says Jane.

Once they are in the garden, and get going, Jane rounds on her husband.

"Fucking hell. Jay and Harriet. Moving out. Cashing in and moving out."

She undoes the straps of the tent case viciously.

"It's very nice of her to have us in her garden, but there is so much fucking schadenfreude in that kitchen you could practically cut it with a knife."

Patrick sighs.

"Jane, do you always have to see the worst in people?"

"Well, I know you don't like what I say, but I have to say that Harriet is a bitch of the first order, and is delighted that a) our house is awash in some Biblical fucking flood and b) she is going to be filthy rich, quite soon."

Jane finds, to her horror, that she is crying. She pushes the tears away furiously.

"Tents have got a lot easier these days, haven't they?" she mutters to Patrick, pushing the long jointed rods through the thin fabric.

"That's the Glastonbury factor for you. Loads more stuff on the market. Maybe we should all go."

Jane shudders.

"To Glastonbury? Fuck off. Even if you have a ready made tent, the loos are like something out of a refugee camp. And I don't know who any of the bands are these days. Nor do I want to live on Pot Noodle for a weekend. I think one night at the neighbours' is quite enough for me."

Patrick crawls inside the tent. He remembers the terrible conversation between them about Jay. He remembers how insistent Jane had been that George was simply making everything up, and how he had chosen to believe it. Did he believe it? Probably not, but the alternative was too horrendous to envisage. And then he had screwed Anya on the kitchen table, so it was evens. Moreover, he was enjoying himself at the moment. And now Jay and Harriet are pissing off, that makes things a lot better. Out of sight, out of mind.

"Can you hand me some of those pegs, darling?"

She crawls in with him.

"If I wasn't so wet, this might be quite fun."

"It's dry as a bone in here," he says, tickling her, and laughing.

Jane finds herself laughing, alongside him, despite herself.

Before supper, the emergency plumber rings. The plumber announces that he has been to the house and sealed the area, prior to 'full boiler and water tank refurbishment'.

"That sounds expensive," says Patrick.

"Of course the whole first floor will have to be redecorated," says Jane gloomily.

"We won't be back for about two months, I should say. We'll have to go and rent somewhere."

"Have some Pinot Noir," says Harriet. "Are you sure you

don't want to sleep in the spare room tonight?" she asks, again.

"No!" shouts Jane, too quickly, and then covers it up by coughing.

She has a dizzying horror of going upstairs, entering the familiar bedroom in which she has been so often, to sleep with her husband. She must have fucked Jay about forty times on that bed.

She doesn't want to go into the room, shortly to be walked into, cleaned, ordered by a woman who will have no idea of the erotic entanglement that it has witnessed. She doesn't want to see that bed. She has torn her clothes off on it and rolled on the sheepskin rug beside it, and been spanked, and sucked, and pressed up against the wall there, in that room.

Going into it now, with Patrick, her husband, would be impossible. She thinks it might actually make her physically sick.

"No, thank you Harriet," says Patrick.

"Thank you so much Harriet," says Jane, recovering. "How lovely to have a spare room, I didn't know you had one. That's going to be a great asset for your estate agent, you know. But no, thanks, we'll be fine. We can't really leave George in the tent on his own. We'll be very happy. In the tent," she repeats.

The fish pie is eaten. The washing machine is put on. George formally hands out the torches. Harriet ventures outside alongside them, puffing on a cigarette, to have a look at the tent.

"Rather you than me," she says.

Jane looks at Harriet. She imagines Harriet is the angel at the Garden of Eden, the cigarette a flaming sword, ordering her and Patrick out. Banished to rental accommodation after a night under canvas.

"Night, then," she says, bending down to enter the tent, flashing the torch around the compact interior, scenting that particular camping aroma of canvas and wet grass. George is already inside, sitting up in his sleeping bag.

"Shoes off by the fly-sheet," he orders.

"Very good, George," whispers Patrick, wrestling his large frame into the space.

"God, Patrick," says Jane, "be careful!"

At midnight, she hears gusts of rain come pattering back. She is with her husband and child, all in separate sleeping containers. In the garden of her lover. There is a faint light outside from the street lights. She can make out their faces, the son's a smaller, rounder version of the father's.

The rain goes on and on.

In the studio, Gilda is slowly swaying around the naked figure of Philip. She is wearing a belly-dancing outfit. He watches her, hypnotised.

In his new, large, properly heated and illuminated vitrine in the Reptile House, the Munchkin moves slowly along a twig and bites the head off a cricket.

At Highpoint, the concrete Caryatids bearing the heavy parapet of the foyer stand immobile in the rain, rivulets of water streaming down their faces and over their naked breasts.

In his apartment, Alan Makin tosses under 1000-thread count sheets tucked over his Emperor-size bed.

Beside him, on the Philippe Starck bedside table is a glossy property pamphlet.

The cover reads as follows:

"For Sale. Four-storey, four-bedroomed family house boasting knock-through kitchen and 100-foot garden in enviable Central London garden square."

On the front of the brochure, there is a large tick.

Acknowledgements

I would like to thank Adam Foulds, who led the Guardian/ UEA fiction writing course, during which *The Square* came into being.

Also I must thank my classmates; Jill Offman, Natascha McElhone, Anjana Shrivastava, Sam Burns, Chris Gawor, Barbara Hudson and Leke Adewole, who laughed in all the right places and stopped me from mad flights of fancy. Thanks also to Philippa Perry for reminding me about smartphones and the need to include references to them.

Huge thanks of course to my wonderful agent Cathryn Summerhayes and Siobhan O'Neill from William Morris Entertainment, who also laughed in the right places, and everyone from Legend Press, particularly Lauren Parsons, Lucy Chamberlain, Lottie Chase, Jessica Reid and Tom Chalmers, thank you so much.

Credit goes to my old friend Nick Gibbs, who makes sculptures of famous golf holes for wealthy enthusiasts, and who was very nice indeed about me stealing his idea.

For my husband Pip Clothier, who always keeps the faith, profound thanks.

I should probably also apologise to my wonderful children Phoebe, Gabriel, Honey and Lucien, for potentially embarrassing them.

For more explanation, see the dedication.

Come and visit us at
www.legendpress.co.uk

Follow us
@legend_press